THE PLAYROOM

JOCELYN DEXTER

BLOODHOUND
— BOOKS —

www.bloodhoundbooks.com

Print ISBN: 978-1-917214-64-3

ONE

Jessica

I ronically, I was only interested in exceptionally handsome men. I enjoyed the spectacle they put on: strutting up and down, all cock and little else. They dressed to better show off their physical attributes, but mostly they just wore vanity. It wasn't a wardrobe that I'd ever worn, but all the men I wanted, they all had it in abundance and wore it well.

It was as though vanity was a figure-hugging second skin for them – perhaps they'd been born with it. As if their baby bodies had been birthed with a film of beauty coating them. Like silk, an arrogant pride covered them from head to foot. It grew with them, a live and tangible thing, nurtured and encouraged by doting and adoring parents.

Against my better judgement, I found I needed one of these ultra-attractive male specimens.

One man: all for myself.

It wasn't a huge thing to ask. All I wanted was my very own beautiful man-toy, that I could play with and do with as I wanted. Like other women did. Being loved by someone, a man – that was something that should happen naturally. It should be a woman's right. It was only a little thing to expect in life.

Problem was – I was ugly. And I didn't mean that I was a bit on the plain side, or not very pretty – I meant I was deep down shit-ugly. Fat-and-ginger-ugly.

For once, I decided to fight back against the world and get what *I* wanted. Proactive – that's what I needed to be. I rolled up my sleeves. I'd get myself a man.

Whether they liked it or not.

In my mind, that was the only way I'd get what I so desperately desired. To be brutal and demanding and unflinching in what I wanted.

Needed.

I'd never had a proper boyfriend before. Not really. Not one all of my own.

At thirty, I thought it really was high time I got what I wanted.

TWO

Jessica
___

Everyone knew, there were women who lunched. I did a whole lot more than that. I breakfasted, brunched, lunched, snacked, dined, and snacked again. Food was my life.

My love of beautiful men, stemmed in part, I thought, from having two very attractive, *slim* parents. To my eternal shame, it wasn't me who'd left home, but instead, my parents had. Jaunted off on some never-ending cruise. They stopped off and visited me infrequently when they were in England, but essentially, *they* had left *me*. When I'd been eighteen.

I hated them. My mother was a bitch and my father was married to her.

The only perk at being effectively parentless, was that they'd left me their house and a handsome income – probably to assuage their guilt at dumping me. Although, I suspected I was being overly generous in my estimation of their motives. It was far more likely they simply wanted me to look after the house, to keep it running, and what I did or didn't do, mattered not at all. I suspected I didn't figure even minimally on their radar.

They'd informed me, often, before their departure, ever

since I'd been a fat child in fact, that I really should do something about my excessive weight. It was a disgusting thing, they'd told me. My mother had said, 'You're fat, Jessica. Really. Not pleasant. Lose some weight. I'm sure you'd be pretty if you'd only let people see you, and not just rolls of flesh.' Mummy had added, for good measure, 'Do try, dear. All that blubber – it's not nice to look at. No, really, it isn't. You're such a *glutton*. You can't always have what you want, Jessica. Life doesn't work like that.'

Well, fuck them.

I'd ignored them when they'd first left, and as good as forgotten them not long after.

We'd never been a tight, loving family unit. Now they were dead to me.

But I did, and with great pleasure, take advantage of the trust fund that they'd set up for me. Slowly but surely, I was literally eating into it. Daily. Every piece of food that I crammed into my mouth tasted somehow even more delicious because *they* were paying for it.

It was my habit, and had been for some years, to dine out alone at my favourite restaurant every night – except on the odd, rare occasion when I dined elsewhere.

As a thirty-year-old eligible, but very fat, single woman, I sometimes allowed myself to entertain thoughts of being noticed by a handsome young man and being asked to join him at his table.

It hadn't happened yet.

Last night, however, things had taken a turn from the ordinary feast fest, and dinner had become a very personal and very real nightmare.

Sitting at my table, tucking into my steak, salivating politely and discreetly gobbling, I'd glanced up at an unexpected noise. Two giggling, shrieking women and one beautiful man had taken a table next to me.

Engrossed as I was in my food, I still couldn't ignore them. They were loud. Drunk. Wrapped in raucous laughter as if their shared humour truly belonged to only them. Uncaring that their overly loud hilarity made heads turn, faces frown and eyes squint in outraged irritation. They remained oblivious, wrapped as they were, in their own beauty. Apparently, it made them immune to the rest of the world. Which wasn't news to me.

The two women fawned over the very handsome man, who lapped up the attention – clearly used to it and loving the adoration. He momentarily glanced my way and our eyes met. His face changed. And I knew, right then, that this wasn't going to be good.

I kept on eating, but my absorption in my meal was stained now with a familiar dread. Because I recognised what was coming from the beautiful man with the scathing expression.

I immediately hated one of the girls – the taller, skinnier one. All bones jutting out at awkward angles; an anatomical leafless tree. She was a collection of stick limbs. I thought she needed a bit of meat on her. To make her human. She smiled at me but the expression was drenched in disdain. I didn't bother returning the greeting. Head back down, I carried on chewing and waited for it to start.

The she-stick clapped her hands, getting the attention of the room, and whispered theatrically loudly so that the entire restaurant would hear her words. 'Wow. I mean, really, wow. Have you seen the size of her, Johnny?' She snorted and I could only imagine the face she'd have inevitably pulled. 'Looks like she's let herself go – just a smidge.'

Turning to glare at her, I saw Stick hold her hands out wide from her body and puffing her cheeks out, she mimicked the shape of me: as if I were a balloon.

At a disadvantage, knowing intuitively that I was now the

very public butt of the joke being played by the beautiful people, I endeavoured to refocus on my steak.

Stick laughed nastily, and Johnny rubbed his palms in pretend excitement. 'Ooh, yes.' I looked up at him and held his stare. Better to face it head-on. Pointing at me, he clicked his fingers repetitively, pretending difficulty at placing me. 'It's… I can't recall your name. Fatty Fatima, isn't it? No, that's not it.' He shook his head. 'Humungous Helen?'

I didn't answer. *They see me and all they see is a joke.* Putting my knife and fork down, I simply waited for the inevitable teasing to really kick in. From past experience, I knew it would gather an awful momentum, an impetus all of its own, and I waited for it to pick up speed.

The women, Stick and her equally slim twiglet-shaped friend, were manufactured and plastic-looking: their lips glossy and wet with anticipation. The female friends were like the mean girls found at every school. They had grown into mean women.

I tried to extricate a piece of steak that had wedged itself in between my teeth. Sucked frantically at it. But it was there to stay.

In my peripheral vision, I saw Johnny cup his perfect chin in strong muscular hands. 'I wonder if she's single. I mean, who'd go out with that? I know I wouldn't, that's for damned sure.'

The non-stick one, who looked as dumb as lettuce, said, 'You only like women my size, don't you, Johnny? *She's* gross.'

I kept my face straight, refusing to show any emotion. Listened to the growing hysterical glee of Stick's friend who laughed drunkenly, and pretended to ignore the look of… well, it could only be described as a horrified repugnance on Johnny's face as he gazed upon me. The women laughed more and more; waiters hovered – unsure whether to intervene. I

watched as Johnny theatrically clapped his two palms to the
side of his cheeks and started to laugh.

'She's a blimp, that's what she is.' He high-fived Stick.
'That's it. A great ginger balloon *blimp*. She's like *the* main
attraction. A walking, talking freak show.'

Stick said, 'She's *cir*cus fat. Do you think she even knows
that?' and took a long drink from her glass. The other girl
remained quiet. Perhaps she'd used up her repertoire of
joined-up sentences.

Johnny laughed and semi-stood, turning to the other guests,
as if in appeal. 'Have you *seen* this woman? Have you?' He
laughed, drunkenly loudly. 'She's so big, you could hardly miss
her.' Throwing back his head, he started making piggy noises.
Loud grunts and snorts.

Leaning on his table, he knocked a glass of wine over.
'Blimp should be ashamed of herself, sitting there, eating. Is
that all she does? Eat?'

'When will she stop? When she explodes?' Stick shrieked.

I turned to face my tormentors again, aware that the whole
dining room had stilled, forks were held suspended in mid-air:
some eyes were lowered, others blatantly stared. One woman
smiled at me. I didn't return it. I didn't want sympathy.

I wanted revenge.

Dumbo-girl made an effort and formed words which she
managed to spit out. 'How could she let herself get like that? It
can't have happened overnight.'

Johnny said, 'Because all she does is eat, that's why.' Now
he acknowledged my presence by addressing me directly. 'How
could you do that? You're disgusting. You dis*gust* me.'

A young man stood up at his table, his arm tugged frantically
by his partner. He shook her off, and spoke loudly to Johnny.
'Stop it. Leave her alone. How dare you speak to her like that.'

His face flushed and I could see my knight in shining

armour tremble as he stood, defiantly, fists balled at his sides. I smiled quickly in thanks although felt he'd only made me more of a living breathing display. Deeply humiliated by so many eyes on me, I momentarily dipped my own. Black shiny shoes and black trousered legs appeared in my line of vision, making a barrier between me and the beautiful people.

'Excuse me,' a blushing young waiter said to Johnny. 'I must ask you to leave.'

'Why's that then? We've hardly started. Our meal, I mean,' Johnny said and snickered, all round-eyed with innocence.

'You're upsetting our guests. I insist you leave.' The waiter stood firm and a fine sweat appeared on his upper lip.

Johnny threw back his chair and looked down at me. Quickly scanned the other diners' faces. For the most part, they looked quickly away, whilst the few and the brave blatantly stared back at him with unapologetic anger. He needed his adoring audience. Angry at the show of defiance from my small defence team, Johnny said to the waiter, his face pressed nose to nose with him, 'Fine. Who wants to eat here, anyway? The fat bitch has probably eaten the best of what you have to offer. Who wants scraps?' He laughed and Stick and Dumbo laughed along with him.

Loudly, the trio gathered their bags and mobiles and threw back their drinks.

Johnny's parting shot was hardly sophisticated, but it made his dwindling fanbase glower at him, safe in the knowledge that he was leaving. 'Bye-bye, fatty. You just carry on eating. Whatever I say, you will, anyway. Because you can't stop yourself. You're out of control.'

After they'd left, I did carry on eating, my face burning with shame.

I raised my head and was in time to see a man giving me a gentle look, his face wrinkled up with pity and sadness. He ventured a smile. It was meant to be kind but it was too little, too late. The damage had been done, and I vowed I'd make someone pay.

I picked up my fork and crammed in a deliberately large bit of meat, opening my mouth in an extra-large O-shape. Behaving as Johnny would have expected me to: like a sow, snuffling at my trough. Because I couldn't think of anything else to do.

I seethed. *Just wait and see. All of you in this restaurant, laughing at the fat bitch, laughing at* me *– I'll get my own Johnny-man, but he won't be cruel.*

Because I'll make *him love me.*

There and then, I swore that the first handsome man who showed me any kindness or showed some basic common decency, who dared to even *smile* at me, I'd pounce and if it killed me, I'd make him mine.

You can't always have what you want, that's what Mummy had always said.

I'd prove bloody Mummy wrong.

THREE

Max

Max went through life, easily and expertly, labelling people. It was more than a hobby. It was a natural gift and he prided himself in identifying and correctly pigeonholing people. It made life so much simpler.

For once you knew what they were, people were almost embarrassingly easy to engage with. And when Max used the word 'engage', he really meant that any of his stereotyped targets, once neatly categorised, could be manipulated. He was a master at it.

It was a knack.

Uniforms always helped. People, especially women – obviously his primary goal – saw a man in a uniform, any uniform, and failed to see *beyond* it. Saw only what it represented. A priest with his collar, a construction worker with his high-vis jacket. And women, *always*, without fail, fell for the 'oh-help-me-I'm-disabled' game. A well-placed bandage, crutches, a wheelchair, a white stick, a needy hopeful smile. The women thought *they* were saving *him*; the wounded little soldier. The irony killed him.

Women were a sucker for shit like that. The ones he

labelled as need-to-be-seen *doing the right thing*. They always fell for the 'Excuse me, Miss, would you mind helping? I can't, you see…' And Max would point out whatever his infirmity that day was, and they'd fall over themselves, desperate to help a person in distress. Thinking their good deed would be noticed and applauded.

And of course, there was the police uniform. Well, you could get away with bloody murder assuming that particular persona.

Over the years, he'd visited and purchased many costumes from various fancy-dress outlets. He didn't use the clothes as fancy dress: to Max they were props. He liked to be dressed appropriately and prepared for everything and anything. There was nothing *fancy* about it.

Max had been prepared to do the old copper routine with the deliciously fat woman who had waddled along the road this morning, looking extremely un-festive. Instead, she'd looked furious; her face screwed up like she was deep in thought. Thinking nothing good. He could change that.

But he'd realised he was without any obvious props. Was dressed only in his normal jeans and a T-shirt. Watching her for some time though, he was confident that he wouldn't need any uniform at all to convince her. He instantly recognised the type. Needy. Wanting attention. *Desperate* for any kindness thrown at her. He was prepared to give her some.

Keeping his speed to a minimum, he'd kerb-crawled behind the walking fat woman. Had pulled over and wound down his window. Asked for directions. Simple was always good.

Max liked his women fat. He liked women, full stop. But especially fat ones. It was his *thing*.

She'd been positively gushing in her efforts to help him. Had said she was going that way. To that very same road. *Yeah, right.* Had said to him, 'Perhaps it would be easier if I got in with you and pointed you in the right direction? I could *take* you there.'

He'd laughed. She'd laughed. It was a right laugh all round.

The real joke of it was that he reckoned she'd labelled *him* immediately. And more to the point, accurately. Tall, dark and handsome stranger. The stuff of dreams.

What a fool she was. She obviously had no idea that to him, she was just a number. Her name didn't matter in the slightest. Why would it? No subtle psychological grooming had been necessary, no coercion needed, no messy physical altercation with woman Number Eight. Just him. Doing what he did best. That usually did the trick anyway. The uniforms he used were a perk. For him. They gave him a strange power.

The woman had got in his car of her own free-will. She'd *leapt* in. He couldn't have stopped her even if he'd wanted.

Stupid bitch. Deserved whatever happened to her.

She hadn't stopped talking from the moment her fat arse had hit the passenger seat and she'd buckled up. Told him her name was Jessica, she was rich, had her own home, and most importantly – *she* thought – she was single. The bitch was actually expecting him to ask her out for a drink at the end of their destination. A meal, maybe. Certainly, a date of *some* description.

As a man, as an exceedingly *handsome* man, Max knew that every woman who was lucky enough to be serviced by him, would experience sex as if it were their first time. There were never any complaints in that department.

He liked to think that he gave his women the *Max*imum carnal treatment. He never failed to laugh and delight in the appropriateness of his name. *I am the Max.*

As proven with Jessica, he didn't always have to use any of his wardrobe repertoire: although he did like playing 'doctors' in the bedroom. Or sometimes, a butcher with a red-stained apron. It was testament to how truly irresistible he was that he could acquire women without any obvious disguise. Without having to put in any real effort.

He'd happily basked in the simple joy of being his natural, charming self with Jessica. Flashing his perfect smile at her, knowing his gold tooth would glint and catch her eye, he'd relaxed and laughed, not really listening to a word she'd said on their short car journey. His thick hair was attractive, he dressed well, his voice was well modulated and sexy.

God, I am great. *I've got it all. How can women resist me?*

This particular woman had been so grateful, so very relieved and thankful that he'd picked her up, that for a moment, he'd felt genuinely overwhelmed with his own virility and masculinity. He was irresistible.

Internally, he'd tuned out her ridiculous prattling and decided it would have been harder to pick up a dog.

She'd made no bones about wanting him.

And deliciously fat Jessica would certainly get him.

Although, not necessarily in the way she was imagining.

But because of her over-eagerness, when they'd got to his house, he had, on principle, left her upstairs in his room – which she'd tripped up in her excitement and haste to reach his bed – and then he'd left her there and let her wait.

He'd tied her, disappointingly easily, to the four corners of the bed. Thick rope bound her; her legs splayed. He'd left her dressed, with a gag in her mouth to drown out her screams for help.

She'd seemed let down, clearly and rabidly wanting him and making no attempt to pretend otherwise. But fear hadn't creased her face, cries and whimpers hadn't fallen from her gagged mouth. Instead, she'd appeared more disappointed than anything that he was leaving her alone in his room.

What is wrong *with her?*

Weirdly, and in truth, her total willingness to be completely obedient and unafraid of him, threw him a little. She'd showed none of the normal terror that he always instilled in his women, and she'd been more than prepared to go along with whatever plans he'd had in mind for her.

It had taken the fun out of it all.

Evidently, she wanted a boyfriend.

Stupid bitch.

Jessica wasn't girlfriend material.

More like a pet, really. A stray, kindly taken in. Temporarily. Nothing more than that.

She was already as good as dead.

After he'd played with her for however long he wanted.

Until he'd seen the whites of her eyes.

Then he'd dispose of her.

I am untouchable, invincible and incredible.

All the women I have murdered, will never be found.

I *will never be found.*

Because I am the best.

She'd disappear like all the others before her.

And good riddance.

FOUR

Jessica

S*hocked.* That was my over-riding emotion as I lay on the bed. Uncertainty at what lay ahead, at what Max might do to me. But I had something secret and powerful that Max didn't know I possessed. Having been teased by most people all of my life, I'd acquired the art of waiting and watching. And learning.

It held fear at bay. No, I was being modest. It did more than that – it made fear something I didn't experience.

The aim of most bullies was to embarrass, to provoke, to upset and to destroy with their unkindnesses. As with Johnny-man, with all of them, I'd found the easiest way to make it all stop and go away quickly, was to *not* give them what they wanted. To not show tears, nor any blushes. On the shaming night, I had carried on eating, accepting the piggy role as given to me by Johnny-man: I hadn't spoken, had given no fight – had just carried on shovelling in food, until it was over.

My throat mottled like a patchwork quilt with an ugly red blotching when I thought of it. Perspiration covered my fat body at the memory, and rivulets of sweat ran and pooled within the folds of my flesh.

Now, instinct and a sense of my own survival, made me aware, very quickly, that what excited and galvanised Max, was the showing of my fear. After we'd entered the bedroom; me, laughing and excited but apprehensive about sex, he'd growled. At first, I'd thought he'd been joking. But he hadn't been. He'd lunged at me, baring his teeth like a comic book monster.

He'd been trying to frighten me. It wasn't subtle, but he'd succeeded in startling me. Without thinking, and from years of habit, I'd automatically made my face go blank, forced my body not to react defensively and had tried to smile. At my non-expected response, his brain short-circuited. I'd taken away his pleasure and he'd immediately been confused. Allowing him to tie and gag me, putting up no resistance, I'd begun to see how to apply my years of torment from all my bullies. Not giving them what they so desired, ultimately made their goal pointless.

Max had clearly wanted, *needed*, to see me scared. Instead, I'd given him calm and willing. It was this ability to read others, my first-hand knowledge of being a victim of beautiful people, that had saved me so far. I'd carry on with this plan of attack as it appeared to be my only option.

I knew, because I wasn't bloody stupid, that I'd come across as desperate when I'd allowed him to pick me up. *I picked him up, let's not be coy.* Far too needy and naked in my ambition to get my man, I'd behaved like a teenager. So over-excited when the handsome man in the car had stopped and asked for directions. Unable to contain my excitement and what I'd viewed as a huge piece of luck, I'd thrown myself at him.

Now, I found myself playing prisoner. With an unpredictable man. But I gave myself a break, recognising the whole situation had been driven by my more desperate self, behaving as if I'd been a truly inexperienced adolescent who'd been tricked by a grown-up. But I refused to beat myself up about my lack of experience – it wasn't my fault I had none when it came to men.

At the moment, all I had was the desire to get out of this alive.

My own stupidity didn't mean I deserved to be treated like this, however. Leaving me tied to the bed and gagged wasn't funny. But I'd *allowed* him to tie me, remained uncomplaining and smiling, even as he'd shoved a cloth into my mouth. My throat had dry clicked: it was difficult to swallow, and I'd concentrated on diluting and eliminating the panic that swelled in my throat. But I'd *permitted* it. I knew that. He didn't. That gave me an element of control that he wasn't aware of.

Instinctively, I'd known that I had to play along. I *had* to. Max's rules, obviously, until I got a better handle on the situation. Anger from the shaming still consumed me, and I was damned if I'd let any man get the better of me again. This time I was better prepared. Johnny-man had been my catalyst, and I thanked him silently for his brutality. It had given me the wherewithal to combat Max.

Because of the rage I had, I knew Max had underestimated me. Feeling as I did: shocked, livid and *indignant* – those emotions allowed me to be pretty damned sure that he'd bitten off far more than he could chew. He'd be sorry he'd treated me like this. Very, very sorry. I might be fat, but I sure as hell wasn't a welcome mat to cruelty, to be trampled upon by every man I met. It was enough. *I'd* had enough.

If I worked it all out properly and prepared mentally, I could turn this situation to my advantage. I needed to play it just right. Against all the odds, I might even win.

I could change this man. I knew that was the premise upon which many women worked: a fundamental belief that they could sculpt and whittle away at a bad man, and make him a good man. The concept worked for me. By changing him, improving him, I could ultimately make him mine. Forever.

That was my plan. I hoped it would work – there was no plan B.

FIVE

Max

H e'd waited long enough. He couldn't put it off any longer. Normally with his lady abductees, the whole performance, from pick-up to death, was a couple of hours. Tops. There was no need to draw it out. Max had honed his artistry to a tightly organised two-hour block of ecstasy.

Now, it annoyed him that he was experiencing a strange and unexpected... *unease* – that was the only word he could come up with. Normally, this was show-time. Going into the captured woman's room, and relishing, bloody re-lish-*ing*, their fear was the high point. It's what it was all about. It was what he enjoyed the most: their fear, their horror, their begging and bleating, their bloody great struggle to survive.

When he took the gag off, the great intake of breath as they prepared to scream, to shout, to fucking bellow, that's what he lived for. And then of course his hand would clamp over their mouths, locking the noise in forever. That was by far the best bit. The bit he really loved and craved. It made him feel good. Better than good. It made him feel alive.

Instinctively, Max was having to re-label Jessica without actually seeing her, as she'd lain upstairs for the whole day.

He'd gone over, again and again, her weird lack of terror when he'd tied her to the bed. Gagged her mouth to stop the screams, which he knew weren't going to come. A sort of calmness clung to her. Like she was fucking used to being kidnapped by men. Like it was all very normal.

He *always* loved the terror from the women he got. It was the whole fucking point. How dare she ruin it for him?

She hadn't even pre*tend*ed to be frightened of him.

So, now he worried this time, this woman, would be different. When he saw her again, he'd have to re-categorise her. He knew intuitively that she was trouble and for a more thorough pigeonholing, he needed more time with her. Face to face. She was complicated and he didn't want to get it any more wrong than he already felt he had.

Max was pissed off.

He hoped he hadn't made a serious bloody mistake with this one.

It was nearly midnight. Max hoped the bitch hadn't pissed herself. He sure as shit wasn't up for changing the sheets. Briefly, he wondered what uniform to put on. Something frightening. He toyed with the butcher's bloodied apron, but his very presence was normally enough to get the desired effect when the time came: total fear – what*ever* he wore. The clothes were obviously just for fun: to deceive, to enthral, to initially capture. But he conceded that this time, he'd feel better if he put a bit more thought into the whole thing than he normally did.

A policeman's uniform was way too authoritarian: not what he was after. A bricklayer, a plumber, a physical trainer? All of them complete with his own muscles on display. A construction worker? *Nah.* None of them was quite right. He tutted and clenched his fists in irritation, temporarily stumped. Jessica would approve of a virile, masculine type, although little acting was required for him there. It was almost too easy for him to be manly. No fun, but she'd managed to suck all the joy out of things so far, so he modified his expectations.

His mother had left Max and his dad soon after his birth, and even though Dad was okay, Max had secretly realised he'd always been the man of the house. He'd taken it one step further. Now he was man of the world. And Jessica needed to understand that. You didn't fuck with a real man.

Feeling more confident, more himself, Max finally decided on the surgeon-in-scrubs outfit. He prepared a metal trolley on wheels, just for a laugh, with medical-looking instruments on it, although the gleaming steel blades were all for show: bought from a toy shop. He had no intention of cutting her. Not his style.

Strangulation was more his thing. It was the feel of his hands on the flesh of their throats that he really loved. How much more intimate a thing could you do?

Still feeling strangely apprehensive but faking a confidence that for the first time was wavering, he put on his blue V-neck cotton short-sleeved top, blue baggy trousers and white clogs. He rolled up the cuff of his top, snugly tight against his shoulder to better show off his biceps. Chicks were a sucker for a bit of rippling flesh. Checking that his knife was strapped to his ankle, he was good to go. He slipped his camera into his pocket then picked up the tool-laden trolley, lifted it and slowly walked up the stairs.

Ignoring the fact that he didn't feel as powerful, nor as excited as he normally did.

He told himself, *I'll show the bitch. I'll bloody show her. Just wait and see.*

Before opening the door, he pulled up his surgical mask which covered his nose and mouth. Wanting to startle her, to make her jump as Dad had made him jump as a boy, to really freak her out and take her by surprise, he threw open the door so hard that it bounced back against the wall with a loud cracking sound. Shouting, he walked briskly into the room, letting go of the trolley and laughing as it clattered across the floor. A triple whammy of noise.

Emergency, emergency coming through here. Stand back, Dr Max to the rescue. 'I'm here, Jessica. Miss me? Did you miss me?' He delighted as she visibly jumped although flat on her back, her eyes rounding and bulging with shock. He couldn't miss the flash of white in her eyes. There. Nothing to worry about after all. She *was* frightened.

He grinned and swelled with his own power. His body reacted physically; growing hard at her helplessness, he forced himself to breathe deeply. No need to hurry. He had all night. Forgetting that he'd been cautious of her, he moved quickly to the base of the bed and stood over her. Pulled down his face mask. Took her gag out. Took his camera from his pocket and pointing it at her face, said, 'Say cheese.'

Her face had taken a while to recover from the brutality of his entrance and she'd swallowed several times – clearly trying to find some saliva. Having seen the camera, her face showed the opposite expression to what he'd been expecting. The response he'd always got from the others. Terror at what lay ahead.

Instead, she smiled.

A calm, relaxed, and he had to admit, rather beautiful, soft smile lit up her face.

The camera wavered in his hands, but he clicked anyway and then tossed it aside. She'd ruined it all with her wrong expression.

Right then and there, his erection withered and disappeared. The life and blood drained from his penis, like a balloon deflating, leaving a wrinkled piece of shrivelled skin. It died right there inside his blue cotton scrubs. With no working tool, he faltered.

Still smiling, Jessica said, 'You took your time. I've been

waiting hours for you. But at least you're here now.' Her appreciative glance swallowed him up whole. All she looked was greedy. Greedy for him. 'You're very handsome. I'm flattered that you picked me.'

Max was completely thrown. *Is she mad? I've tied her to the bed* and *gagged her. What is she expecting? Dinner and a show?*

He knew that his initial labelling of her had been correct: she was needy and wanted a boyfriend. But he was also horribly aware that he'd missed something else about her. She wouldn't be leaving before he'd correctly labelled her.

Standing over her, he was unsure what to do next. At this point, there was usually a lot of snivelling from his female hostage; tears would be spilling from her eyes, and her lips would be trembling. *This* reaction was all wrong. It made him nervous and unsure.

He watched as she licked her dry lips. 'Why don't you come and sit down on the bed, Max. Here, next to me. We can talk. Or we can do whatever you want to do – either way, I'm game.' Her grin got bigger and his dick got smaller.

He knew then that he would not get to see the whites of her eyes again. Not tonight, not with this one.

Completely unnerved, he wanted to slap her, needing her to be frightened. Her calmness confused him. His mind flew around his head, trying to find something to hold on to, trying desperately to regain control. This had never happened before.

He closed his eyes, striving to recall, word for word, exactly what Dad had always said. It wasn't difficult – he'd heard it almost daily for as long as he could remember. 'You are the best, my little man. My big *strong* Max. You can do anything. Anything at all. My beautiful, beautiful boy. No woman will ever be good enough for you, Max, and don't you ever forget that.'

Yes, no woman will ever *be good enough for me. I bloody* can *do anything. Why am I worrying? It's just some stupid bitch – no different from any of the others.*

Planting his legs further apart, bending his knees against the bed frame, he thrust his groin into her face, and made himself laugh. Ignored the hollow ring it had to it and the way it echoed emptily around him. 'Undo my scrubs. I know you want to. Pull the cord. Right here.'

Her smile put him off. Changing his mind, he instead decided to untie one of her arms. Thinking that she'd plead for him to stop, beg him not to hurt her, hit out at him pathetically and weakly – and so get his dick working again – he was bewildered that she smiled more broadly than ever before. Hoping that her stupid smile would break in two as it stretched right across her face, he still felt no stirring of life in his groin.

Fury took over and he welcomed it. Leaving her arm free, he threw himself on top of her, pinning her to the bed. The feeble beating of her arm against his muscular back never came. Instead, he felt her fingers as she snaked them around his shoulders, drawing him closer, pulling him tightly to her around the back of his neck, fucking *hugging* him to her. What was the bitch doing?

She made a soft sort of noise which threw him further into downright fucking panic, not knowing how to deal with her. She whispered in his ear. 'Come on, Max. Please. I'm yours. I'll do anything you want.'

That's when he slapped her. Not that hard – more of a way of silencing her, than with any intent to knock her out. Although that was tempting. Her hand flew to her cheek, cupping the instant pinkness that spread across her face. 'There was no need for that, Max. What are you thinking? I'm here. You're here. Let's have some fun.'

His equipment had never failed him before. He'd *never* not been able to get it up. Not ever. Not in his entire bloody life. It was all her fault. His cock had always been his weapon. Now he imagined that he could actually *hear* it, as it seemed to scream out its failure, as it dangled pathetically in between his legs. Soft. Completely bloody flaccid. He hoped to fuck it was a one-off.

Max rolled off her and sat with his back to her and felt like weeping.

It was too late to use his knife. He often used it because he liked to threaten with it – not because he wanted to actually cut his women. Max wasn't overly fond of blood.

Instead, turning quickly, lunging, he thrust his hands towards her and tightened them around her neck, and felt a bit better. A bit more bloody normal.

But she wouldn't stop looking at him – her big brown eyes fixed on his. Slowly she blinked.

And then she fucking smiled again.

When he kidnapped women, Max thought of it as a three-course meal. There was the starter: the initial pick-up; the beginning of the entire proceedings. Jessica had already ruined that – she'd picked *him* up.

Then, and obviously this was a given, there was the main course. The one around which the whole meal revolved. It was the time for the frightening of Max's guest – that's what really got his juices flowing, and was the highlight of the whole event. The raping of a terrified woman – the cherry on the cake.

Jessica had denied him all of that, with her cooing and clucking. Put him right off: destroyed his ever-ready tool. So, even a quick rape was a total bloody write-off.

Normally, everything was finished off with pudding. 'You can't leave the table until you've finished pudding,' his dad always said. Simple as that. It was the very literal finishing off – the end of, the stopping of the latest woman: the final goodbye to a time enjoyed together as he strangled her.

And now he couldn't even finish his fucking pudding. There *was* no pudding.

All because of *her*.

He couldn't really get going on strangling her properly. His heart wasn't in it. And it was her stupid smile that stopped him squeezing tighter, and he eventually stopped – all pleasure gone.

She wouldn't even let him enjoy killing her.

Selfish bitch.

Max didn't know what to do next.

It wasn't fair.

His skin goose-pimpled as he felt her free hand clasp itself around his wrist. 'Don't worry, Max. We'll be okay. You and me. Don't worry. Honest. We'll be just fine. We'll work it out – just you see.'

'What the bloody hell is wrong with you?' he said, his voice flat. He could hear the confusion and deflation in his own voice. 'I've kidnapped you. Why aren't you frightened?'

'Have you kidnapped me, Max? Have you, really? Perhaps I've kidnapped you.'

As he sat on the edge of the bed, he felt himself become ghostlike, as if he'd lost his whole personality in one go. The very core of himself – the very thing that made him Max, had deserted him. She'd stripped him of his identity.

He panicked. *Who am I?*

SIX

Jessica

'I'm here, Jessica. Miss me? Did you miss me?'

I'd almost suffered a cardiac event when he'd burst through the door. Sleep had been coming and going, dragging me under for a minute, and then releasing me abruptly back into life.

After slapping me, he'd seemed confused, as if everything wasn't going to plan. I didn't know what had been going through his mind, but I realised I'd stopped him dead. Brought him up short. That was my plan. *Change how he sees me.*

I believed it had worked. Finishing off his weird little macho display, dressed up in his theatre gown, I'd rounded off the new game I'd started, with, 'Don't worry, Max. We'll be okay. You and me. Don't worry. Honest. We'll be just fine. We'll work it out – just you see.'

He'd looked like a boy. A child. A child on the verge of crying, having not got his way. That, in itself, gave me strength.

See. I might be inexperienced in the ways of men, but I'm no fool.

'Perhaps I've kidnapped you.' That had been my finest line, and he'd looked broken by my words. Startled, but most definitely broken. Now, I really had the opportunity to take advantage of his wavering and fast-disappearing confidence. Time to start changing him for the better.

I had the time to ponder how a man could seem so in control, so very manly, when in fact, at this very moment, it certainly appeared that he was as frail as me. But I had the upper hand. Because he hadn't seen it coming.

I had always seen humiliation and failure coming my way. But this was the first time I'd been prepared and been able to pre-empt it. Without even meaning to, I was the one humiliating *him*.

When Max had first burst into the room, throwing his medical trolley rattling across the floor, I could hardly fail to see the bulge in his trousers. Equally, I couldn't fail to notice that when he'd said, 'Undo my scrubs,' his trousers had been without any bulge. For which I'd been eternally grateful. I knew he was expecting oral sex and I'd found the idea repellent having never taken a penis in my mouth before.

Plus the obvious fact that I had no idea *how* to suck a dick – it had never come up before, and I'd no idea where to start. Our relationship, when the time was right, would be sexual – of course it would. I wasn't *frigid*, for God's sake. But sucking his dick would not immediately be added to my 'to-do' list. I assumed it wasn't dissimilar to sucking an ice lolly, but less cold on the teeth.

It astonished me how easy it had been to avoid immediately succumbing to Max's behaviour. Were all handsome men this easy to manipulate, or had I just got lucky? Perhaps I should have done this years ago – got myself my own Johnny-man instead of waiting for a miracle to happen. If it was as easy as it so far had been, it irritated that I'd been so unconfident as to not be more assertive before this.

But here was my chance. I was giddy with my own success and amazed at my coolness in what had most definitely been a high-risk situation. Having diffused any immediate danger, I put my mind to what I did best. Still lying with one hand and two legs tied to the bed, I said, 'Would you do me a favour, Max?' I talked to his hunched and I hoped, still defeated back. 'I need a pee. You left me for ages, after all.' Waiting, giving it several seconds, I got no reply. 'And then, maybe, we could get something to eat? I'm starving.'

Suggesting something as normal as a meal, I hoped would set the scene for a cosier mood – with no threat of violence. Perhaps he'd realise that I was worth being nice to.

To my relief, he finally shrugged and wordlessly untied me, led me down the hall and opened the door to a small lavatory. 'I'll be here when you're finished.'

Rustling up a giggle I patted my hair. 'I wouldn't expect you to be anywhere else, Max.'

I clasped his elbow as I squeezed past him.

As I pulled down my knickers and squatted over the lavatory, it occurred to me.

Maybe he picked me because *I'm fat. Maybe he really is* the one.

My smile broadened – it had never been bigger nor happier.

SEVEN

Max

As Max had stood outside the bog waiting for Jessica, he'd considered killing her straight away. It would have been so easy to strangle her as soon as she'd stepped out into his waiting arms. Strangled her where she'd stood. Just to make it all go away.

But he'd stopped himself because he'd known that he'd have been killing her for all the wrong reasons: murdering out of fury and his own inadequacy. And there was no triumph in that.

She'd have won if he'd given into the temptation to end it all there and then.

Because he wouldn't have enjoyed it without her fear. Her death would have been on her terms. Pride wouldn't allow him to do that. He refused to be beaten by her.

And so he'd brought her down to the kitchen. Let her nose around in the fridge. Of course it was full. Dad had been around yesterday and brought him supplies. He always did. 'Just looking after my bestest boy,' he'd say. He'd come every two or three days – asked or not. Max didn't think he needed looking after but wasn't about to turn his nose up at free food. He wasn't a fool. Knew he was on to a good thing.

Initially, he'd hovered at Jessica's shoulder, but quickly realised there was no need to guard her. If anything, he'd have trouble getting *rid* of her. And he knew he couldn't do that. She might report him if he let her go. He smiled to himself. *I might fucking report* her *if* she *doesn't go.*

He couldn't believe the position he was in.

She'd opened the fridge, seeing what was available. He pointed at a Tupperware dish.

'What is it?' she'd asked.

'I haven't checked. It'll be one of Dad's stews I expect. Heat that up.'

'No, that's okay. I'll cook something special. Just for us.'

This whole set-up: a woman cooking for him, busying herself around the kitchen as if it were all very familiar and she belonged there, all this was very new. Only his dad cooked for him – if he couldn't be arsed to do it himself. He didn't even have to ask nicely. Dad would always offer to cook for him. *Because I'm his little Max.*

This was different though. Very different. He was at a disadvantage, as he assumed she was used to cooking for and feeding her men. Used to this cosy scene.

Why is she so desperate then? Is she desperate for all men, or is it only me?

That thought made him instantly feel better. That must be it. It was *him*. All women wanted him and that was a fact. He allowed himself to relax.

'Got any soya sauce, Max?'

'Somewhere in there. No…' He pointed. 'That cupboard.'

'I'm just throwing everything into a pan – bit of a one-pot wonder type of thing. That suit?'

'Yeah, whatever.'

It was like she was suddenly fucking living here with him.

As if this was some nice little domestic scene. He shivered.

'Cold?' she asked.

She didn't miss a trick, this one. Watching her move smoothly around the room, calm and confident, doing something which she was obviously good at, he thought she was a sly one. Definitely needed to keep a very close eye on her. Find out what made her tick.

Jessica wasn't normal. That much he already knew.

Sitting at the table, he opened a bottle of beer. Didn't bother offering her one. Kidded himself he was biding his time, not afraid of her at all. All he needed was to find a chink in her personality. A weakness which he could exploit. Because that's what he did best, and all women had weaknesses. And plenty of them. It was just a question of finding and identifying them correctly.

At the moment, he was struggling. Breathing deeply, he got a grip of himself. 'Cook for all your boyfriends, do you? Why do you do that? To fatten them up?'

With her back to him, he could see her body tense. So, there you go, she was paranoid about being fat. That was something worth knowing but wasn't the greatest bloody revelation going. Most women didn't like being fat.

They didn't know that's precisely how he liked them.

She didn't answer but started humming instead. He gritted his teeth in annoyance.

'Had many boyfriends, Jess?'

'Not loads, no. How about you?' She laughed. 'I mean girlfriends.'

He laughed too, pretending to join in this happy romance. Simultaneously, he fisted his hands under the table. Not ready yet to show he still had every intention of inflicting violence on her. When *he* was ready. When it was right.

His brain worked busily, attempting to get a handle on her.

Shrugging, he answered her. 'Girlfriends? Me?' He made

himself holler loudly. 'Whoa. Too many to count, babe.' Holding his arms out on either side of his body, he waved his hands at himself. 'Look. What's not to love? Have to beat women off with a bloody stick.' He leered. 'Keep your eyes on the prize, hun.'

'Why did you pick me up then?'

'I didn't. I asked for directions, and you took it from there. You said so, yourself. *You* picked *me* up. Not the other way round. And don't you forget that.'

She turned and looked him square in the face. 'Oh, I don't forget anything, Max. You'll discover that, once we get to know each other better. I never forget a thing.'

Her words chilled him. His cock turned itself inside out, cowering and completely fucking disappearing. Angry, he stood. Did something Max-like. Strode over to her and took her chin in his hand. Made his fingers pinch her double chin. Forced his nails into her flesh. Hurt her. 'Don't push your luck, Jessica. Don't try being all clever with me. You can't outsmart me, so don't even try, because you'll lose.'

Squeezing her skin tightly, he watched her wince. Keeping her head in a fixed position, she had no choice but to look him straight in the eye. She didn't blink. Neither did he. And belatedly discovered he was playing some stupid bloody childish game of 'who blinks first, loses'. Opening his eyes wider, he glared at her, expecting her to dip her gaze. But she didn't. Just glared straight back at him. All the time, with that fucking smile plastered over her stupid face. He was tempted to knock it off but was concentrating on not blinking. Feeling a fool even as he did so.

And knowing that he'd lose.

There was something about this particular bitch that was beginning to completely weird him out.

His eyes started watering.

He blinked.

She smiled.

'Ready to eat now, Max? I found some chocolate éclairs in the back of the fridge. You must have known I was coming.'

Angling away from her so she wouldn't catch the bewilderment which he knew was spoiling his handsome face, he was unexpectedly struck with a thought. *Play to your strengths. Don't let her get to you. Don't lose your nerve.* He turned back and made himself soften his face. 'Give us a kiss, Jess.'

She didn't need telling twice. Swivelling her head, stirring spoon still in hand, she turned her expectant face to his: her lips parted, her eyes semi-closed in anticipation.

He wasn't overly confident with this scene: the promise of sex being so easily given up by the woman. He only liked *taking* it. It was all the better the more the woman *didn't* want to give it up. But he worked with what he had.

Smirking now, he bent forward and then abruptly swerved her pursed up ready-to-kiss lips – making a point of it. Left her hanging in the air, mouth waiting: she actually tottered forward – off balance. Her expression of dismay wasn't as good as fear, but it was a start. In that moment, he caught her expression like a photographic snap: disappointment. She was *upset*. Caught on the hop and emotionally flat-footed.

This was definitely moving in the right direction.

She was dis*gustingly* desperate. For *him*. She really truly wanted him and only him.

That was her frailty.

He knew instinctively that if he played along, pretended he really liked her, she wouldn't say 'no' to him. Not ever. He was sure of it. She'd do anything for him. And that made him wonder how far she would *actually* go – when push came to shove. He'd labelled her correctly after all, but had missed the fact that she was a complete whack-job. For reasons which he didn't yet know, she had picked him, and wasn't about to let go. She'd decided. Her decision was him.

Plenty of fun and games to be had here. Lots of options.

Instantly, Max was back in control.

He'd made progress. But her despair and unhappiness at his refusal to kiss her, wasn't the same as making her frightened. That still remained his ultimate goal.

Now he knew her weaknesses better, had re-categorised her as fixated on him – *and who could fucking blame her?* – he was sure he could attain that goal. She needed a little work, but he'd have her eventually. On his terms.

Having come off a six-night graveyard shift, he now had a week off. The week before Christmas. Yesterday had been day one. Plenty of time to sort out Jess. One way or another.

If all else failed, he could always kill her. Only if everything went tits-up.

He was confidently back in the driving seat: all systems go.

Knowing it would be rude, considering the bitch was cooking, he took a chocolate éclair from the fridge and swallowed it in one. Wiping the cream from his lips, deliberately licking every finger in the most sexual way possible, he turned away from her, dismissing her again.

Keep her keen. Keep her wanting more. No probs there.

He smiled to himself, delighted to have caught that momentary sadness on her face when he'd swerved her lips. It had made her more beautiful in that one moment. Made her almost perfect. Her pathetic-ness almost turned him on. But not quite.

Not as much as her terror would, but it was enough to be getting on with.

Back on fucking track now.

Maybe this could still work.

But it would be different this time.

He could do different.

Different was his middle name.

EIGHT

Barry

B arry had always been proud of his Max. His son had never been anything other than the perfect child, the perfect boy and was now the perfect man. Barry never stopped bragging about his son: the best thing in his life by a long shot. There was nothing that could beat that very special bond they had. They were kindred spirits and Max belonged to Barry. Like father, like son.

Max's useless mother had done a runner not long after giving birth to her baby. Said she was just popping out for a packet of fags, and she'd never returned. Barry was better off without the slag – he'd said it then, and still thought it now. With the cheap tart gone, that only meant even more time for him and Max. It was a chance that Barry had grabbed with both greedy hands. He'd swallowed up his son with fatherly love. And pride. Lots and lots of pride.

With no woman about the place, Barry had had to be both disciplinarian and care-giver. Secretly, he'd loved every minute of it and didn't feel any less of a man for his obsession with his son.

Barry had invented the White Eye game to keep Max

under control as he developed from young boy to teenager. Barry had nipped misbehaviour in the bud before Max had a chance to even think about being bad. 'If you're a naughty boy, Max, you know what? I'll frighten you to death until you're a good boy.' He'd smiled when he'd said it, and Max had understood. Quickly.

It was better this way. This way, Barry didn't have to raise his hand to the boy to discipline him. That would have been too easy. Something in Barry made him think that beating a child wasn't right. His game was much better. Much more effective. Much more thrilling.

For both of them.

The full title of the game was the 'Whites of Their Eyes'. It had been a good game. The first and only rule was to make his son frightened. Easy enough. At any given time, he'd jump out at his unsuspecting child, shouting at the top of his voice, 'I'm coming to get you. Here I come, you bad, bad boy.' Barry would hide behind doors, hide behind closed curtains, hide behind leafy shrubs on the path up to the house, and surprise Max by jumping out and bellowing at him. His favourite place to conceal himself was under his son's bed and he'd grab Max's ankles, shouting, 'Gotcha. There – I can see the whites of your eyes.'

Barry had found it very satisfying.

With the fat slag long gone, Barry, in sole care of his son, had gone to his GP, who was aware and congratulatory that he was bringing up Max alone. Barry had learnt a lot from his GP, and when he'd taken in Max for one of his very early post-natal checks, Barry's eyes had been opened. The doctor had held Max's tiny form, and whilst still cradling him, had then dropped him in mid-air, catching him before he'd fallen more than an inch in his arms. Barry had shouted angrily, and the doctor had explained that he was only carrying out necessary tests. He'd added that there were only two real basic human fears: the fear of falling and the fear of loud noises. Babies had both. Max had reacted normally to the two tests.

Any other fear was learnt, the doctor explained further.

If it was good enough for his GP, it was good enough for Barry. The fear of unexpected loud sound. He'd tried it out on Max.

Turned out, his doctor was completely right. When Barry shouted at Max, it did make him frightened. It worked. It was great. It was Barry's way of being the right sort of father, creating the right sort of boy.

Once he'd seen the white of Max's eyes, Barry had made it all better by hugging his son tightly to him, squeezing the air out of the boy's tiny chest. Holding him close to his own body, feeling his son's breath gasping, he'd tell Max how much he loved him. Loved him to bits. Told him what a real little man he was.

Max had learnt pretty quickly not to fuck with his old dad. Barry had frightened the bad and the naughtiness right out of him. He'd done a good job of it too, if he did say so himself.

But Barry hadn't raised a stupid boy. He'd raised a boy who'd become an admirable man. A strong, tough man. A real man's man.

That's my *boy.*

Anyway, it had all worked out for the best. Barry had tired of the game, as it had worked a treat and there was no point in continuing to play it just for the sake of it. He had succeeded in instilling structure and obedience, and now his Max was the most well-adjusted man he knew.

He had it all, and Barry felt he'd been repaid as a father, in full.

It had always been like that. The two of them together – inseparable. The child had never wanted for anything, because Barry had given him everything he could possibly want. Whether he could afford it or not. It had been tough. Barry had been forced to give up his lorry driving to look after his son, and they'd scraped through life surviving on benefits. But it had all been worth it.

Max's first legal drink at the pub at the age of eighteen with his father, had been a real joy. A coming together of young and old, naïve and experienced in the ways of the world. They'd sat together at a bench outside, and Barry had said, 'See those four girls over there? Look at the two fat ones. That's what your mother looked like. I know I've never shown you photographs because I got rid of them all, but that's what she looked like. Just like those fat ones. A useless fat slag.'

His son's eyes had stared, his eyebrows lifted a little. 'Really?'

'Yeah, really. And don't forget, she left us. You and me, both. We're better off without her though, right?'

Max hadn't really responded, had only carried on gazing at the girls and sipping his pint.

Barry had felt uncomfortable with his son's disinterest and leaning in close, he'd said, 'Why haven't you ever asked about your mother before? I've sort of been waiting for the question.'

Max had looked at Barry, his face unreadable. He'd shrugged. 'What's the point? She's not here. So what?'

Looking at his beautiful son's blank face, Barry had nodded. 'Yeah, right. So what?'

Something in Max's lack of interest, briefly chilled Barry. But then he reminded himself: *My son is a* real *man. He's tough and mean, like I taught him to be. Bloody women. They're more trouble than they're worth.* And his son was beautiful and brave. He'd be a real lady-killer when he grew up.

Later, out of a sense of duty, Barry had shown Max the one picture of his mum, that he'd kept – in case Max had ever asked. Mainly to show what his son *wasn't* missing. Max had stared at the old photograph, had studied it carefully, and shrugging, had given it back. Barry had burnt it and wondered why he'd bothered.

Now that Barry was an older man, living on his own, he needed and missed his son more and more. Relied on his presence. And Max never failed him, always making sure that he was there for his father.

Max liked to look after and include his old dad – although Barry wasn't *that* old. Not by a long shot. But he was lonely without Max. Not that he ever admitted that. He was a man, and men don't complain. So it was nice, just knowing Max was there. Waiting to help, if it was help Barry wanted.

Which was rare.

Like never.

I am the father and I *do the mentoring, the sheltering, the helping-out. Even the caring. Because that's my job. That's what a good strong father does.*

Barry knew that he'd smothered Max in love, and what the bloody hell was wrong with that? Max was his son. His possession. Barry had taught him everything he knew. Especially about women. The slags. Better off without them.

Max belonged to Barry and always would.

Barry was proud that he had always, and still did, make sure Max was okay. Nothing was too much trouble. Anything to make him happy. After all, it was his job, his *duty*, to make sure his son was happy and well fed and had clean clothes and a tidy home. Obviously, without his slag of a wife, and in charge of a baby, Barry had learnt quickly how to cook. But he was also always on hand for the manly stuff: fixing a broken tap, redecorating a tired old room, repairing a broken cupboard. Always eager and grateful for a man-to-man chat with his offspring.

He even had his own personal key to his son's house now, which Max had given to him so Barry could pop in and out as he pleased and make sure that everything that Max could possibly want, was there, on hand, waiting. He never went without. Not with his old dad around. Keeping his eyes firmly on Max was a pleasure and most definitely not a chore. It was a privilege and one that Barry took very, very seriously.

Barry adored Max. And he didn't give a rat's arse what other people thought of his devotion. He'd created a man in his own image – what was there to be ashamed of?

Bugger all.

Max never actually thanked his dad. For anything. Max was his own man, but Barry knew that his son wouldn't be the man he was, if it hadn't been for his old dad's input.

Barry wanted to boast to everyone when Max had got that special job. It was a great job – a job with bloody knobs on. Something to really brag about. But Max had told him to keep schtum, so Barry kept his lips buttoned. Bursting inside with pride that he had to keep to himself. It was a secret he kept with his son, and he was happy to be included. All the intrigue, the hurried and hushed mum's-the-word nature of Max's work – it excited both of them and he'd sit for hours, if Max had the time, and listen to his son as he told him the more dangerous and riskier aspects of his work. Who'd have thought he'd go and get himself a grand job like that. Barry was so impressed it took his breath away.

And of course, it was important to Barry, that Max found himself a nice young woman to share his successful life with.

Not a fucking slag like his mother had been.

But Max was very private about his love life. It was funny that. The fact that he'd never introduced any girlfriends to Barry. Not even once. Perhaps he was shy. Perhaps he knew that they would never be good enough, could never match up to his own perfection. Or perhaps he simply hadn't found Miss Right yet. There were an awful lot of slags to sift through, that was for sure.

Maybe he didn't want to make his old dad feel left out and abandoned.

But of course Barry would never be left out, because Max would always need him.

Max would always be the best thing Barry had ever done. And his son would never desert him, whether he found himself a slag or not.

Barry would always be there to support his son, and would happily die for him.

NINE

Jessica

I felt myself slip into my new role as *pretend girlfriend*. Not dissimilar to putting on a new dress in front of my bedroom mirror and luxuriating in its fit as it clung to my curves, smoothed down by my pudgy fingers. Obviously, that had always been a private performance: unseen by anyone else.

But this time, my display was public. Max was my audience. I allowed my new persona to sit tightly and snugly around me, as if it truly belonged. It was surprisingly easy: I was the perfect size for it.

It hadn't been as hard as I'd thought – the transition from going to the loo, to cooking merrily in the kitchen. But I wasn't a fool. Knew I was still on a very slippery surface with Max.

I thought I'd broken him; but I wasn't stupid enough to think, entirely. Not even nearly. I had some serious work to do still. He hadn't disintegrated into anything even remotely resembling submission – but he was definitely not as cocksure as he had been. And that was obviously a good thing. For me. It meant progress.

It had all been going so well. I'd felt in control in the kitchen: cutting, chopping, dicing, slicing. And then he'd mentioned the word 'fat'. Asking about my boyfriends, asking if I liked to *fatten them up*. It had been uncalled for. Intentionally cruel. I didn't have to remind myself that I was new to all this, but I'd still been taken aback by his unpredictable venom. He'd been violent in the bedroom, but not spiteful. I'd been shocked by it, as was his intent.

Humming, I'd pretended to ignore him. Breathed deeply. Tried not to think of spiteful Johnny-man. Hoping this wouldn't all run away from me before I had the opportunity to grab the reins tightly in my hands and steer the play. For play it was.

I absolutely refused to give any ground now that I was nearly winning this battle. Knowing I'd unnerved him in the bedroom, gave me the confidence to carry on cooking – *I'm fine. Absolutely bloody fine. I am in control. And I am worth it.*

And then, the nearly-kiss. That had threatened to derail me completely. I'd felt such a fool. He'd caught me off guard, and I'd allowed myself to really believe that he liked me. That he really wanted to kiss me.

What a bastard.

And what an idiot I was to think it would be *that* easy. Nothing in life was ever that simple or clear cut. I'd never got what I'd wanted without hard work.

Max had left me there, like some acne-pocked virgin: all eager and desperate, all full of pouty lips with no tongue to fill my oh-so-ready mouth, my face hanging in space.

To add insult to injury, he'd turned away from me and inhaled an éclair. *And it wasn't even time for pudding.*

It was too embarrassing and too shaming. Again, *shaming*. I must naturally attract humiliation like shit attracts flies. I'd blushed and dithered and stumbled awkwardly before I'd regained my equilibrium and a little something else – but thankfully he'd missed all of that – too intent on shoving the creamy chocolate patisserie into his mouth. Not even bothering to look at me.

He sat there, sneering and smirking at me and so obscenely sure of himself.

*I'm sure of my*self. *You don't know who you're dealing with.* Suddenly, my belief rang a little truer now that I had a little something extra. My faith in myself reawakened. I concentrated on ignoring the brief and thankfully temporary desertion of my strength, as if it hadn't happened. Still, I found myself upset that he'd gone from being confused and beaten, to éclair-eating confident. *What had changed?*

It was the non-kiss that had changed everything.

Keeping my emotions in check, not wanting any of my personality to leak out and be on display, I bit my lip and served up his supper with a smile. Swayed my hips as I placed his plate in front of him with one hand. As if everything was all as it should be. I knew my control had returned but was careful not to let him see that I was stronger now. He had no idea just how stronger I'd become since he'd nearly kissed me. I'd recovered well. And cleverly.

'How's your food? Good?'

He didn't answer: only bent his head to better shovel his food from fork to mouth. Watching him, my stomach turned a little and I was surprised to find myself cringing. He was only human after all, I reminded myself, but just there, for a minute, as he'd scooped and failed and re-scooped an escaping noodle which had stuck to his chin, he'd looked less than beautiful. His face covered in dripping vegetable stir-fry, he'd given a good impression of something like ugly. Dribbling, sucking and slurping, he'd lost his handsome coating, and seemed, just for a second, very plain and average.

It pulled me up short.

For perhaps two seconds, we'd been the same. Ugly. Not nice to look at. Ordinary, as we each battled through the daily grind of being. I was damn sure he wasn't aware of his fleeting ordinariness, but having seen it in him, I couldn't unsee it.

At first, I thought I'd broken the bubble of his perfection. Ruined everything. But then I saw it for what it really was. Normal. He wasn't so special after all. He was certainly dressed in a prettier package than I, but when it came right down to it, we were the same. I, wrapped in plain brown paper, he swathed in sparkles – but if you only took the time to look deeper, there really was no difference between us.

It was superficial trickery.

That knowledge, although unhappy and unwanted, changed everything. Right there and then. I felt my heart break a little as I realised how juvenile I'd been for far too many years. Starry-eyed and star-struck by only centimetres of skin that was simply differently arranged than mine. His appearance had been sculpted by Gods; mine, by warehouse workers, hurrying to get home and uncaring as to how the finished job looked.

It didn't mean I didn't want him. I wanted him even more now.

Now that I knew he was attainable.

Grinning, I said, 'So, how come your fridge is so well-stocked?'

'My dad. He brings me stuff.'

'Well, lucky old you. A daddy's boy.'

He wiped his mouth with the back of his hand and sat back. 'Fuck off. Don't be stupid. Course I'm not. You don't know what you're talking about.'

'So you can cook then? All that food in the fridge, if I hadn't been here, you'd have been able to rustle up a decent meal?'

'Course I bloody could.'

Forcing my eyes to non-blink mode again – always effective and unnerving for the recipient – I said, 'You're lying.'

Something in his face gave a little. A quick dip of his eyes, an unconscious lift of his shoulder. I'd got him. 'I reckon your *daddy* comes and cooks for you. Unless you have a girlfriend? Do you?'

Thinking himself back on safer ground now, he straightened his back higher in his chair, and glared at her. 'Told you already, didn't I? Got loads of them.'

'But obviously no one special. Because where are they?' I waited and let the silence lengthen. 'I'm not stupid you know. I'll prove it. What I know, for a fact, is that when you brought me here, irrespective of how foolishly eager I was, you were prepared for me. The ties were all ready and waiting, along with the gag. Your moves were practised and smooth – no panic. Which means, Max, that you'd done it before. Taken women. Kidnapped women. Bloody stolen women right off the street or from their homes. Wherever you found them, if you wanted them, you'd take them. Right?'

'That's bollocks. Don't be stupid. Look at me. Why on earth would I have to steal women? I could have any woman I wanted. All I have to do is click my fingers and they come running. You're a fat stupid slag, talking complete shite. Why don't you fuck off back where you came from. Go on. Off you waddle.'

But he didn't move. If I was that wrong, he'd have stood up and thrown me out. But he didn't. He continued to sit and was waiting to see what I did next. I was in command, because I'd been right.

That made things interesting. Changed the landscape. Bending my head, I calmly started to eat. Carried on eating and saying nothing. Knowing that silence would further unnerve him if he didn't know what I was going to do or say. It was rare for me to be in such a position of control. Over a real live Johnny-man no less.

No, I told myself. Max was far worse than a bullying and

cruel Johnny-man. Max was a whole lot more than a bully. He was a psychopath. A high-functioning psychopath.

Wiping at the corners of my mouth with a paper napkin which I'd taken from a pile on the worktop, I put down my fork and put my hands in my lap. 'So, what do you do with them? The women you take. Do you kill them?' I nodded wisely. 'I rather think that's precisely what you do. You *have* to. Having treated them like that, probably raped them purely because they were there, how could you possibly let them go?'

I smiled, knowing it annoyed him. 'Which leaves us in something of a novel situation. You didn't kill me. I wonder why.' I stroked my chin, mocking him, as I made a theatre of giving this question deep consideration.

Max had stopped moving. It was as if he'd stopped breathing – caught out by the fat bitch who'd thwarted him.

'Why don't you kill me now, Max? Go on. I dare you.'

I was playing for my life here. He didn't know that I'd slipped a carving knife from the block when he'd been stuffing his face with the éclair. It was wedged between my thighs under the table; the fingers of my right hand held its handle tightly.

His move, when he made it, was unexpected but unoriginal. He stood quickly, making the chair behind him fall to the floor. 'Go on then, bitch. Go. Go now. Walk away and don't come back.'

I also stood. Not wanting to stay seated – it made me too vulnerable: the proverbial sitting duck.

Considering my weight, people were often surprised at how light on my feet I was, but when I needed to, I could really move. I did so now. In a couple of strides, I stood in front of him. Not near enough for him to get me, but near enough to show who was leading this performance.

Holding the knife out in front of me, I was pleased to see that it was bigger than I'd realised. I was even more pleased when I saw Max's face change from all bluff-and-bluster, to fear. Real, honest-to-goodness fear. It made me feel special.

'You're not going to let me go, Max, because I know all about you. You took me for a fool and the only reason I'm not dead is that I did something that the other girls didn't do. I stood up to you. I didn't let you bully me. I didn't let you frighten me to death. That's your thing, isn't it? You like creating fear. You *enjoy* a woman's fear. So I'm not going anywhere. Do you want to know why?'

'Surprise me.'

His voice didn't match his words now. It seemed reedier in tone, and I was delighted to discover that *I* enjoyed seeing *his* fear.

'I think perhaps we're more alike than you might imagine. I'm staying right here, Max. Because I want you. For all the wrong reasons, I'm sure. Nevertheless, it remains the case. I want you for myself. Which means ...' I swished the blade through the air. 'It means we've reached an impasse. A stand-off, if you will.' I grinned. 'Seems all has changed at the not-so-okay corral.' I laughed. 'What a bloody pair we make. I rather think we'll have to sit down and discuss terms, don't you?'

I was pleased to see that for several seconds he remained stumped, at a complete bloody loss for words.

'There's nothing to discuss, Jess. Fuck off. I mean it.'

'No. You don't mean it. We're too alike for you to pass up this chance. Perhaps it would change things if I said I'd kill for you. And in return, we'd *have* to stay together. Quid pro quo.'

My words had surprised me as much as they had Max. I couldn't fail but notice that his eyebrows reared up in shock at my words. But I thought my words were true. Might be true. In this exact minute, they could be true. I felt like I'd arrived somewhere, and it was a destination I'd never considered visiting before.

Not even for a day trip.

For the first time, I found myself thinking about a long-term stay in this strange new land I'd discovered. A much-deserved all-inclusive activity holiday. Mentally I started unpacking.

I don't believe I'm in Kansas anymore.

TEN

Eve

Eve's face was so cold she could feel the iced chill on her cheeks with her chapped and red-raw hands. Her feet and toes were numb, and her fingers stung as if bitten by the wind, but still she carried on walking, head down, pretending none of it was happening.

It all seemed extra cruel as everywhere around her, it was Christmas. And yet, here she was, cold, hungry, dirty, alone. And homeless. Fa-la-la-la-lah.

She'd had her mobile nicked on her first night on the streets, and worried about being cut off from everyone in the world. It emphasised her solitude. Not of course that anyone had texted or rang her recently; nor her, anyone. Anyway, it had needed charging and had no credit. But still. It really pissed her off. It was the final insult. The total cutting off from the world as she'd known it.

Eve's life up until this point, couldn't be described as exemplary. After her death, her eulogy would definitely not be full of comments about how bubbly and friendly she was, how she lit up any room she walked into, how everyone loved her like a sister, a mother, a daughter – nor how she wanted world peace. She was just her. Flaws and all. But she was tough, so hadn't been *too* freaked out at the prospect of being on the streets. Hadn't welcomed it with open arms, but she'd been through worse and assumed she'd be able to look after herself and terrify people into leaving her alone.

It wasn't easy.

The other homeless were a pain in the arse and she didn't trust any of them. Eve didn't suppose they trusted her either, but it wasn't really a making-friends type of environment. They didn't gather around the canapes and chatter mindlessly whilst supping champagne in a convivial fashion.

It was more like huddling around a makeshift fire and keeping your back to the wall, and your eyes alert to the first flash of potential violence and making damned sure you kept hold of your pennies in your grubby little mitt.

A few of them, Eve knew by name. There was Pissy John – named for obvious reasons. Most days she'd see him and every day his trousers would be re-stained with urine, overlaying his previous day's efforts. Weirdly, his damp patches always seemed to resemble a geographical region. This morning his groin had been an almost perfect replica of the coastline of Italy, as he'd peed over yesterday's now-lost map of South America.

Then there was Big Bella. Again, no mystery as to why she'd been named so. Bella wasn't fat, just very big. A square block of a woman, whose torso was so large, it made her limbs look small. Her head sat firmly on her shoulders like a ball teetering on a shelf, as if she had no discernible neck. Bella steam-rollered her way along, her face grim, but her eyes scared. Eve wondered who she was running away from and if she'd truly escaped whatever or whoever frightened her. Occasionally, Eve would nod at her, if she was feeling friendly.

Eve actively avoided Shitty Sharon. Again, no need to

explain. All in all, there was way too much unnecessary bodily excretion on the street, and she steered well clear of it.

Choosing the easier path, Eve kept to herself. It was the cold that was killing her. She could handle the non-interaction with people as, in a way, she was used to being on her own. It was the physical brutality of being homeless that was destroying her.

She was relatively new to this situation. Two months. But already Eve hated it and knew she couldn't survive it. Wouldn't survive it. She refused to stay begging on the pavements, hiding and sleeping behind bushes in people's front gardens as darkness fell. She'd worked out that a house with a flowerbed and some bushes in the front gave her at least a semblance of safety. Away from all the nutters, the drinkers, the druggies, and the prostitutes. She didn't have a personal issue with any of these people, just couldn't be arsed to put up with the emotional torment that travelled with them.

Eve had stolen a sleeping bag from a young naïve girl on her third night sleeping rough and had felt bad. But she couldn't afford to be all sweetness and light – that attitude was wasted on the street. Being nice here would be misinterpreted and would get her nowhere, other than further away from normal.

The rule on the street appeared to be straightforward: fuck everyone else. And Eve could do *that*.

Other than the lack of food, the lack of washing, the lack of everything, it was a very, very boring existence: traipsing along every day, keeping moving and the blood pumping: constantly avoiding the police who occasionally did blitz attacks on beggars. It was soul-destroying and shameful. She couldn't really accept that at the age of twenty-nine, this was where she'd ended up.

Instead of whining and bitching about it though, she stuck to her routine, and kept her eyes peeled for ways to escape.

She wanted to be rescued, because she'd had enough.

But who would rescue her?

Life didn't work like that. It wasn't that kind.

That's why Eve carried on walking, head down, and pretended that none of it was happening.

Horribly aware that it still was.

ELEVEN

Max
___

Max and the completely mad fat woman, sat in the kitchen: him with his hands clasped on the table and pretending a casualness he didn't really yet feel, and Jessica still holding the knife.

At first, he'd seriously bloody panicked when everything had gone tits-up and she'd brandished the knife at him. He'd considered getting his ankle blade out but wasn't sure he'd be quick enough. More importantly, her knife was a lot bigger than his. So, he sat there and sucked it up.

She freaked him out more than he liked to admit. He was beginning to wish he'd killed her when he'd had the chance. With or without her showing fear. That bit seemed less important now. But he still could easily overpower her and *then* kill her, and that made him feel much better. Safer.

Although, he couldn't move past the fact that if it went down like that, she'd have won. He'd have been forced to kill her, with her pulling all the strings, and she'd have succeeded in sucking all the fun out of it. He refused to be beaten by a girl. It wasn't how it worked.

He could get any woman he wanted.

Anyway, interestingly, for the moment, he found himself intrigued with how it was all playing out. He convinced himself it would make it all the more exciting. When he *did* win – and there was never any doubt that he would – it would make this shite all the more worth it.

So, for the time being, he'd humour the slag. That's what he told himself, although he was surprised, and a bit put out, that his mouth remained dry and he had difficulty swallowing.

He stood up and was pissed off that she didn't jump or seem even remotely startled at his movement. 'I'm getting a beer. Want one?'

'Yes, please. That sounds nice, thanks.'

Handing her a bottle and not bothering with a glass, he said, 'Just shove it in your mouth and suck. Sure you've heard that instruction before.'

She looked at him, her eyes cold and angry. 'Must you be so coarse? You don't have to prove anything to me anymore. I'm still here, which is proof positive that you've worked your magic on me.' She smirked. 'And remember who's holding the knife.'

'What are you going do? Hold me at knifepoint all night? You won't be getting any sleep that way.'

He watched with interest as she put the neck of the bottle to her lips and downed a good third of the beer. 'I was thinking…' she said, wiping froth delicately from her lips with a clean napkin, '…that we should have that chat now. As it's the middle of the night and I don't intend on sitting up in bed with a knife to your throat, we need to finalise some details before sleeping. I'll tell you how it's going to be, shall I? Seems a good starting point. I mean, me taking command.'

'You're very sure of yourself. What's to stop me taking the knife off you and killing you. It would be easy. And it would put an end to all this bollocks right now.'

Jess laughed, her chins tumbling over themselves, joining in the merriment. 'Don't be ridiculous. If you were going to kill me, you would have done so already. Yet, here you are, still sitting next to me. And you know why? Because you want to know what I'm proposing.'

The bitch had a point.

He sat back down again. 'Go on, then. What's your proposal?'

'My plan is, we can work together. Team up, if you like that term better. I'm prepared to make certain sacrifices for you. In other words, I will do whatever is necessary in order to keep you. That way, we'll both get what we want.'

'But what's in it for me? Are you going to kidnap and kill for me? You've never killed anyone before – I can tell. You're too soft.'

She's not *soft. She's a nutter. She's a stone-cold, cruel whack-job. I recognise the type. If she hasn't killed before, I know she could – if she wanted to. I don't know how I missed it.*

'Oh, I certainly come across as soft, Max, but believe me, deep down where it matters, I'm not soft at all. I couldn't be harder. I've put up with a lot of shit in my life. Now, I've finished being nice. I'm getting what I want. And I want you. As previously stated.' She see-sawed the knife in the air. 'I'm presuming your penchant is women only. Any women? Do you have a particular criterion, or will any female who is breathing do the job? You'll have to give me some sort of a hint: I can't be expected to know your type.'

Max was well and truly fucking freaked out. He'd made a very big mistake with this one, but even so, he couldn't bring himself to let her go. He wanted to see what she'd be willing to do, in order to stay with him. Max took more than a minute to think about it – he was about to put himself out there – a risky move. But he argued, *if*, and it was a big *if*, in the extremely unlikely event that she escaped, or more accurately, if she decided to leave, it would be a 'he said, she said' thing and who'd believe her over him? *He kidnapped me, tried to rape me, changed his mind and let me go.*

No one would believe that. Not in a million years. So he leant forward into her space, their knees touching, and whispered, '*You're* my type, stupid. Women who look like you. That's what I like.'

Looking at her expression, he suddenly felt like laughing. He'd still got it. The stupid bitch was *flattered*. Jesus Christ. She'd taken it as a compliment. Sitting back, still in his scrubs, he planted his clogs on the kitchen table. Belatedly he realised they weren't the butchest footwear going. He put them back on the ground, but kept his thighs spread wide, reasserting himself. Her fat face was all aglow and she couldn't wipe the smile from her lips. Her hand touched her hair, and she tipped her head in a girly way.

It took him a moment to realise he *had* fucking complimented her. He'd admitted he liked her. Liked how she looked. He *never* complimented women. Or if he did, they wouldn't be breathing for much longer. Mentally, he kicked himself, but it was too late. Jess was still smiling. Showing her teeth in sheer delight. Couldn't stop beaming like a child at Christmas. Like it was the first nice thing anyone had ever said to her.

She'd outwitted him. That easily. He wanted to take it back but couldn't think of a way of doing it without being too obvious. Glaring at her, he waited to hear what she had to say.

'Really, Max? I'm your type? Tell me why. I need to hear it.' She tittered. 'For research purposes only, naturally.'

Shrugging, giving her this one, he slithered his eyes over her. 'You're fat. I like my women fat.'

Her knife-less hand flew to her chest. 'Really? Max, really?' Not waiting for an answer her face clouded. 'But I'm ginger.'

'Hair colour doesn't bother me one way or another. It's just hair. Who gives a fuck?'

Amazingly, that went down as well as the first free compliment. Christ. What a saddo. Wanting to deflate her, he said, 'So, again, Jess, who are you going to kill for me?'

Now she looked confused. Silent, she gave it some thought. Spoke slowly and avoided directly answering his question. 'You want me to just go up to any old fat woman, irrespective of hair colour, and kidnap her and bring her to you? Is that it? There are no other parameters?'

'What do you mean? Like, rules? Course there are bloody rules. You have to be very careful when you…' He waited, thinking of a non-incriminating term to use, but knew it was a bit bloody late to be worrying about that. 'You have to be careful when and why you take a woman. And who you take,' he added. 'Needs a bit of watching and waiting and most importantly, you need to get it right first time.'

'Like you got it right with me?'

She giggled in what she no doubt thought was a sweet and sugary way, and he wanted to smash her in the face. 'Yeah. Just like you. I agree, you were a mistake. And I don't make them very often. Never make them, actually. You're my first.'

'There's a first for everything, Max, and I'm delighted to *be* your first.'

'What do you expect will happen once you've kidnapped a woman for me? I'd be allowed to do what I want with her, right? Seeing as how that's the whole fucking point. That's our agreement. You're doing it for me, so I get to do whatever I like with whatever woman you bring home. You sure you'd be all right with that?'

To give her credit, she managed to keep her face a blank, although he could see the first doubts as they hit home. He grinned and leant forward again. 'You'd be fucking jealous, Jess. You couldn't handle it. Me, with another woman. Not you. You'd be kicked into touch. Surplus to requirements.'

A silence settled and Max felt superior. He didn't bother

hiding it and let his lips curl up into a sneer. He'd got her on that one.

Jess ignored the fact that she had just lost that point and said, 'Let's be clear about this. I bring them back, one at a time obviously, and hand them over to you, and leave you to it? You rape them and then you kill them? You think that's the deal?'

He nodded, smug. 'That's the deal. Why? What did you have in mind?'

'I'm not watching you defile a woman. It's one thing me bringing a female to you; quite another to actually watch. I'm not a voyeur.'

Max grinned. Shrugged. 'I repeat, that's the deal.'

'Or what? What are you going to do if I don't follow your rules? You can't kill me.'

'Can't I?'

'No.'

Just like that. *No.* Who did she think she was? He let it go; mostly because she was right. The longer the conversation went on, as much as she weirded him out, he was fascinated by her.

And her idea of teaming up had possibilities. Really good ones. He balanced his elbows on his knees, showing that he was being serious. 'Maybe I need to give you some advice, Jess. Picking up unsuspecting women isn't as easy as it may sound. It's an art. You have to be able to identify their weaknesses and adjust your behaviour accordingly. You pick up on their frailty and then you exploit it. You have to be able to spot a–'

'A victim. Yes, I know. It's not a very complicated system, Max. You pick victims, different types of victims, and cater for their individual needs. Needs being the operative word: not wants. I can do that easily. Because I *was* a victim. But thanks to a man called Johnny, and of course you – how can I not thank you – I'm not any longer. I will never be a victim again. But I am *not* watching you rape a woman. I do have standards.'

He ignored her drivel about being a victim. Knew it all anyway and frankly didn't care how she felt. It was all about him. But he was surprised and a little put out that she'd so easily grasped the concept of capitalising on a victim's fragility. She was definitely a sly one. Making his tone persuasive and appealing, he flashed his gold tooth at her and winked.

'Think of it as hunting. You go out on the hunt. Bring your catch back to me. And I do as I like with them. It's not difficult. It's not complicated. Them's the rules. If you don't like them, you can fuck off. Simple as.'

'Hunting.' He watched, mesmerised, as she licked her lips, making them shine and glisten. 'I like the idea of hunting,' she said. 'But we both go. Because, you know... I'm new at this. And after all, you're the serial kidnapper here. You'll have to show me how to go about it. You teach and I'll learn. As you say, simple as.'

She got up. Looking up at the ceiling, her eyes glazed over as she thought about his rules. 'You're imagining me as a slave to you, catering for you, doing your bidding, am I right? Feel free to correct me if I'm wrong.'

She was waiting for his answer, so he gave her none, and Jess was forced to continue. 'We'll have to finesse the finer details tomorrow. But now, now I'm tired and you don't seem up to really listening and understanding the actual ins-and-outs of this show. Let's call it a night. You've obviously had enough for now. Show me to my room.'

She got up and stood over him, touched the knife to his chin. 'We won't be sharing a bed tonight, Max. You can sleep wherever. And don't you be getting any funny ideas in the night. I'm a light sleeper and we need each other. Remember that.' Kissing him lightly on the cheek, she waited for him to stand up.

He thought about stamping his authority on the situation,

maybe giving her a slap to keep her in line, but there it was again. That scary niggle of fear.

He walked out of the kitchen and up the stairs, confident, without having to check, that she'd follow. He threw open the spare room door. Tutting, he went back to the small closet in the hall where his father had put his clean and laundered sheets, duvet and pillowcases. He tossed them at her. 'Here, catch.'

She didn't bother attempting to catch them but gathered them up neatly where they'd fallen at her feet.

'See you tomorrow, Jess. And do sleep well. I know I will.' Going for a swagger, sure she was watching him, he sauntered to his own room – the room where he'd left her tied and gagged to his bed. Seemed an age ago. Before closing his door, he waited until he heard her close hers. Waited a few minutes more, standing there in his blue operating scrubs, feeling stupid and oddly vulnerable.

Quietly, he took a chair and wedged it under the doorknob, before getting undressed.

TWELVE

Jessica

The next morning, unwedging the chair from under the doorknob, I walked out into the hallway. I had to go downstairs to find my mobile. It was in my handbag which was still slung over the newel post where I'd thrown it coming into the house yesterday. Thrown it haphazardly and in excitement, tripping up the stairs to Max's bedroom. What a fool I'd been.

Shaking my head in disbelief at my own stupidity, I quickened my pace back upstairs. It was nine o'clock already. Late. But it had been a late night, so I didn't worry too much. I had all day. *With Max.* Lots of days. *With Max.*

I found the bathroom after opening two wrong doors and washed my face and squirted toothpaste onto my finger. Rubbed vigorously at my teeth until they squeaked. I'd have to do some shopping for essentials today. Looking at my reflection in the mirror above the sink, I studied my face. It wasn't *that* bad. Well, if you squished up your eyes and didn't look too closely. But however hard I squinted, I could still see the shape of my cheeks: like two big round balls, stretched to capacity. One very small nose and two piggy eyes. Curly ginger hair. I closed my eyes and inhaled slowly.

Opening them, I stuck my tongue out: pink and white and frothy with toothpaste. Laughing silently, I did a little dance of excitement. I couldn't get over it. Max liked me. I was his type. Not able to really believe it, I sucked up water from the running tap and rinsing my mouth, spat out the toothpaste.

Max is a very stupid man. But I can't be greedy. How can I expect brains and beauty? This isn't some magic land. This is real life and I'll take what I'm given.

I found myself slightly confused. On the face of it, I had no intention of kidnapping any woman, be they fat or thin, and certainly wouldn't dream of killing one. Not really, whatever I'd said. I'd simply got carried away last night. Had allowed myself to get sucked down to his level.

But on an academic level, it did have some appeal. Kidnap and murder. I couldn't really get my head around the whole thing. Even thinking about taking the life of another human being I knew was a wicked and evil thing, but I'd planted the seed in my own mind. And now I couldn't fully rid myself of the thought. The idea was like a weed. A living thing, but growing in the wrong place: inside my brain. When alone, like now, I questioned it and acknowledged it as alien to me.

The problem was, when I was with Max, within touching distance of him, all rational thinking and common sense deserted me, and I'd do anything for him in that moment. Desperation: that's what it was. I was so painfully desperate to have my own man all for myself, I knew I'd do whatever was required to keep him. I couldn't help myself.

Hoping that my saner self would prohibit me from being really bad, I was aware that ultimately, I'd always been greedy. That had always been my downfall. I was uncomfortable with this unsavoury truth but accepted it as I must. When I wanted something, I'd always take it. With both grasping hands.

Shaking my head, I decided to go looking for my man.

Max was in the kitchen, reading the newspaper. The radio

blared out music into the stuffy room. I switched it off and opened the window. He didn't look up. As if I didn't exist. Nodding to myself, I realised he was playing a child's game. Trying to make me feel uncomfortable by pretending I wasn't there.

'Morning, Max. Breakfast?'

Still not looking up, he nodded. More of a grunt, really.

'What are we playing this morning? Old married couple who no longer speak to each other?'

He snorted at that. 'You wish, babe, you wish. In your dreams. An old married couple. Ha fucking ha.'

'Full English?'

'Great.'

Part of me thought, *What an arsehole*. The other part, the bigger part, thought, *He's mine, all mine*.

I didn't speak again, busying myself quietly: getting lost in the joy of domesticity – preparing, touching, smelling and cooking food. It was all a prelude to the grand finale: eating. I found two mugs and made a pot of tea.

'Coffee. I like coffee. I don't do tea.'

'Your father's not here. I am. If you want coffee, make it yourself. I've made tea. Drink it or don't.'

Putting two plates on the table, each heaped with sausages, bacon, two eggs, beans, tomato and frozen hash browns – I preferred making my own, but was too hungry to make the effort – I sat down and tucked in. I watched, pleased, as Max picked up his knife and fork and started shovelling the food in. It was nice to share my food, to not eat on my own for once. I rather thought I could get quite used to it.

Swallowing a piece of tomato, I said, 'I need to get a few things from home, as I'll be staying here for some time. Can you give me a lift later and I'll drive my own car back here with all my stuff.'

He shrugged. 'Why not?'

I'd expected more of an argument on this point, but took his response in the spirit it was given. I was in charge. Good. I held my fork in the air. 'I've gathered that you like to take your women from the street, is that right? I'm guessing here, but I think I'm correct. But as we're now a team, we could afford to mix things up a little. Go out as a couple. No one will suspect a couple, will they?'

I hoped I wasn't laying it on too thick, but Max was thick, so I thought thick was the way to go.

He didn't answer for a while. Like he was thinking. Hard. As if it were a new thing for him. I imagined I could see the cogs turning slowly as his mind created thoughts, which in turn, he'd translate into speech and eventually he'd get it out, using words. Instead of irritating me, his stupidity endeared him to me. I was the brains; he the beauty.

'I thought you weren't up for hunting and kidnapping anyone for me to rape. Thought you had standards.'

'I do have standards. But if we're going to do this, we'll do it together. And I'll have a say in who we take. Tonight, though, I have something I must do. On my own.'

He shrugged again and seemed not to be interested in what I might be doing later. That suited me just fine. Max made a sort of derisory sound. 'I can guarantee we'll have different types. Can't see you picking a really nice fat juicy woman for me. As I said, jealousy will stop you. And I'm not putting up with you choosing some super thin girl, just to make yourself feel better. That's not going to happen.'

'No. I wouldn't do that. That wouldn't be fair on you. I like to play fair. And stop saying that I'm simply here to "pick up" a woman. I'm here for much more than that. Then, we can talk, Max. *Then*, we'll decide what it is we're actually doing together. Together, Max. We do the women to-ge-ther.'

He stared at me; a bit of yolk stuck in the corner of his mouth.

'What are you doing tonight that's so important?'

'Never you mind. Think of it as a surprise.'

He raised his eyes but didn't bite. I carried on, making myself sound needy and reliant on him. 'But I'd really appreciate you showing me how you go about it. I've never kidnapped anyone before, especially not with the goal of ultimately raping or murdering them. Be patient with me, Max. I need time.'

Appealing to his superiority in these matters would do the trick. He was so arrogant he wouldn't be able to resist showing off his talents – as he saw them.

And here I go again, raring to go with the whole murdering thing. What is wrong with me? I can't seem to help myself. Max gives me the killing bug.

'You're really serious about this, aren't you? I couldn't have got you more wrong. You do know you're mad, don't you, Jess?'

'I'm as mad as you want me to be, Max.'

'Don't I know it. But if we're going to do this, we'll do it properly. You need training, and I'm prepared to do that. Today, for as long as it takes, you'll sit there and I'll tell you about correctly labelling people. It's not just about identifying victims. It's way, way more than that. You need to recognise what will appeal to people, what they want, and give it to them. That's an art.'

I concentrated on not showing my impatience at Max's patronising tone. He was making kidnapping sound far more complicated and sophisticated than it was. But I'd play along. For him. I'd do anything to keep him. It was just a little wobble that I'd had in the bathroom. *Of course I can kidnap and kill for my Max.* Nodding in agreement, I stood and started cleaning up. 'Okay. That sounds like a plan. You're the boss. Reporting for duty. Sir, yes sir.'

When I saluted, he looked at me blankly, so I carried on regardless, enjoying the fact that he seemed to have accepted me as a partner. Of some kind. Any kind would do. Tea towel in hand, I tried to hide my delight at the way things were going.

I laughed. 'We can spend the afternoon planning. Going over the basics, for me, and then the finer details, again for me, but it'll be an opportunity for you to train me. Consider me your student.'

'Whatever you say, babe.'

Babe. He called me babe.

'We're not going out together, until you're properly qualified and I say you're good enough to work with me.' He put his hand on mine. 'But we will. Promise. When you're ready. And anyway, I'm letting you out on your own tonight, so I'm showing trust. You should be flattered.'

'I am, Max. Very flattered.'

I rather thought *he* should be the flattered one, me even entertaining playing his sick kidnapping game. *Maybe I have the same sickness as you, Max. I rather think you've awakened something vile deep inside me.*

Oh, you, Max. You are a naughty boy.

Unsettled by what I was actually considering doing tonight, my confidence momentarily wavered. Not too much, but enough to make me uncomfortable. I'd been so swept along with his saying that I was his type, I'd lost track of the bigger picture. And that was stupid and dangerous. We were planning a kidnap and murder. *I* was planning a kidnap and murder.

What the bloody hell was I thinking?

I'm thinking I want to keep my man. Am I prepared to go to these lengths to keep my stupid, beautiful man?

Ask me tomorrow.

I couldn't keep up with my rapidly changing thoughts: killer or non-killer? Kidnapper or saviour? Beautiful or ugly? Excited or appalled? Eager or reluctant? Captor or captive? Good or bad?

Again, ask me tomorrow.

THIRTEEN

Bella

B ella popped her head out from her red tent and checked
it was safe to come out. Her red tent made her safe. She
wasn't stupid and knew it was a paper-thin covering and not an
armoured tank that would keep out the bad people, but still, it
made her *feel* safe.

Saf*er*.

Bella had been living on the streets for years now. She'd lost
count, but it must be five, six years, or thereabouts. And she
still couldn't really believe it. She was a nice girl, with a nice
family, and no real excuse for being homeless.

Pride kept her from telling her parents.

Every week, she'd borrow a phone and call her mother and
tell her how her non-existent job was going, with her non-
existent live-in quarters with all her non-existent friends. She'd
even invented a boyfriend, Dominic, who over the years, had
become almost real in her mind.

Over the years, Bella had made a string of excuses. Once
she'd explained regretfully to her parents, that she wouldn't be
able to come home for Christmas as she was spending it with
Dominic, and then the following year, she'd been invited for

Christmas lunch to meet his parents. Also, Bella often insisted work was too much, and as she moved up the ranks, her timetable didn't allow her enough time to take days off and leave London to travel back to Ludlow – she just didn't have the time.

Bella was deeply embarrassed about her lifestyle and would die if her mother could see the shit she lived in. But she lived for the day, every week, when she called Mum and Dad and lied and lied, and listened to the news from home. The dog was still alive – alive but old, same for Dad who was ill now, but not dying. Her mother worked hard and Bella felt guilty that she'd let her own life slip away from her.

And she had no excuse.

Most of the people she met on the street came from bad homes, with bad parents, bad marriages, violence, domestic abuse – Bella had heard it all. And avoided the really sad cases, the ones who drank and took drugs. The sad, frightening people.

Instead, she hid away in her red tent in the tunnel and kept to herself.

And imagined in so much detail, she could almost touch him, brown-haired, brown-eyed Dominic with his long dark eyelashes, who worked in banking, and who adored her. In her mind, they were always holding hands and smiling at each other. Sometimes, she talked out loud to him, in her red tent, whispering and chatting about all sorts of things. Dominic was gentle and a very good listener.

On the street, Bella thought she had one thing going for her. She was big. Big went a long way if you were alone and a woman with only a red tent for protection, and a pretend boyfriend. Bella had tried making friends, but it had proved too difficult and risky, and in the end, she'd decided she was much better off on her own.

So, she tried to look fierce and gave it a don't-mess-with-me attitude, and mostly, especially now she was a regular on this particular patch, mostly people did leave her alone. She was on nodding terms with lots of the other homeless people, Her Majesty, Pissy John, The Monster – a big, tall man with long arms and an even longer beard. He was harmless but she preferred to keep her distance. Just in case.

Bella was lonely and missed her family. Every day she'd make her way to the entrance to the Tube station and sit down, holding up a bent old bit of cardboard on which she'd written 'Please help me, I'm hungry'. She didn't do too badly. She thought that, although she was big and plain, she looked innocent.

Because she was.

However hard she tried, she couldn't hide that. Living rough didn't change who you were inside. It made you pretend who you were on the outside. And Bella pretended with the best of them. Most of the time, everyone left her alone because she hadn't got anything worth stealing, and she wasn't any trouble. To anyone. She made it her business to merge into the background.

I am a shadow.

A shadow who lives in my very own red tent.

Thank God for my red tent.

It's my home and it's all mine.

Just occasionally, I allow myself the fantasy of talking to Dominic who is safe and kind. What's wrong with that?

Dominic is never far from my thoughts.

It was a nice fantasy, Bella thought. She wished it was true.

FOURTEEN

Jessica

The idea had come to me last night in bed, as easily and as smoothly as a raindrop falling down a windowpane. I hadn't even been concentrating or consciously thinking about anything in particular.

Why had I let myself get carried away with Max's insane needs, involving myself too quickly and putting myself into an untenable position? It was stupid and dangerous. I'd immediately fallen headlong into the possibility of committing murder for Max. *What am I even thinking? I am not* that *desperate. Am I?*

Instead of jumping into something which was obviously an abomination of an idea, I realised it would be far better to ease myself into this game, for game it was, by committing the crime of kidnapping. I certainly wasn't about to murder anyone, nor stand by and watch the act of rape from my front row seat – whatever I'd allowed Max to believe.

But I could choose the victim and I would choose wisely. I need not have anything to do with rape and murder, because I wasn't a psychopath, and it might not come to that. The possibilities were endless, after all. I had brains and, I liked to think, a certain sense of right and wrong.

My idea was now cemented and grounded inside my head. And I knew my choice of victim was a good one. Good, being the operative word. I convinced myself I would genuinely be saving a girl, not abusing her, but saving her – giving her a second chance at life.

And I had the perfect hiding place to keep her rescued soul, safe from prying eyes.

Mummy and Daddy, before they'd given up on me as a child, and before I had got really fat, had renovated a room in anticipation of showing off their child to their grotesquely simpering friends. It had been vigorously refurbished: showcased with a glass ceiling which looked down from the open-plan sitting room into the cellar. The simple and utilitarian windowless basement was now a ta-dah centrepiece when viewed from above.

It had, in effect, become an observation room; a vantage point from which my parents could look down with pride on their peachy daughter and showcase me to anyone who cared to see. *Look what we made.*

My parents had officially named it 'The Playroom' – a place where I could play quietly with all my school chums, neatly packaged safely away in a room, but always visible through the glass floor above. My parents wanted to be able to exclaim over their perfect creation, from the viewing gallery. *See how nicely she plays. See how beautiful she is. See how she resembles us. Aren't we so clever?*

But I never brought any friends home down the wrought-iron spiral staircase into the ever-ready-and-waiting playroom, to play, because I had none, preferring my own company. I had never played nicely with anyone other than myself. I wasn't beautiful and I bore no physical resemblance to either parent.

The Playroom quickly became a beautiful and solitary

space, used by me playing on my own – unwatched by my parents. There was no need. After all, how could you show off your child when all she did was sit on her own and read books? That wasn't good enough. I wasn't pretty enough. And more to the point – I was fat. Frankly, that was too embarrassing for Mummy to even contemplate parading me.

In bed, last night, when I had remembered the room, the type of victim who would happily fit into it, seemed obvious. It would be the perfect place to keep a lost soul, rescued by me and brought to this sanctuary. A person who would truly appreciate the playroom, but whom Max and I could keep a beady eye on through the glass floor that looked down on my private room from the sitting room above.

It would give Max and me time to think what to do with my first hostage.

FIFTEEN

Felicity

Felicity laid down her stripey beach towel on the cream canvas seat and clipped it to the back of the sun lounger on the top deck, to make sure it didn't get whisked away by the wind.

She decided to enjoy her time alone without her husband, Christopher, and took pleasure in ordering herself a daiquiri. Lying back, she settled under the blue sky to enjoy the sun and think about her life. Or more specifically, the life of her daughter, Jessica.

It's not my fault. I am blameless.

Certainly happy enough now, she realised that her contentment stemmed from being away from her child. It was an evil and very unmotherly sentiment to entertain, but entertain it she did. And why shouldn't she? She couldn't ignore it altogether – although she'd spent most of her life trying.

Neither she nor Christopher had ever really wanted a baby. It had been a sort of happy-at-first accident. And very quickly, when their daughter had come along, there had been no happiness at all. Instead, it had all been rather a shock: an extraordinarily alarming one. It wasn't a joyful time, nor celebratory in any way. It had proved to be bone-crushingly melancholy. Felicity had drifted further and further away from her baby, as she battled her way through post-natal depression.

Trying to be fair and generous in her assessment of Jessica, Felicity attempted to find her redeeming qualities. It was a game she often played, knowing that surely it should be an easy task. And always discovering, disappointingly, that it wasn't. Felicity should be stuffed full of happy lifetime moments and memories filled with her and Jessica. But there was nothing. Not really.

There was, however, a feeling of guilt when she thought back to when she'd been a mother. *And I'm* still *a mother*, she had to remind herself. Although she didn't feel like one. *I am an imposter.*

Taking another sip from her glass, she lit up her cigarette and watched as the breeze stole the smoke, much like her daughter had stolen Felicity's soul from her. Had thieved the very life from her. Leaving Felicity no option but to escape.

Even after her recovery from her depression, Felicity and Jessica had never bonded.

They'd never got on. Never laughed together. It had been one long and very tedious argument. Jessica had been a grizzly baby, a petulant child and a recalcitrant and wilful adolescent.

Inhaling deeply, Felicity knew that she didn't even think of herself as a mother. She'd been purely the receptacle that had carried the embryo, and then pushed it out into life as a screaming and wailing crinkled-up baby.

Her child had made things worse for herself by intentionally over-eating and making herself an easy target for bullies. Had made herself a victim. Felicity had tried to encourage her to lose weight, but her chubby little girl had ignored her. Had looked straight through her, as if her mother didn't exist. Greed had always plagued Jessica: not just when it came to food, but to everything put in front of her. If Jessica wanted something, she'd go out of her way to get it. Nothing would stop her.

A contrary and disobedient girl, sullen and charmless, she was chilling in her strength of belief. When she'd identified a need, she was frighteningly determined, and never failed in her quest for whatever it was that she so desired.

A surprising candidate then to become a victim of bullying. Felicity often thought perhaps it was the attention she craved and fed on – devouring it hungrily: putting herself shamelessly in the 'poor-me' category.

There was never anything poor-me about my daughter. I was never fooled by that game.

Felicity didn't and had never really liked Jessica. It was as simple as that. And after all, it wasn't a legal requirement that one had to love one's family. It was nothing more than a bonus if you got on.

It is not my fault. It really isn't.

Ever since Jessica had been old enough to talk, Felicity had noticed something disturbing about her, found herself a little nervous around her own child. If she were being entirely truthful with herself, she'd have to say that there was most definitely something not-quite-right about her daughter.

But it was so much more than that. Deep down, she'd always known that Jessica's personality was a little… off. There was something wrong with her. She wasn't *right*.

Felicity had been frightened of Jessica since her child had learnt to speak and become her own person. More than frightened. Bloody terrified.

I am scared of my own daughter. Is that my fault?

Never being able to pinpoint the exact nature of what ailed her child, unable to identify categorically why Jessica scared her so, with her blank stares and lack of empathy, Felicity stopped thinking of her entirely for the moment. It was the only thing she could do.

She had to frequently pretend to herself that she'd done the right thing by her daughter. After all, she and Christopher had as near as damn it given her their house in which to live – free of charge, along with a most handsome allowance. What Jessica chose to do with her life, was entirely up to her. She'd been given everything. What more could they do for her? They'd given her everything for a good start in life.

I am guilty of noth*ing.*

Felicity needed another drink to better rid herself of her knowledge that Jessica was truly bad.

Thank God, I'm not there to have to pick up the pieces.

I've done my job as mother as well as could have been expected.

I am totally *blameless.*

Having convinced herself that she wasn't at fault, yet again, and relieved she was far enough away on a boat to avoid the inevitable fall-out which would come purely from the stark fact that Jessica breathed and walked the earth, she stubbed out her cigarette and ordered another drink.

Anyone meeting her daughter needed to take a great deal of care.

Felicity had always been very careful to avoid her daughter as much as was humanly possible.

Good luck, everyone else.

SIXTEEN

Jessica
_____

Looking fascinated at everything Max says is killing me. I swear to God it is.

Max and I had spent all day 'in training'. I felt slightly mortified at the ridiculousness of it all, and thankful that no one could see me, sitting at Max's feet, my back leaning on the sofa, taking earnest notes as he went through his dos and don'ts of how to pick up a woman. The right woman. In the right place. In the right way. Wearing the correct apparel.

I'd got it after about ten minutes. Could comprehend the intricacies of his dastardly methods, but didn't like to say so and was loath to interrupt the copious lists he dictated, smiling as he was. Really, he sat there, giving a monologue on the greatness and wonder of being Max. His narcissism made me smile. Like a showing-off little boy.

I wished I had narcissistic tendencies. Thinking that _I_ was great, that _I_ had the adoration of others, that _I_ was important. I admitted the unkind truth that I envied him his self-love.

What I did have, however – and it's a strange contradiction in terms – was self-belief. Quite different but just as useful. I knew I was in command of this situation. Max hadn't come to that realisation – not yet. His narcissism stopped him from seeing anything positive in someone else.

But I enjoyed listening to him speak and perhaps I was being a bit unfair. And they weren't dos and don'ts: they were *laws* that could not be broken – according to Max. 'You have to have the knack, Jess. It's all about capitalising on people's weaknesses and destroying them. Simple as. Simple for me, but you'll learn. I think you'll be a natural at it.'

Nodding demurely, I mumbled my thanks, eager to please. His 'teachings' were in fact incredibly juvenile and simplistic. I could have told *him* most of what he'd said in half the time. His so-called laws-that-must-be-followed, were obvious and required no finesse at all.

'You've either got it, hun, or you haven't. And I've got it. In oodles.'

A narcissist *and* stupid. An odd combination. Neither took away his handsomeness. Nothing could take that away. So, I smiled and bobbed my head, showing that I was taking it all in.

Arching my back and stretching out my legs in front of me, I scrunched up my toes. They were cramping. 'How about some food, Max? We've been at this for hours. You must be famished. I know I am.' I waited a beat before reminding him that I was doing my own thing tonight. 'You don't mind, do you? It's just something that I must do, and I know you'll approve. I'd go so far as to say, I think you'll like what I'm doing tonight. It will impress you.'

He looked down at me and put his hand on my head as if I were a child, asking for a break. 'Whatever, Jess, do whatever you want. It's not like I have to worry that you won't come back, is it? So, yeah, heat up Dad's stew. We'll eat before you go. It's in the Tupperware in the fridge.'

'I can knock something up.'

He shook his head. 'No, I want Dad's stew. He'll be upset if

I don't eat it. Go on, Jess, cook me what I want. You'll like it too, promise.'

'Do you care if he's upset?'

'No, not really, but do as I say, because I'm the man, and that's a good enough reason.'

Heaving myself to my feet, having to reach vertical by going at it sideways, I finally and triumphantly stood above him. 'Okay. This time, for you, we'll eat your father's food. But I'm telling you now, I can guarantee you'll prefer my stew when I make it for you.'

'I bet I will.'

He flashed his gold tooth at me. Unaware that every time he manoeuvred his mouth to achieve the desired glint, he had to slightly contort his face in order to intentionally show off the sparkle of yellow metal. His upper lip had to be retracted just that extra bit to make the gold molar visible. *Silly man. Sweet, though.*

I tousled his hair before leaving the room. It was three o'clock and I was starving. Passing a big square tin on the kitchen worktop, I opened it and was thrilled to find it full of custard creams. My favourite. Max's favourite as well, obviously. We even liked the same biscuits.

I scoffed at myself. We were only talking custard bloody creams here. Not an obscure shared love of something weirdly esoteric. But still.

We were like a real couple. Max and Jessica. It even sounded right. Grinning inanely to myself like a lovesick schoolgirl, I warmed two bowls and got out bloody Daddy's fan*tastic* stew. I was pretty sure it wouldn't be a patch on mine, but for Max, I'd happily serve it. Humming, I waited for the microwave to ping.

Max and Jessica, sitting in a tree.

K-I-L-L-I-N-G

Laughing delightedly at my own joke, I hurried back to the

sitting room, bowls and napkins on a tray. I felt we'd really bonded throughout the day, but allowing him to be in control was killing me. Obedience and playing nice wasn't an instinctive thing.

Only one of us was in charge, and it wasn't Max.

Before I went into the sitting room, I arranged my face into something resembling docile. Wiped the smile from my mouth as I thought of how he'd told me, all hush-hush, that he worked as a codebreaker for MI5. *Pffft. What a crock.* How stupid did he think I was? I'd nodded and ooohed and aaahed in a suitable way. 'I'm impressed, Max. But not surprised. I just knew you'd have an exciting job. A real man's job. And don't worry, I won't tell anyone.' I'd kept my expression respectful, showing a touch of awe, but concluded that curtseying would be too much.

Shrugging, I decided that for the moment I'd let him think he was in charge. I'd let him know later that he wasn't. Tomorrow, after I'd successfully carried out my first really bad thing. I was doing it for Max, but had to admit, I was looking forward to tonight. For myself.

If I'd only known how easy it was to get a man, I'd have done it years ago. Smiling – outwardly adoring, inwardly triumphant – I took the master his food.

I've been a good girl all day because I want to go and be naughty tonight and impress my very own Johnny-man.

SEVENTEEN

Max

'No, don't come round, Dad. I've got some workmates here. Colleagues, you know? Yeah, all day. What? Yes, all night and tomorrow. And the next day actually. I've got plenty of food.'

Max gazed up at the ceiling, running his fingers over his chin, careful not to dislodge his mobile wedged between ear and shoulder. 'No, Dad, really. It's top-secret stuff. Confidential. Yeah, that's right. Government work. And you're not to tell anyone, right? You're sworn to secrecy.' He laughed. 'I might have to kill you if you say anything.'

He picked his boxers out of his arse crack as they'd ridden up, and nodded. 'Okay, cool, Dad. Yes. So, don't come over, right? I'm being serious. It's not convenient. I'll give you a bell as soon as the coast's clear.' He smiled and nodded, pretending exasperation. 'I promise, okay? Talk to you later. What? Yes, it was great, Dad. No, really, I loved it. You make the best stew ever. Yup, yup. Laters, Dad, bye. Yeah, bye.'

Why wouldn't anyone leave him in peace? *Because I'm me, that's why.* He grinned to himself and realised, surprised, he was enjoying his day so far.

Long ago, Max had told Dad that he worked for MI5. Had said it as a joke, but Dad had been so impressed, so proud of his achievement, that Max hadn't the heart to tell him he was lying. And the lie had grown over the years, Max enjoying the intrigue and secret squirrel misinformation that he fed his father. Max said he did it as a side-line to his day job. Moonlighting. Sometimes, he found himself actually believing his own big fat lie.

But now, job done – he'd told Dad not to come to the house and Max knew he'd obey him. He didn't want bloody Dad turning up and letting himself in with his key, while Jessica was here. That reminded him – he'd have to give Jess his spare key as she was going out tonight. He definitely wasn't waiting up for her. It meant nothing giving her his key – it wasn't like she was going to run away, screaming to the police. Max wished she would just bugger off, but knew she was here to stay.

Even if he'd offered to pay her, she was so smitten with him, so desperate to be with him, she'd always come back. She'd come back until he killed her: it would be the only way to rid himself of her.

Jess would think the key symbolic of something that wasn't. She could shove it up her arse as far as he was concerned.

I wonder what the mad bitch is doing. I could follow her, but I can't be arsed, because I know she'll be back and she'll tell me. It would be a waste of my precious time.

It was more important that Dad and Jess didn't meet. The thought made him break out in a sweat.

Maybe it would be funny though. If it came right down to it, a real punch-up between the two of them, fighting over him, he wasn't quite sure who he'd put his money on. Usually, Dad would be a dead cert. But with Jess... He really hadn't entirely got her sussed out yet.

But he'd strangely enjoyed their teaching session. He was

used to doing it at work: explaining the bleeding obvious to the newbies, the underlings. And he loved those times – all those young, innocent, *stupid* faces, hanging on his every word as if he were a god. Lapping it all up. All of them knowing that he had all the answers to their thick-as-shit questions, and they were so eager to learn.

Max couldn't get enough of teaching those beneath him in the hierarchy, because it confirmed his superiority. He was the best, and it was right and proper that people looked up to him and listened and realised that if they wanted to learn anything, they'd better sit up and listen very carefully to everything he had to say. And they did listen. Always. Teaching, mentoring – whatever you wanted to call it, came naturally to him; he had everything that was required – patience, calmness, kindness.

Jess had proved a very quick learner, and as his protégé, he'd been proud of her.

And of course, himself.

Putting the mobile back in his pocket, he smiled as Jessica came in bearing food. It was like having a fucking dinner lady on hand. Fucking brilliant or what.

'Here you go, Max. Your father's stew.' Jess smiled, clearly enjoying the day as much as he. It wasn't how he'd seen things playing out when he'd lain in his bed last night, barricaded in with his chair under the doorknob. But priding himself on his ability to adapt, he now took the bowl from her and dived in, not giving a toss what she thought of his manners. He certainly wasn't putting on any airs and graces for the bitch. Why the bloody hell should he? Aware that she was posher than him, was probably used to napkins and silver fucking spoons, he didn't give a flying fuck. She'd already made it obvious that she'd do anything for him, so he sat back and enjoyed the ride.

Jess sat on the sofa, bowl delicately positioned on her lap, and daintily spooned stew into the gaping hole in her face that was her mouth. Not *that* daintily. Max sniggered.

She looked up. 'What's funny, Max?'

'You and me, babe. That's what's funny. Who'da fucking thought we'd be sitting here, eating my dad's stew together, all friendly and not arguing. I haven't killed you and you, politely, haven't killed me yet. Thank fuck for that.'

'Yeah, Max, I'm beside myself with relief.'

Now the tutoring had finished, and they'd both relaxed, Jess seemed to have gone back to her weirder, colder self. The woman who made him nervous. There was a disconnect about her that made his flesh creep. Shrugging off the doubt that whispered around him, he concentrated on getting back to being the real Max. The one most definitely in charge here, whatever the silly bitch believed.

He reminded himself that there was nothing to worry about. Jess was as good as dead – it was a matter of when, not if. So, he didn't mind allowing her the illusion that all was fine and dandy. Everything was only as good as he permitted it. Her days were numbered, and the real joy of it was she had no fucking idea that she was playing into his hands. Thinking herself all superior to him. That was a joke.

Having given her the full Max-treatment, all smiles and compliments and endearments, he thought he could get used to this. A maid, at his beck and call, catering for him, doing his bidding.

Next, she'd be killing for him. She didn't think so but he knew so, because he was never wrong. Slowly he was getting a better feel for her, and once she was totally his, she'd do whatever he told her to. Without question.

It was a shame that he didn't want to shag her. However hard he tried, he couldn't see her in a sexual way. She wasn't subservient enough. She wasn't frightened enough. She wasn't even frightened a bit. It pissed him off. But at the same time, because he had absolutely no desire to give her one, he put it to one side in his brain. He'd get her. When she was truly scared.

And she would be. Then she'd be very, very sorry that she'd ever fucked with him.

He didn't doubt that he could terrify her. Burping loudly, he attempted to drown out the voice that niggled in his head: *she* could terrify *him*. Max shrugged it off. He was in control. No bloody question.

She had no idea who she was dealing with here. Sitting back in his chair, he balanced the bowl on his knee. Maybe he should have got a girlfriend years ago. Meals on wheels and the promise of a whole lot more. He was happy to see how it played out – in no hurry.

'When we've finished eating, I need to go, Max. Are you still okay with giving me a lift? When I've done what I have to do, I'll pack up the car and bring my stuff over here. And then maybe tomorrow night, we could go to the pub, and I can put into practise everything you've taught me today. Like a dry run. A rehearsal. Okay?'

Max thought about telling her to fuck off and just who the hell did she think she was, telling him they were going out together tomorrow night. But what the hell? Why not? It would be a laugh seeing her trying to apply what he'd so painstakingly taught her today. He'd watch and laugh at her inevitable failure.

'Okay. Whatever you want. We'll go to a pub I've never been to. No point shitting on my own doorstep, right? Yeah, that works – a new place that neither of us has been to. Makes it fairer.'

'Great. Sounds perfect. And fair. And Max, don't treat me like I'm an idiot. Don't think I don't know you'll be sitting there waiting for me to fail. I don't want you to worry. I can guarantee you, I'll surprise you.'

His appetite left him.

His good mood evaporated.

His self-belief wavered.

What was it about Jessica that so freaked him out?

EIGHTEEN

Jessica

M ax dropped me off outside my house and pretended not to be impressed with the size and grandeur of my parental home. I didn't care how it made his eyes round in shock and admiration. My parents' wealth meant nothing to me, but I wasn't surprised that Max was enthralled by the house. It was like physical beauty, I thought. It was all about how a thing was presented; everyone missing the point that what lay beneath might not match the exterior ribbons and bows in which it was gift-wrapped.

Finally, Max left and I had to move fast. First, I contacted a locksmith and told him to come to the house, explaining exactly what was required of him. He'd complained it was the end of his working day, so I promised to make it financially worth his while.

He was working at the playroom door within thirty minutes.

I had already got a sleeping bag down from the attic, making me *not* nostalgic in the least at the memory of an ill-fated camping holiday spent as a child with Mummy and Daddy. It had rained every day; my parents had hated all the nature that had rudely surrounded them, and especially hated having to piss in what was not really much more than a bucket in a cold stone shower block. It had proved too much for them. Then I'd got measles: it had been the spotty infectious disease that had tipped the holiday into catastrophe.

As I dressed for tonight, I snorted as I remembered that particular domestic disaster. Happy days. Ha bloody ha. I looked at my reflection in the mirror. Patting my hair, I took out my earrings, took off my necklace and unstrapped my watch. It was important that I looked the part, and appeared kind, sensible and approachable. Business-like, simply dressed but humourless. I could do that.

Finally ready, I took down what I needed to the playroom, and stood quietly for a while, remembering. It was a happy place for me – not for my parents, but for me it had been secure and warm and a comfortable place to be alone. It had been all mine and I had liked it.

Especially after Mummy had put a large dark rug over the glass floor. Then it had definitely belonged to me. I'd become invisible to my parents. They'd effectively blocked out my presence, blacked me out, preferring not to look at their daughter at all, and that had suited me fine.

Now it would belong to someone else, and I hoped they'd appreciate the space as much as I had. They'd have no choice but to like it.

Or God help them.

Before leaving, I patted the key which Max had given me so I wouldn't disturb him when I got back to his place – our place now – and checked the clock again. Midnight. That felt right to me, but really I was winging it. Flap flap. I grinned and got into my car.

I spent hours driving slowly along kerbs where I knew the homeless were. They weren't hard to find in London and stood in messy clumps, littering the streets, like a forgotten tribe.

Driving slowly, I worried I might get arrested for kerb crawling. So I parked the car and holding the hammer tightly in my fist, hidden in my bag, I walked along the road, alert to danger, but courting it at the same time.

For reasons I couldn't identify, I felt absurdly powerful and lethal. The unexpectedness of the emotion made me want to snigger, but I toned it down, hiding it underneath my adopted looking-to-help-the-needy *gentle* smile. It wasn't a great fit, like wearing someone else's false teeth, but I thought the demurely upturned mouth would fool most people. It was tricky to keep it from falling from my lips with a rude crash of laughter, so I concentrated hard on looking caring and trustworthy, whilst enjoying myself tremendously. Now, I was *really* living.

I am me and I'm ready to make you fuckers pay for how I've been treated all my life.

It was soon very cold. The wind gusted and freezing rain spat at me. I felt like spitting back, and hurried, refusing to leave without a woman.

Surprisingly, the odd assortment of homeless people that I did see, didn't approach me and weren't confrontational, but instead gave me a wide berth. I wondered why that should be. Perhaps I looked too much like Authority with a capital A.

Fuck them.

But they should consider themselves lucky – they'd made the right choice by ignoring me.

Then I saw the woman, who skirted a main huddle of ragged people, avoiding eye contact. She was one of them, except she wasn't. Her solitude made her stand out. I thought the woman maintained a certain dignity, an individuality, although obviously dirty and living rough.

Immediately, I made my choice. This was the woman I'd take.

Whispering along the pavement, hugging the shadows, I walked quietly but determinedly behind the woman. Both of us walked for some time, getting further from the main drag, and intrigued now, I realised the woman had a specific destination in mind. Her head remained down, but her strides were strong and she never wavered nor dithered in her mission – getting from A to B with intent. Surprised at my excitement, I wondered where B would turn out to be.

The woman stopped with no warning and turned quickly, looking over her shoulder, checking, I assumed, that no one was watching her. Her body language screamed out: *Keep away. Leave me alone.*

Or you'll be sorry.

I didn't stop, wasn't fazed by the woman's not-so subtle aggression, and carried on walking. It made me seem innocent and I hardly posed an obvious physical threat: it wouldn't occur to the woman that I was indeed coming for her. Like a double bluff, I strode purposefully up to the woman and stopped about three feet from her.

The woman's eyes squinted in query. 'What do you want?'

I smiled. A genuine smile – strangely. I realised I really meant the smile. I was here to help. To save. To kidnap with kindness.

I want you and I shall have you.

'I'm Jessica.'

The woman put her weight on one hip and adjusted her orange backpack on her shoulders, slipping her thumbs under the straps and taking the weight off her back. 'Good for you.'

'What's your name?'

'What's it to you?'

'Nothing. Just trying to be nice, that's all. You look cold.'

'Because I am.'

Silence. Neither of us dropped our gaze and I refused to speak again. I was good at this game. I could out-silence anyone. Eventually, the woman sighed.

'Eve. My name's Eve. There. Feel better?'

'Not especially. This isn't a contest. I don't want anything from you. Nothing at all.' I spoke truthfully and was pleased with myself. I'd got this. It was child's play.

Eve shrugged and turned to leave. 'Bye then. It's been a real pleasure meeting you.' Her words dripped with sarcasm and I laughed.

'Are you hungry?'

Sitting down suddenly on a brick wall in front of a tall Edwardian house, Eve manhandled her backpack to the ground and said, 'Of course I'm hungry.'

'Would you like something to eat and a warm room for the night?'

Eve laughed and tucked her hands under her armpits. 'I know it's Christmas so either you're the archangel Gabriel or you're a psycho. Which is it?'

'Definitely a psycho.' I smiled my least psycho smile but felt it falter on my lips. *Am I a nutter, who's been tipped over the edge? Am I on the precipice of doing something I'll forever regret? All for a Johnny-man? Am I really that shallow?* 'No, really, Eve. It's Christmas and I was thinking how nice it would be if I could help someone by doing something simple. Offering kindness. It seemed like a good idea at the time. But I can see why you might mistake me for a nutter. Who knows? I might have a hammer in my bag and want to beat you to death with it.'

'*Do* you have a hammer in your bag?'

'No. *Are* you hungry and cold?'

Shrugging, Eve said, 'Yes, I'm starving and freezing.' She bent to pick up her rucksack. 'And you know what, I am so hungry and cold, I'll take a chance that you're not a lunatic, so if you're offering, I'm accepting.'

I clapped my gloved hands like a child. 'I'm so pleased. You can stay the night, and have a bath as well, if you like. I'll cook us something and then you can sleep in your own room. That's my gift to you, this Christmas.'

God, I really am a fucking angel. My wings are so heavy, I am weighed down by my own goodness and benevolence.

Other than telling Eve that my car wasn't far, we didn't speak again as we walked back the way we had come. I didn't want to dispel the aura of goodwill to all men that I seemed to have generated and Eve seemed happy in her silence.

But on her guard.

She is no fool, I thought. *She is also not fat. Boohoo, Max. But better than being slim, Eve has a brain. That makes it all much* much *more interesting all round.*

And *her name is Eve. How appropriate. The first woman and she is being led into temptation.*

NINETEEN

Eve

E ve couldn't really believe her luck. She'd prayed to be rescued and rescue had come. Albeit in the form of a woman, who was definitely lying about something. But fuck it, she was willing to put up with whatever was coming, for food and warmth. What was the worst that could happen?

They didn't speak much on the drive to her house. Eve appreciated that as she wasn't willing to answer facile questions like, 'What's a nice girl like you... et cetera, et cetera.' Even nice girls had shit lives.

And anyway, who said I was nice?

She'd take what Jessica was offering, sleep in a warm room and be on her way. Unless circumstances meant she could somehow lengthen her stay. Presuming Jessica wasn't a nutter. There was definitely something a bit off about the woman driving, but Eve couldn't put her finger on it. As a rule, she liked to know exactly who and what she was dealing with. And at this precise moment, Eve wasn't truly convinced by Jessica's selfless act of charity towards her.

But she knew she deserved this piece of good luck. If good luck it was. She prayed she hadn't made one of her famous errors of judgement, because those never ended well for anyone.

'Here we are, Eve. This is my home.'

Eve refused to gasp at the enormous house – more like a mansion. Much grander than anything she'd been anticipating. 'Nice,' she said, being polite and making sure she didn't gush all over the place. She didn't want to look like an idiot who'd never seen a big house before.

Jessica led the way and flicking on lights as they walked through the front door, she said, 'I left the heating on, so it's nice and warm. Would you like a hot drink, while I cook us something to eat, or would you prefer a bath first?'

'A bath, please. That would be lovely.'

She trailed after Jessica, feeling like a tradesperson who'd taken a wrong turn, and Jessica showed her to the bathroom and gave her a pile of fluffy towels. 'Could I get you something clean to put on afterwards? Maybe I could wash what you're wearing, and it will be dry by the morning?'

Jessica was implying that she was filthy and stank. And Jessica would be right. 'Yes, thanks.' Eve put her rucksack down next to the bath and felt obliged to say something more. 'I really appreciate this, you know. It's very kind of you.'

Jessica flapped her hand dismissively, as if she was in the habit of picking up waifs and strays on a regular basis. Maybe she was. 'When you've finished, put your clothes in that basket there, and then come back down the stairs and the kitchen is the big room next to the front door. You'll smell the food, so just follow your nose.'

Jessica smiled at Eve and Eve smiled back. She realised she hadn't smiled for so long that the expression felt out of place on her face. She stopped what was fast becoming a rictus-grin, and nodding, waited for Jessica to leave.

Eve took her time and used every lotion and potion to hand. It was like dying and going to heaven in a fluffy sudsy cloud of perfumed bubbles. But she was also starving, so reluctantly she got out, dumped her clothes in the basket and trotted down to the kitchen in a snowy white fleece one-piece which poppered up the front. It even had padded feet which made her feel like a five-year-old, but she didn't care. Because for the first time in months she was squeaky clean and warm.

'Hope spaghetti bolognese is all right with you?'

'Perfect. Thanks.' Eve shoved her rucksack under the table and bent to eat from the bowl in front of her. It was difficult not to shovel it down, but she managed to remember her manners, and ate at a rate she thought passed for passionate eating. 'It's delicious. You can cook,' she said.

Jessica laughed and looked flattered. 'I love eating.' She waved at her own body. 'As you can see, but what the fuck? If people don't like me because I'm fat, then screw them, is what I say.'

Shocked, Eve hadn't expected her to swear but she liked her for it. It made her seem more normal. 'Good for you. People are obsessed with stupid things that mean nothing when you get right down to it. It's what's in your heart that counts. It doesn't matter what anyone looks like. It's just how you perceive things. One person's ugly is another person's beauty. It's all meaningless.'

Jessica stopped eating and stared at her, as if she'd spoken in tongues. 'You're not what I was expecting, Eve.'

'What, because I live on the streets, you thought I'd be horribly uncouth and unable to form whole sentences? That's like me assuming because you picked me up and fed me, you must somehow be blessed and good. You really might be a complete bitch and hiding inside your beautiful house with a dirty little secret, just waiting to come out as a monster.'

Eve stopped. Thought she'd gone too far. She usually did. She did blunt. A lot. Sometimes too much. Normally, she was less public with her stark views on life. *I am me, and I can't help saying what I think and doing what I want. One of the reasons I ended up on the streets.* 'Sorry,' Eve said. 'I was born without a filter. Gets me into all sorts of trouble. I'm not suggesting you're anything other than you appear. I couldn't be more grateful for the bath, the food and you letting me stay the night. Really. I mean it.'

'No, not at all. You surprised me, that's all. You're refreshing. Pity we didn't meet under different circumstances.'

'Yeah, well. There you go. A missed opportunity. Who knows, we might have been best friends if we'd met over a drink at some party instead of me being homeless and you helping me.'

Now Eve was being polite. She didn't think her and Jessica would have ever been friends – whatever the circumstances. Eve didn't really *do* friends – preferred her own company. Until she got bored. But Jessica lapped it all up, as if Eve had spoken some cosmic truth.

Having said something kind to her, unaccountably, Jessica's manner suddenly changed, and she shifted in her chair and became all buttoned up and business-like, as if in self-defence.

'Have I upset you?' Eve said. 'I hope not. You'll have to excuse me. I never think before I speak.'

'Not at all. I'm not used to people who are honest. People usually lie to get what they want, don't you think?'

'Yeah, most people are shits. I'm not a great fan of people in general. Usually, they're bastards and only interested in themselves.' She put her fork down. 'And then they get you when you're least expecting it, so I leave them alone and stick to my own company. Safer all round.'

Jessica's face creased, and Eve realised she'd touched a nerve. For a moment, she saw understanding and compassion dance across her features. Jessica's mouth moved, ready to frame a question. And then she changed her mind. In the sudden silence, Eve turned her gaze downwards, her default position, and stared into her empty bowl.

'Shall I show you to your room?'

'Thank you. That'd be great.' Eve had obviously said something Jessica didn't like or had offended her in some way. Eve hadn't meant to and felt bad.

'Follow me,' Jessica said, and so Eve did, trusty rucksack dangling from her hand and dragging along the floor.

It really was a beautiful house, with fine art on the walls, which Eve suspected wasn't reproduction, and silk rugs on thick pile carpets, and soft muted lighting bounced from the walls, discreetly and quietly glowing.

They walked through a door which was standing open, and Eve had to side-step down a spiral staircase, feeling inelegant and oafish in mastering the correct foot position to best negotiate the black wrought-iron steps. The room she found herself in was a child's room filled with beanbags and not much else. Again, the lighting was muted and Eve looked around for a bed.

No bed.

Jessica went to a cupboard and got out a sleeping bag. 'Sorry, this will have to do, but it's new and you can snuggle into the beanbags. It's very comfortable. I used to sleep here when I was a child. It's a lovely room and I hope you'll be very happy in it.'

'I'm only staying one night, Jessica. It's fine. Perfect.'

'Shall I wash your sleeping bag for you, so it's nice and fresh for when you leave? It's no trouble and I'll make sure it's dry by the morning. I have an excellent tumble dryer.'

Bang went any chance of Eve staying here for any longer. It was obviously a one-night-only deal. Perhaps she could persuade Jessica that she was worth keeping around. If not for Eve's amazing wit and intellect, then maybe Jessica would like to carry on do-gooding. Although she didn't look the type.

Jessica said, 'Or you could just keep that one when you go. It's yours.'

'Thank you very much. For everything.'

'No problem. I'll leave you to it then. It's late. Goodnight.'

Jessica was halfway up the stairs before Eve thought to ask, 'If I need the loo, where is it?'

Standing at the top of the spiral staircase, Jessica looked down at her and for a second, Eve thought she saw a flicker of sadness cross the other woman's face.

'Use the bucket. It's in the corner. And there's lavatory paper as well. Goodnight, it's been lovely meeting you. See you tomorrow.'

And then she was gone.

TWENTY

Max

It had been the right thing to do, getting Jessica to move into his house with all her crap. Now he had not only a cook on hand, but a chauffeur. And this way, he could keep an eye on her. She was draining in her strange neediness of him; in contradiction with her odd and cold assertiveness. Her confidence. Although it unnerved and disturbed him, he felt safer having her close at hand, where he could watch her.

Constantly.

And this is where all the decisions he'd made so far, had brought him.

At first, Max told himself he was pleased to be rid of Jess for the evening, but as the night wore on, he started to feel anxious. It took him a while to identify the emotion as it wasn't something he was used to experiencing. But it was definitely bloody anxiety, and he didn't like it.

When the bitch had said she'd be going out on her own, he hadn't bothered to over-analyse it – keen to be on his own. Her company unsettled him. The whole situation unsettled him.

But there had been an unexpected bonus. He'd seen her house, and it turned out old Jess was a rich bitch. That could come in handy. Never one to pass up an opportunity, Max thought of ways of spending her money. She was so besotted with him, she'd hand over her cash to him, no question, and he'd spend it on anything he wanted.

It might give him the chance to move in different circles and go for a different type of woman altogether. Of course, labelling very wealthy women would be much harder for him, because it was a world which he wasn't familiar with. But Max was up for broadening his horizons, never one to shirk away from something purely because it was hard to achieve.

It would also make the achievement of kidnapping and murdering a woman with money all the sweeter, because it would be new and different. But shit, women were women, right? So he didn't see any immediate problems. He'd got bloody Jess, hadn't he?

He closed his eyes and tried to fantasise about taking a better class of women, but looking at the clock he realised it was one o'clock in the morning. Where the bloody hell was she?

Standing up from the sofa, he paced up and down, getting increasingly angry. He should go to bed and definitely not be sitting here when Jess came in. It would look like he was waiting for her, and he didn't like the image of that at all, as it popped into his head and stayed there, taunting him.

But she'd love it. It would make her think he cared.

What was the stupid bitch *doing*?

Furious and increasingly worried, he went to the fridge and opened a bottle of beer. Turned the radio on. Turned the radio off. Went back to the sofa. Lay down. Closed his eyes. Opened his eyes and stared at the ceiling. Fucking *bitch*.

And then he heard the key turn in the front door and he closed his eyes, aware that it would still look like he'd fallen asleep, waiting for her. Fuck it. Fuck her.

The sitting room door opened and before he could stop

himself, all pretence of sleep gone, the words spilled from his mouth. 'Where the bloody hell have you been?'

Christ, he might as well be her bloody mother. What was he thinking? He should have gone to bed. He turned from her, not wanting to see any more of her smiling and triumphant face as she peeped around the door. She'd done something, he could tell, and was bursting to tell him. Whatever it was, she saw it as a success. He recognised the self-adoration which shone from her.

'Wouldn't you like to know,' she said, as she sashayed across the room, oozing confidence all over the place. Like a snail leaving a trail of slime, she walked over to the armchair, leaving a shiny wet line of victory behind her, and sat down.

Max waited. She didn't speak. Tutting, he said, 'You've obviously done something which you're proud of, so come on, now's your time to show off.'

'I did it, Max.'

He wanted to hit her. 'Did what?'

'I got a woman. For you. For us. I got one.'

His heart rate quickened and his mouth went dry. 'Without telling me? What the bloody hell were you thinking? Where is she?'

'Aren't you pleased?'

'Where is she?'

'At my place. Safe and sound.'

'Where did you get her?'

'Off the street. It was easy. I didn't need any of your silly rules and systems. I asked her to come with me, and she came with me, and now I've got her.' She patted her hair. '*We've* got her.'

'Are you mad? You can't just take someone like that. You don't know what you're doing. And now you've got me involved. I'm an accessory.'

She grinned at him. Laughed. 'Puh-lease, Max. You're a

killer. A little bit of accessorising won't tarnish your reputation.'

Despite himself, Max wanted to see the woman for himself, but didn't want to give Jess the satisfaction of asking her if he could. 'Will she be missed? You've got to know who to take and—'

'She won't be missed. By anyone. She's homeless and her name's Eve. She's perfect. And don't worry.' Jess got up, placing both her hands on the armrests to give herself some leverage. 'She's all scrubbed clean after her bath, she's been fed and watered and is under lock and key. The perfect kidnap.' She curtseyed and stood over him, full of herself. 'I thank you.'

Needing to take the wind from her sails, Max lifted the leg nearest to her and farted. He waved at the air and pulled a face. 'What a fucking good one. A real stink bomb.' Grinning as she wrinkled her face in disgust, he said, 'And what makes you the expert in human behaviour all of a sudden?'

'Life experience makes me an expert, Max. You don't need a degree in kidnapping. To some of us, it comes naturally. It appears I'm in that category.' She bent down and put her hand on the arm of the sofa, her face inches from his. 'Would you like to see her? I can't quite work out if she'll be sleeping now, or wide awake and worrying. Either way, I'll show her to you, if you like.'

She straightened up again, and only then did he notice the suitcase in the doorway. 'I'll go and unpack while you make your mind up.'

'Knock your socks off.'

There, Max thought, that would show her. He'd take his time in asking to see the woman. He absolutely refused to be controlled by Jess. This was his domain, his skill, his fucking *craft*, and she was trying to take over. He wouldn't put up with it.

Stretching out again on the sofa, he closed his eyes as if sleeping.

He heard her as she shut the door and gritted his teeth as the sound of her squeaking suitcase on wheels went down the hall, and then bumped up the stairs.

Thirty minutes later, he was still lying on his back and trying to work out how he could see the woman in Jess's house without looking too eager. But if he knew women, he was pretty fucking certain that Jess would give in first, unable to keep her prize a secret from him. She'd beg him to come with her so he could see for himself what she'd done and how clever she'd been.

Sure enough, the door of the sitting room eventually opened. Keeping his eyes closed, he feigned sleep. Nothing happened. Max wasn't even sure Jess was in the room. She must be – the door hadn't opened itself. But still, there was only silence.

And then he felt her presence right next to him. It was an effort not to open his eyes. Not seeing her made him nervous. The silence was oppressive and suddenly he couldn't bear it. Sitting up quickly, he found he was panting. Pride rescued him and he got his breathing under control.

Jess stepped back a few paces and stood in the middle of the room. She smoothed down her hair, fiddled with her bra strap, and jiggled her massive chest back into place. Walking right up to him, she slipped her hand into his, gently squeezed it and pulled him off the sofa, towards the door. 'Come on, Max. I'll take you to her.' Her fingers intertwined with his like tiny clinging limbs – holding on tight: not letting go. Her thumb moved softly on the back of his knuckles, making circles on his skin.

She the spider, he the fly.

Max felt like screaming.

TWENTY-ONE

Eve

—————

E ve couldn't really believe how she hadn't seen how mad
Jessica was. Her, of all people, taken in so easily. Furious,
but definitely at a disadvantage locked in this room, she
concentrated on her outrage at having to piss in a bucket. She
might be homeless, but that didn't mean she'd sink that low.

She hadn't turned off the little lamp and walking carefully
around, she inspected her cage. Jessica hadn't been lying – it
had definitely been a child's room at some point. Everything
was soft – no hard corners. Other than beanbags, a lamp, her
new sleeping bag from Jessica, her rucksack and the fucking
bucket, there was nothing else. It might as well have been a
padded cell. It didn't take long to examine every corner,
wishing like hell that she'd find something useful.

But there was nothing.

Finally, she thought to look up, noticing light coming from
above. It took her a while to understand what she was seeing. It
was a glass ceiling and on the other side, on what would be the
floor of the room above this one, Eve saw Jessica's feet. She
watched as Jessica slowly bent at the knees until she was on all

fours. Her face peered down at Eve. Jessica raised her hand as if in greeting and smiled as she waved.

Eve was on display. Like a spider in a glass.

For the first time, real concern kicked in and Eve stared blankly up at the woman who had saved her. Refusing to acknowledge Jessica, keeping her expression completely neutral, Eve didn't move. Her head remained tilted up. Jessica laughed and got up, and the soles of her feet walked slowly away, and the light went off, and Eve was left with only her lamp.

Not wanting to think about the situation she was in, Eve focused on the positive. The only good thing she had going for her, was the fact that at least she had her rucksack. And in her rucksack was her trusty knife. No self-sufficient homeless woman left home without one. She'd often slept with it clasped in her hand, waiting for a man to creep up on her while she slept. Jessica hadn't thought to confiscate her rucksack, nor even thought to search it. Jessica's foolishness.

The knife was all Eve had.

Wondering if it was enough, the thought then occurred – did Jessica have a boyfriend? Eve tried to imagine why a woman on her own might want to kidnap a single woman, and couldn't come up with anything sensible. But of course, her reason for taking Eve, would never be anywhere near sensible.

Eve prayed that Jessica was on her own.

It would mean she might stand a chance.

Bring a man into the equation, and Eve knew the game wouldn't last long.

Two against one. Didn't seem fair. But her life hadn't been fair. In fact, it had been extremely *un*fair, and she lived with that knowledge and what she had done, every day of her life.

Eve didn't want a repeat performance.

After all, killing somebody wasn't a nice thing to do.

But if push came to shove, she knew she'd do it again. Who wouldn't, if their life depended on it?

Survival, Eve knew, was a very real thing. It made you do things that you'd never thought yourself capable of. But she hadn't liked taking the life of someone.

She was also a liar. To herself. Of course she'd enjoyed killing. Because the bastard had started it and Eve had finished it. In her world, that made it fair.

TWENTY-TWO

Jessica

A lot of my stuff from home – everything I needed anyway; I could always come back for more if necessary – was now at Max's place. *I've moved in. I'm co-habiting with Max. Whether he likes it or not and I know he doesn't like it. At the moment, he hates it. But I like it, and that's what's important.*

Now he was here with me in my house. I was pleased with myself at how I'd managed to get the upper hand in this relationship. But I refused to allow myself to think that Max was enamoured with our strange and unexpected partnership. I was well aware that he certainly didn't consider me a romantic interest, but was more than confident that he would. Especially now I'd kidnapped a woman for him.

I was going to make myself fucking indispensable to him.

Max was beautiful, he was weak, but mostly, he was mine.

I could and would change him, and he'd eventually come to realise that I was quite a catch. I was going to enhance and enrich his life and he'd learn to happily accept his fate.

But he didn't look happy now. Max was nervous, which surprised me. *Why isn't he excited? Is he jealous that I've so easily accomplished something that he obviously has to work so hard at? Is he that childish?*

'Would you like a drink to settle your nerves, Max? A beer?'

'What do you mean? I'm not nervous. I'm quietly eager, that's all.' He rolled his shoulders. 'Lead the way, Jess.'

Slowly, I walked out of the kitchen and through the hall. I put one foot in front of the other deliberately slowly, wanting him to beg me to hurry. But he followed without speaking and we moved through the house in silence.

When we reached the sitting room, I slowed my steps and then stopped and turning, looked at Max. He quickly glanced around, confused. 'Where is she, then?'

As if I were on stage, rolling my hips as I walked, I went and stood on the glass floor where the light from below, shone up and into the room where Max and I were. Max didn't move but stood dumbly in the same position. 'Come here, Max. Look through the glass. She's down there. See, she's looking up. I wonder why she's not tucked up in her nice new sleeping bag yet.' I smiled and waved and sang out, 'Hello, Eve.'

Max joined me and sinking to his knees, he pressed his hands against the glass. His breath misted it as he peered down, his hands cupping his eyes, and he rubbed it clear with his arm.

'You don't have to put your face to it. It's just normal glass.' I patted his shoulder. 'Eve can't hear us, unless we shout. Just so you know.'

Max rocked back so that he was squatting on his heels. 'What's with this set-up? Why do you have a glass room?'

'Glass ceiling, glass floor, depending on where you are, obviously. It's my old playroom. My parents liked to watch me playing with my friends from up here; made sure I was safe. It's not that special.'

Max stared at me and raised his eyebrows. 'Bit odd.'

'What's odd?'

'The whole glass room thing. Your parents were odd, and you're odder.' He twizzled his finger at the side of his temple and showed her his gold tooth. 'But it makes a good kidnap room, I'll give you that.'

He only looked quickly at me, before turning his eyes downward again, unable to tear his gaze from Eve. 'What happens if she turns off her lamp and I still want to see?'

I flicked a switch. 'This happens. There are four spotlights in the top corners of the room for precisely that reason. My parents were real worriers: always liked keeping a beady eye on me.' I laughed but Max still wasn't paying me much attention. He seemed fascinated by Eve, who's pale face still gazed upward. She'd flinched at the harsh glare of the spotlights, but hadn't changed her stance, standing in the middle of the room. I couldn't really blame her; she must be shocked at how her evening had ended.

Ignoring the guilt at admitting this to myself, and knowing I'd made everything worse for Eve, I also shook off the genuine empathy I'd felt for her when we'd eaten together. I wondered what I was doing. Without Max, alone with the girl, I had thought clearly and normally, and hadn't been able to ignore the wrongness of my actions.

When I was with Max, I had a tendency to be swept along by his madness, and almost unwillingly, I'd get caught up in his game – and become intent upon impressing him. I worried at what lurked within me, and why Max had the power to unleash whatever darkness I had inside me.

But I refused to dwell on my own very short shortcomings. It amazed me that now I had my very first man firmly within my grasp, I had actually kidnapped another human being and was even entertaining the idea of murder. But it was only at the entertaining stage – it definitely hadn't morphed into a solid date. It remained unconfirmed.

The longer I was in the presence of Max, the more likely it

was that murder would become a tangible thing. The realisation amazed me but I couldn't deny it was also a bit of a turn-on.

Sooner or later, I'd have to decide which side I was coming down on: good or bad.

'Why isn't she doing anything? Why's she just standing there, looking up?' Max quickly flicked his eyes at me and then back at Eve. 'And why's she dressed like a fucking snowman?'

'She isn't – it's something for sleeping in. And just what exactly were you expecting, Max? A song and dance from her? She's not about to perform for you.'

'Is she locked in?'

I had to stop myself from sighing. 'Of course she's locked in. She's not roaming about the house, admiring the fixtures and fittings, is she?'

'Can she breathe? It looks like a box down there.' He stared at me. 'I wouldn't want her suffocating before it's playtime with Max.'

'There's plenty of air vents in the room, and the door up here will be open and shut often enough. Because we won't just be watching her, Max. She will be fed and watered.'

He giggled. 'She'll be more than fed and watered.' He went quiet for a minute. 'She's looks nice. What I can see of her.' Glancing quickly again at me, he smiled, and I took it as a compliment, and allowed myself to feel pride in a job well done.

Max spoke with his face glued to the statue that was Eve. 'She's not fat, but she's not bad looking either. And she's frightened, I can tell. Good.'

He couldn't take his eyes off her, and Eve carried on standing there, staring up, keeping her eyes on his. She looked challenging, I thought, but didn't think Max noticed. His dick was doing all the thinking, and he thought he saw terror because that's what he expected.

That's what he wanted.

I thought he was wrong.

'Nice,' Max said. 'Fat or frightened. Either will do. But both would be perfect.'

He never looked like that at me. Max was just Max with me. Now, he's really interested. He's in love with fear. It doesn't matter she isn't fat. Female terror is enough to arouse him. Seeing it play out live on his face, I recognise how truly perverse it is – he is.

Max moved his still kneeling body and bent nearer the glass. 'What's that on the floor next to her?'

Still standing, I dipped my eyes and peered down in between my shoes. *Shit. I forgot Eve's rucksack.*

'Is that *her* bag? Why's she still got that with her? Did you search it? What's inside it?'

I closed my eyes. I'd made a mistake; it would be pointless to lie about it. 'It's her rucksack and I don't know what's inside it. So, no, obviously I didn't search it.'

Max stood up, his shoulders hunched in anger and his hands curled in fists. 'See. Bloody, see. That's what happens when you don't know what you're doing. You make stupid fucking mistakes. How do you know she's not armed and dangerous? Jesus, Jess, I told you to wait for me to show you how it's done, but you wouldn't wait, would you?' He stood in front of me, and I felt his breath on my cheeks. 'And now look what's fucking happened.'

'Armed and dangerous – I think you're getting carried away here. There's no need to panic. There's two of us, we can see where she is in the room – it's not like she can leap out at us unexpectedly. Hence the beauty of using this room. We'll sort it, don't worry.' I smiled, but it didn't soothe either my irregular heartbeat, or Max.

'No, Jess. *I'll* sort it. You've done enough, going off half-cocked, trying to prove yourself to me. You should have waited. Now, I'll have to make sure she's safe to be with.'

I tried out a laugh. 'Stop over-reacting, Max. I doubt she's got a gun.'

'How the fuck do you know?'

He jutted his chin out at me, and his hot breath smelt stale. Max jabbed his finger hard into the middle of my chest. 'Show me how to get down there.'

I didn't speak until I'd unlocked and opened the door. Stepping back, I couldn't resist saying, 'I'll stay here and watch how it's done – always good to watch a maestro at work.'

'Don't test me, Jess.' Grabbing my wrist, he said, 'You're coming with me. I wouldn't want you to miss anything.'

He grinned at me, and for a second, I was caught off guard. Max was excited, whilst my excitement had definitely waned. I wondered what level of excitement Eve was currently experiencing.

I led the way down the spiral staircase and we walked into the playroom and stood opposite Eve. She still hadn't moved and was attempting to look fierce in her fleecy footed onesie.

'Hello, babe. I'm Max. I'm here to help you. I'm sorry you were locked in this room. You'll be all right now I'm here. Don't you worry. Why don't we go and sit on that beanbag together, and we can have a chat.'

'We don't need a chat. Let me out, if you're that concerned for my welfare.'

'I will let you out, sweetheart. In a minute. Come on now, sit down with me and we'll talk.'

Eve took a step towards Max, and keeping her eyes on him, she nodded in my direction. 'Thanks a bunch, Jessica. You *tricked* me. No one tricks me.'

I heard the outrage and watched, fascinated as a furious Eve slapped Max across the face. Left him flat-footed in shock.

Pushing past him, she ran straight at me.

Instinctively, and without any thought, I pulled back my arm and punched her, connecting with her face. There was a loud crack and some blood. Not a lot, but enough for it to be shocking. The snow-girl, dressed in white, was now spotted in red.

It was the first time I had ever hit anyone.

Turned out I had a killer right hook.

TWENTY-THREE

Eve

W hen Eve opened her eyes, it took her awhile to work out where she was.

Then she saw Jessica. And him. And she remembered.

She was lying on the floor and the man squatted over her, dangling her knife in his hand. 'Who's a naughty girl, then?'

'That's mine. Give it back.'

'I don't think so. It's mine now.'

Eve shrugged, pretending a coolness she didn't feel. 'Keep it then.' Ignoring the glass ceiling above her, imagining it a window into something better than here, she used a polite conversational tone. 'Would you mind telling me what's going on?'

Jessica loomed into view over his shoulder. 'You've got blood all over your nice new onesie, Eve. Wait.' She held her finger in the air and crossed the room to the bucket. Wrapping toilet paper around and around her hand, she gave it to Eve. 'Here, press on the cut. That should do it. You won't die.' Jessica smiled. 'Promise.'

Pushing up with her palms on the floor, Eve sat up and the

blood dripped from the side of her face. A trickle of red from her cheekbone. Pressing with her wad of paper, she said, 'I can't believe you made me bleed.' Gingerly, she massaged the bone, and felt all around it, wincing in pain.

What Eve couldn't work out, was who, out of the two of them, would be more satisfied by her injured state? Her vulnerability? This situation? Bum shuffling away from both of them, she landed in a beanbag and inspected the pair who had captured her.

They were an unlikely couple: Max all blatantly false and Jessica… *Jessica* was more frightening. Although Eve didn't think Jessica knew quite what was going on. The woman was winging it, unsure of the order of things – if order there was – and, most terrifying of all, Jessica couldn't quite hide the fact that on some level she was enjoying herself.

But she was definitely the one in control. Eve could tell. She recognised the signs.

Max just thought he was in control.

As a social observation, all this was very interesting. As a reality, it was a serious mind-fuck.

The one in control didn't know what was happening, and the idiot man looked very much at home. Totally comfortable with the way things had progressed.

This clearly wasn't his first time at female abuse as he moved with a comfortable and casual ease. Eve guessed he'd done it before. She also guessed that it was Jessica's first time – and yet, oddly, it was she who pulled the strings, and unwittingly, Max followed without realising it. Strange. And very unsettling. *And let's not forget, she* did *kidnap me.* Jessica had already proved herself as no angel.

Eve gathered from the set-up that she had plenty of time – the woman had brought her here and given her to Max. Hand delivered. And he was ready. Ready to… what? Eve didn't know what he was ready to do, but you didn't have to be a mastermind of psychology to work out the most obvious reason.

'Are you going to rape me, Max?'

He smiled. He was astonishingly handsome but because he knew it, played on it, assumed it would get him through life for free, his good looks self-combusted. He was an ugly man wanting ugly things.

All in all, Eve thought that this wouldn't be a quick rape. No, nothing so simple. It would be a thing that lasted some time. Days, perhaps. Why else the glass ceiling to watch her? Why else bathe her and feed her, if only to rape and kill her as soon as Max turned up? That didn't make any sense at all.

'I'm for keeps, aren't I, Jessica?'

Jessica and Eve's gaze met, and Jessica's didn't waver: not too much anyway. But enough for Eve to know that Jessica wasn't yet sure. Unaware of the silent communication between the women, Max said, 'You asked me a very interesting question, which I haven't answered yet, Eve. Eve? That's your name, right?'

Eve saw Jessica roll her eyes, but Eve nodded, playing the game.

'You asked me if I was going to rape you.'

Nodding again, Eve couldn't yet decide on an appropriate expression so kept it all neutral. But furious inside.

Intellectualising was the best distancing-from-emotion tool she had. Eve wasn't sure how long she could keep it up: it appeared to have a very short shelf life – especially when anger was next in line for an outing, and was already pushing, eager to get to the front of the queue.

Or was she terrified? She knew she should be, and of course she was afraid. But she'd done this before. And then, fear had worked for her – as a positive thing. So, she started her own performance. Eve made herself tremble. To all outward appearances, she must have looked a pathetic, terrified victim.

Max's eyes shone, and smiling he said, 'The answer is, most definitely, yes. I am going to rape you.'

However tough Eve thought she was, she was frightened, but not *that* frightened. But she allowed her face to leak fear. She milked it, making sure her bottom lip quivered. That was something she'd learnt to show before, when she'd been at risk of losing; when she'd wanted the beating to stop. She thought it was always a good thing to show terror to a man like Max. Not showing fear would mean she was in deep trouble. That's what Eve thought.

And I'm an expert in this field.

Jessica went up to Max and they both stood there, looking down at her. He, greedy, and she quietly calculating. Eve imagined and hoped she could see Jessica's brain sprinting along, trying to come up with something to derail Max. Eve didn't know why, but she realised Jessica had chosen to be her saviour and as their eyes met again, Eve very gently dipped her eyes in acknowledgement of Jessica's decision. Making it real, instead of a desperate childish wish.

The silent interaction between them was too subtle for Max. He missed it and edged closer to Eve, unbuttoning his jeans. Although she was his focal point, he couldn't stop glancing over his shoulder at Jessica, checking she was watching him. Hoping he was impressing her. Satisfied he had Jessica's attention, he swaggered ever closer to Eve.

When Jessica placed her hand on his arm, he shook it off, but she grabbed it again, harder this time, bringing him to a halt. 'No, Max. I've got a better idea. A much *much* better idea. I promise you'll love it.'

'Fuck off, Jess. Leave me alone with the snowman/woman. The flake.' He laughed. 'You're not needed.'

'We could get another one.'

Eve knew what she meant, but Max lowered his eyebrows in confusion. 'Get another what, for Christ's sake?'

'Another woman. Then you'd have two to play with. And this time, we can make sure she's fat. Then you'd have the best of both worlds – fat *and* frightened. Don't waste your time on Eve now. She'll keep. She's not going anywhere.' Jessica turned to Eve. 'You'll wait for Max, won't you, Eve? After all, the longer you wait, the more frightened you'll be, right?'

Bobbing her head up and down frantically, Eve realised she'd got it all wrong. Max *liked* fear. That wasn't how it was supposed to be. She'd expected her display of fear to calm him, to placate him – like she'd been used to. It had always worked well before. But not now. Eve had made a big mistake. Having to carry on the game, Eve forced herself, all meek and feeble, to say, 'Yes. It'll make it worse. The wait, I mean. Imagining what's coming. It'll be terrifying.'

'Really?' said Max, grinning. 'If I leave you, will you lie there, all bloodied and crushed, and get more and more frightened? Really?'

'Really,' Eve said, knowing, that for the moment, she had to carry on this façade. She made an effort to put a tremor into her voice. 'The longer I have to wait for you to rape me, the more terrified I'll be.'

Jessica put her hand on the back of Max's neck and gave it a little squeeze. 'You've got a lot to learn, Max. I'd have thought, from your own experience in your chosen labelling and pigeonholing career, that you'd understand how to ratchet up the fear. Perhaps you were always too impatient and *couldn't* wait. Maybe you've always been a little premature, if I can put it that way. Everyone knows, if you're already frightened of something, it becomes more frightening, if you have to wait for it.'

He shook his head and pointed at his groin. 'I'm ready now, ladies. Why wait?'

This would be a hard sell for Jessica. Closing her eyes, Eve quietly prayed Jessica would come up with something that would stop a psychopath with an erection.

'Eve's got a friend, haven't you, Eve? A fat friend. You could tell us where to find her, couldn't you? If Max can keep his penis in his pants long enough, then he could have two frightened women, for the price of one.'

Opening her eyes, Eve saw Jessica's expression was almost beseeching. Eve's mind rattled around her head, no coherent thoughts coalescing into anything sensible. Under the pretext of holding her cheekbone, Eve covered her eyes with her hand. Forcing her survival instinct to remain intact, she tried to relax her brain cells as they rolled around in her head, like a bag of frozen peas, dropped from a vast height.

'Yeah, I know someone.' And Eve did. A part of her died at the betrayal. 'If you really want scared, you want my friend, Bella. Big Bella. She'd faint with even the threat of you raping her.'

'I don't believe you. You're just trying to save yourself,' Max said.

'She's not lying,' Jessica said. 'I was going to bring Bella as well. She was hanging around when I invited Eve here, but I didn't think you'd be able to handle two women. Thought it might be a bit much for you. But no worries. You go ahead. Have at her, Max. Go on, rape Eve. You're right. She's here and she's frightened. Well, frightened *enough* anyway. Why wait for two scared little girls, when obviously it would be too much for you?'

Jessica turned to go and Eve almost puked she was so scared at not having a grip on the situation.

At having got it so wrong.

'Course I could bloody handle two women, what are you even talking about, Jess? Fuck's sake. Course I could.'

His face had turned pink and Eve realised he was embarrassed. She also realised he was frightened of Jessica and was desperate to prove he wasn't. Max did his jeans up and pointed at Eve. 'You, bitch, stay there and I'll be back with your mate, Bella. And then we'll have a fucking ball. I'll prove to you all just how good I am.' He sing-songed Jessica's words '*Can't handle two?* Christ almighty. Course I fucking can. Bring it on.'

Trying not to exhale with relief too obviously, Eve managed a small meek nod and scrunched her knees up to her face, carrying on the lie, her words sounding tearful. 'I'm not going anywhere.'

Max suddenly crossed the room and thrust his face into Eve's. 'I know you're fucking not. Because you're locked up, you stupid cow. See you later, *Eeeve.*'

He was a couple of steps up the spiral staircase, when Jessica stopped him. 'Aren't you forgetting something, Max?'

'What?'

Jessica sighed and said to me, 'Where is Bella now? Where can we find her?' She waited a beat. 'And don't even think of lying, Eve, because then *I'll* be pissed off and you wouldn't want that, would you?'

No, Eve really didn't want to piss off Jessica. Eve had got that right at least. Jessica was the one to watch. And Eve liked her a little bit more now. She suspected they shared a commonality, but it was too soon to know for sure if indeed they were both predominantly out for themselves.

And Big Bella *was* frightened of everything. Eve would look after her though. Honest, she would. If she couldn't save herself, Eve could save Bella. 'She'll be under the disused bridge, just up from where your car was, Jessica. She always sleeps at the end, in a red tent. You can't miss her.'

Eve watched them leave the room, an excited Max in front, hyped up, pumped up and fucked up. Jessica risked a quick glance at her, and Eve couldn't really read her expression.

But she thought it was disappointment.

And Eve couldn't really blame her.

TWENTY-FOUR

Jessica

*S*eems *I've come down on the side of good after all.*
For the time being.

I was surprised at how angry I was at Eve for so easily giving up a fellow human being. Poor Big Bella.

But I wasn't a complete fool. I knew that I had behaved badly, to put it mildly, but I had a very good reason for my actions. There was nothing complicated about it: I wanted to keep my man. Eve was a means to an end, that was all.

But I draw the line at rape. I didn't think I would. But apparently I'm nicer than I thought.

What was Eve's excuse for betraying Bella? Perhaps Eve and Bella weren't good friends, but merely acquaintances. In that case, Eve could possibly argue her point. But snow-girl was on thin ice with highly dubious morals, if she'd so easily given any woman up to a rapist. Even if that rapist was Max. I wouldn't dream of doing anything so under-handed and cheap.

To give Eve her due, she'd been quick on the uptake and had given them a name and a location for the girl. It had been a risk asking Eve if she had a friend, pretending that it was someone I had already met and discarded, as Eve might not have understood. Or indeed, she might not have known anyone suitable, although that last was unlikely. There was a glut of choice out there on the homeless streets of London.

Thankfully, Eve had come good. At least she'd better have been telling the truth. If I didn't find Big Bella in a red tent, if Bella was a figment of Eve's imagination, I wasn't sure how to proceed next.

But I knew Eve had been telling the truth. Guilt had made Eve's eyes brim with her own treachery and I had been oddly disappointed in her. I was surprised to find I actually liked Eve and had expected more from her. More in the way of loyalty. *Weird, right, under the circumstances?*

'Do you even know where you're going?' Max's voice was overly loud in the car and I leaned away from him.

'Don't shout, and yes, here we are. Let me park and then you follow.'

As I unstrapped my seat belt, Max startled me by holding me in place, his arm across my chest. 'Stop telling me what to do. You are not taking over my kidnap and raping. You are not. I'm in charge here, so stop interfering. Let me do my thing.'

I nodded and said, 'I'll stay here, then, shall I? Good luck getting Bella to come with you. I get the impression, women on the street aren't that keen on strange men approaching them in the middle of the night. You can't just *take* her – there'll be too many people who'll see you.' Smiling, I added, 'And if she's anything like Eve, she might have a knife on her.'

Max's jaw clenched and he quickly closed his eyes. He took the time to breathe in and out a few times, before opening them. 'You go first, Jess, but I'm right behind you.'

Satisfied, I got out of the car and walked briskly down the road and under the disused bridge. Sleeping bags and a few tents scattered the underpass and a smell, a dying rotting smell, hung in the air.

I trotted quickly down the littered tunnel until I could see the end. And there it was, as promised, in all its magnificence. A red tent.

Glancing around me, there was little movement from the other under-the-bridge people, and only two men were visible from here. They were approximately twenty feet apart, and a good distance from the red tent. They both sat with their backs against the wall, knees up to their chests. One drank from a bottle. The other stared into some abyss that waited only for him. Both of them ignored Max and me. I could hear his breathing at my shoulder.

We were still some way from the tent.

Max grabbed my wrist. Hissed at me. 'Stop. What are you going to say? You haven't even thought about it. You don't know what she'll respond to.'

'Did you think my mind was empty driving here? It wasn't. I know what I'm doing.'

I didn't. I was simply hoping my natural civility would be sufficient for the task in hand, not allowing myself to get bogged down with complications and unnecessary details. But I faltered now, knowing I'd be better without him. 'Why don't you go and wait in the car, Max. Hide behind the driver's seat and put the blanket from the back seat over you. No self-respecting woman is going to come with me if you're here. She'll only come if I'm on my own.'

'Who wants a self-respecting woman?' He laughed. I didn't. 'Pretty sure of yourself, aren't you, Jess?'

I stared at him until he sighed, understanding that I was right, and pushing off from the wall, he held his hand out. 'Keys.'

'And when we get home, don't get out of the car until she's inside. I'll let you know when she's in the bath.'

'A bath? Fuck's sake, Jess. What are you giving her a bath for? You're not running a spa.'

'If you want to rape filth and get fleas, then go ahead. Otherwise stay in the car until I come and get you.'

He walked away, and I could see he was furious by the straightness of his back, his stiff gait and his fists swinging at his side. His breath billowed out from his mouth in wispy bursts of white condensation in the cold air – short little angry puffs of exhaled anger.

Smiling, I approached the one spot of colour in the underpass, and stood within touching distance of the tent. Instinctively, I softened my own breathing. Gently does it. Crouching, I rested on my heels, not wanting to frighten the girl inside and make her scream. Quietly, I reached my hand out and touched the zip at the top of the flap.

I pulled at it. Slowly. Only an inch. I stopped. *I* wouldn't like it if someone unzipped me without asking. It would frighten me. Instead, I spoke quietly. 'Hello? Bella? Are you in there?'

Silence.

'Don't be frightened. My name's Jessica.'

Nothing. I put a bit of extra warmth into my voice. 'There's another girl staying with me tonight already, who told me about you. Wouldn't you like to join her? A bath, food and a bed – as it's Christmas. Come on, open up.' I tried to fill my voice with kindness, but it was difficult as I couldn't see who I was talking to. And it was difficult because it was a long time since I'd been kind. I was out of practice.

Waiting patiently, I was finally rewarded with an answer. 'Who's the girl?'

'Eve.'

'What's she look like? I don't know no one called Eve.'

I hadn't really noticed Eve's appearance. It hadn't mattered. 'About my height, although that's not helpful, as you can't see me.' I added a hint of laughter to my words as an extra tempting festive twinkle. 'Dark hair, thin-ish. In her thirties, I think.'

'There are a million women on the street who look like that.'

I was temporarily stumped.

'Did she have anything with her?' The zip opened and I saw that Big Bella was indeed big. Her hair was blonde and matted but her eyes were clear on a face that sat on broad shoulders.

'Yes, she had a rucksack. An orange one. Looked pretty heavy.'

'What's she talk like?'

I had to think before answering. 'Well, I suppose she talks a bit like me.'

Bella came out on all fours, her big head coming out of the tent like a baby being birthed. A very big baby.

'You must mean Her Majesty. Don't know her name, but it sounds like her. With her poncy accent and her orange rucksack. Must be her.' Bella shrugged. 'And she's with you? In your house, you mean?'

'Yes, in the spare room. Bathed, fed and warm. Do you want to come?'

'Why did she pick me?'

Probably, between you and me: as one large woman to another, because you're the only fattish person she knows and that was the requirement.

I shrugged at her. 'No idea. Look, if you don't want to come, I'll find someone else. But Eve said you were okay and could do with a break, so take it or leave it.'

A wily expression crossed Bella's features. 'I don't have to pay?'

'No.'

'You sure Her Majesty is there? You're not shitting me?'

'I shit you not.'

Bella licked her chapped lips and stared at me, her eyes

round – trying to pick up on any clues I might be giving away. The big woman was unable to hide her nerves, and didn't say anything for a moment, while she studied my face. Nodding to herself, Bella made a costly mistake and unaware of her bad choice, she smiled, showing a missing tooth. 'Right, if Eve's there, it must be okay. I'm coming.'

Turning around to check if she needed anything from her tent, Bella finally stood, empty-handed. 'All right then. And I eat meat, just so you know.'

I beamed my beamiest beam. 'No problem. And I'm so pleased. Eve will like the company, I'm sure. You're lucky she picked you.'

So lucky you won't believe it. Just you wait, Big Bella. You're in for more than you could ever dream.

TWENTY-FIVE

Max
___

S crunched up in a ball, Max was so angry he didn't know what to do with himself. It was humiliating hiding under a bloody blanket. But he was the first to admit that he'd be seen as a threat in this scenario. Best leave Jessica to do it.

As much as that rankled.

But it was the best way to handle this particular situation. A big virile *clean* man, picking up a woman from the street. It would look… odd. And women weren't *that* thick. Even homeless ones. Especially homeless ones. He assumed they'd be more aware of the dangers of the world, and of Max in particular.

But he still thought he could have won this Big Bella over by being himself. Like he'd got Jess. And like Jess, this Bella would have thought she'd died and gone to heaven. But big bossy Jess had taken that away from him. And for that, he'd show her.

Show Jess and Eve and Big Bad Bella the time of their lives.

That made him smile, and he settled down feeling calmer, and waited.

131

When his minion, as Max liked to think of Jess – but not out loud – opened the car door, he kept very still and listened.

Listened to not a lot of talking between his go-getter and the got. He kept his eyes shut, imagining the delights of Big Bella. The car seat had groaned satisfyingly under her weight and his raping tool responded in a very back-to-normal Max way.

He couldn't wait.

He'd give all his slags something to really scream about.

They'd all scream until their throats were sore.

They'd all scream until their throats were squeezed shut and their breathing stopped.

Max put his hands over his mouth, barely able to contain his excitement.

Jess would see just who was in charge around here.

She'd played right into his hands.

Finally, he had more than he'd ever dreamed of. *Three* women, all locked up. It was a fantasy come true. Well, strictly two women, but in theory, three women at his disposal.

And all thanks to his knowing when to delegate, and when to take control.

Max was lying to himself, and he knew it. But he luxuriated in the untruth, letting it take away the horror that was Jess, embracing himself in his own warm lies. But he'd get her in the end. When she'd served her purpose.

He snickered under his breath.

Max carried on, trying and failing to ignore the power that Jess had over him, worrying at it like a loose thread. He couldn't comprehend his strange fear of her. Still struggling to fully understand why Jessica frightened him so much, he tried to label it, give it a name. Once he'd identified the origin of the terror she made him feel, he'd be able to destroy it – take away her power over him.

Jess filled him with a childhood monstrous dread – all

darkness and everything unknown. Unable for the moment to correctly pigeonhole her, he refused to admit how weak she made him feel, how horribly scared, and instead, buried his terror of her, deep down where it couldn't get him. Much easier to concentrate on the positives here, and there were three of them.

Three.

TWENTY-SIX

Bella

B ella sat in the bath, really warm for the first time in
weeks, and scanned the room for anything worth stealing.
She could shove an expensive bottle of shampoo up inside her
before she left, but that was all: there was nothing of any value.
Nothing she could sell.

Shit.

She wondered why hoity-toity Her Majesty had agreed to
come here. Bella supposed it was the promise of free hot food.
Home cooked. That Jessica woman was fat so it stood to reason
she must know how to knock up a decent meal. She was fatter
than Bella, but Bella thought her own body was stronger
overall, with a bit of real solid meat on her. Muscle meat. A
handy thing to have on the street. She could take Jessica,
any day.

The thought of food made Bella hurry and she changed
into a pair of striped pyjamas that Jessica explained had been
her father's, *and* a towelling dressing gown. Posh, or what? Still
a bit damp as she couldn't wait any longer to eat and hadn't
bothered drying herself properly, she padded downstairs, after
she'd put her dirty clothes in a basket. Bella had landed on her

feet for once, and now they were feet with clean socks on, and hurrying, she trotted quickly down to the kitchen.

'Hello, Bella. Do sit down. I've got shepherd's pie, I hope that's all right?'

'Sounds great.' Sitting, she picked up her knife and fork, eager to start, before it had even been served up. Jessica looked at her and seemed a bit pissed off, so Bella put the cutlery down. Fuck's sake. Why the ceremony? She lived on the streets. *I'm so sorry I don't come up to scratch. The bath didn't wash all the filth off me, so this is me. I can't help it.*

Bella hadn't been born yesterday and knew the dangers of going home with strangers. You just never knew what they might really have in mind. But she could flatten Jessica, because Bella was very strong, so that knowledge made her not worry too much.

And Eve was here. She was clever and Bella couldn't see her being taken for a mug by anyone.

No, everything was going to be fine. But still, despite the food, she was nervous. Just a bit.

She didn't wait for Jessica to sit down before she started eating the huge portion of shepherd's pie that was put in front of her. Not bad at all. She had to stifle a burp, and bending her head nearer the plate, she finished it off.

'More?' Jessica said.

'Please.'

The same size portion went down the hatch. She wanted to ask for tomato ketchup but knew Jessica would be offended. They didn't talk at all, but Bella was aware that Jessica watched her. A lot. She wanted to say, *What are you looking at?* but didn't quite dare. Finally, she sat back and trying hard to be polite, she said, 'Thank you, that was very nice.'

'Good, I'm pleased you enjoyed it.'

Jessica cleared the table and put the plates in the sink. 'I'm sure you'd like to see Eve now, wouldn't you?'

Bella nodded. At least she knew Eve, sort of, and she'd never had any trouble with the woman. They were on nodding terms. And Eve was the same as Bella. A street person. It didn't matter how Her Majesty spoke, all la-di-dah – Bella would feel safer once she was with her.

'Here, take this,' Jessica said, grabbing a zipped-up nylon bag from a cupboard. 'It's a sleeping bag, as clean as clean could be. Sorry, I've run out of beds, but you'll be nice and snug in that.'

'That's fine, thanks.'

Bella trailed behind Jessica, through the hall and past lots of different rooms, her jaw hanging open at all the rich stuff, everywhere. She'd never seen anything like it and normally, she might have made some smart remark, but the wealth silenced her and made her feel small.

Without knowing it, Bella's steps had got shorter and slower and she was surprised when she looked up, to see Jessica waiting by an open door. 'Sorry,' Bella mumbled. Her socked feet sank into a thick carpet of air, and for a minute she thought she was floating. Her nose was filled with a clean smell – like flowers.

Bella felt dirty and out of place – she didn't belong. The paintings on the wall looked like children's squiggles but she knew they were expensive. Anything that shite had to be expensive, but she didn't understand it.

This was a world she'd never visited; magical and unknown to her. It made her aware of her size, her voice, her bad education. Her mouth was dry with awkwardness and shyness and just being Bella. She tripped and stumbled, big and ugly in a strange and elegant, *beautiful* place that wasn't meant for people like her. She didn't fit in, and she shouldn't be here. She didn't belong. She didn't like it and wanted to cry with the shame of not fitting in here. Bella quickened up, suddenly desperate to see Eve.

It will all be better when I'm with Eve. She's clever but I'm the physically strong one.

Trotting again, Bella smiled and hugging the wall, avoiding a large glass thing on the ground in the middle of the room, found herself walking through the door and down a staircase.

It went round and round and round.

Cool, or what?

Dominic won't believe what's happened to me when I tell him later.

TWENTY-SEVEN

Eve

The sound of the door opening from above made Eve jump. She'd been lying on top of her sleeping bag, thinking it wouldn't be wise to get into it. She'd be trapped. Trapped again. She heard the thump of feet coming down the stairs, and Bella loomed into view.

Eve had kept the lamp on as she hadn't fancied being in the dark – although she knew it made her horribly naked and visible to Max and Jessica through the glass ceiling. Anyway, even if she turned the lamp off, Jessica could turn on the spotlights, and that was somehow worse.

As if the four beams shone only on Eve, as if highlighting her – prepping her for a post-mortem. That's what the lights felt like – a prelude to something medical – so Eve kept the lamp on.

Guilt temporarily strangled her, and she couldn't think how best to greet Bella. She needn't have worried. Bella, all big and brash and pretending to be bold, said, 'Well, look who we have here. Your Majesty.'

Eve knew this was her nickname on the street, but didn't

care; there were more important things to worry about at this minute.

Bella curtseyed and sniggered. 'Who'da thought you and me would end up kipping in the same place.' She looked around the room and then up at Jessica who stood at the top of the stairs.

'Goodnight, ladies. Bella, Eve will tell you what to expect, won't you, Eve? You won't be sorry you accepted my offer, Bella. Welcome to fear.'

Jessica smiled and slammed the door shut, and Eve listened to the turn of the keys, and as before, the sounds of bolts being scraped across the door. Bella didn't seem to hear the very final clicks and scrapes of keys and bolts. And Bella pointedly ignored Jessica's words. As if she really hadn't heard them. Or preferred to pretend she hadn't. Instead, she feigned a fascination with the room itself.

'It's a bit empty, isn't it? I was expecting a bed. I mean, I know I've got a sleeping bag and all, but where am I meant to put it? On one of them squishy things. That's a bit odd, isn't it?'

'It's all a lot odder than you could ever imagine.'

Looking at Eve properly for the first time, Bella came closer and said, 'You're bleeding. What happened?'

Bella's big face was shocked and she turned around twice on the spot, taking in everything. Eve decided to lie about the origins of her cut face. 'I slipped coming down the spiral staircase. Hit my cheek on the handrail.'

'Poor you.'

But Eve could tell Bella wasn't really interested in Eve's bloodied face, and the red drops had dried where they lay – like Eve had been stained forever for her betrayal of Bella. Exposed for everyone to see her treachery in blood. *I am a traitor to all women.*

'What's going on? This doesn't feel right. I don't want to stay. What's the bucket for? And don't say, pissing in.'

'It's for pissing in.'

'What are you talking about?' Bella had dropped her sleeping bag and was going back up the stairs.

'There's no point,' Eve said. 'The door's locked. We can't get out.'

Bella glared down at her and reaching the door, she rattled the doorknob and pushed and pounded on the solid wood. She kicked at it angrily, panicking.

Eve went and stood at the bottom of the steps. 'Come down, Bella. There's no point. Honest, I've tried. There's no way out. Please come down, I need to explain what's happening.'

It wasn't until Bella was standing next to her, that Eve realised Bella was crying. Her face had come out in red blotches of panic, and Eve hadn't even told her about Max yet.

Nor the fact that Eve had told Jessica about her. About the red tent. About how Bella was always frightened. How could Eve admit to Bella what a shit she'd been? She found her eyes wouldn't meet Bella's and shame overwhelmed her. Eve had always prided herself in doing the right thing, if it suited her, and here was poor old Bella, uncomprehending of what lay ahead, and it was all Eve's fault. She'd dragged her into her nightmare which should be only hers. She'd involved a true innocent.

'Welcome to fear? What did Jessica mean, by that, Eve? Was it a joke?' Ever hopeful – if Bella wished something hard enough, perhaps it would come true, and all this would turn out to be a wildly amusing hoax.

Deciding that for the time being, she wouldn't mention her glorious role in Bella being here but needing her to accept the seriousness of their situation, Eve said, 'Look up, Bella.'

Bella stared up in incomprehension, her strong neck craning back. 'What's that? Is it feet? Who's up there?'

'It's a glass ceiling and that's Jessica and Max watching us.'

'Who's Max?'

'I'm not sure. I don't think he's Jessica's boyfriend, and I'm not sure which of them is in control, but I think it's her. She's the really dangerous one.'

Bella turned around and punched Eve in the arm. 'What have you got me into, you bitch? Why did you ask that woman to come and get me? She told me you asked for me to come. You told her my name. Why me? What have I ever done to you?'

So, Bella already knew of Eve's cowardice and the giving of her name to the enemy. 'Nothing. Really, nothing. I'm so sorry and I know that's not enough. There aren't words to explain how much I regret getting you into this, but I can't change it. We're both here.' Eve took her hand. 'We'll have to stick together. Perhaps we can think of a way out.' Eve shrugged. 'It was unforgivable. All I can say is, I'll do my very best to protect you.'

As apologies went, it fell very short, but Eve couldn't think of anything to add which would be helpful. She didn't want to lie to her and say it wasn't her fault, because it was, and she wasn't a liar. She was only a coward, apparently. Saving herself from making it worse with more useless words, the spotlights came on and they both looked up. Max was now lying face down, spread-eagled on the glass like a starfish, and they could both see his face – laughing. Eva had no choice but to warn Bella. She had to be prepared for what was coming.

'Max wanted to rape me. He'll want to rape you. He wants to rape both of us, but you need to pretend you're not frightened. That's apparently his thing. It's what he likes.' She shrugged helplessly. 'I'm sorry, Bella. Truly, I am.'

Bella's face was dough-coloured, and her mouth hung open

in disbelief. She carried on looking at Eve, speechless, and then she looked up at Jessica and Max again. Back to Eve. Then up.

Her voice, when she did speak, came out in a cracked whisper. 'But, Eve, I'm always frightened. I'm frightened of fucking life. Of everything. How can I not be frightened of rape?'

She punched Eve in the arm again, and shouted, '*How can I not be frightened of rape?*' Then she collapsed onto the floor and started crying. Wailing, her whole body trembled and shook.

Eve couldn't bear to watch, and turning away from Bella, she looked up through the glass at Max.

He gave her a thumbs-up.

TWENTY-EIGHT

Jessica

'No, Max. Not yet. Haven't you learnt anything? Weren't you listening to everything I've said to you?'

Max's face was shocked, as if he couldn't quite understand my words. My audacious and patronising words, as he saw them. 'Do what, Jess? Everything you know, *I've* taught you, so don't you dare question whether I've learnt anything. Who do you think you are? You're just a woman who I kidnapped and then, because you're a nutter, you fell in love with me. That makes you the biggest idiot here.' He lifted his shoulders and grinned. 'But who could blame you falling in love with me? It happens all the time. Almost an occupational hazard.'

I clasped my hands, tightly, so hard that my fingers ached. Max might very well be the most handsome man I'd ever met, but he was beginning to more than annoy me. 'This is important, Max, and I'm not repeating it again. No, you are not going down to rape the women yet. I thought you understood that's why I got Bella. To make *both* of them frightened. Double the fun, in your language.'

As both Max and I were standing on the glass floor, I

bowed my head and closed my legs, so that the two women beneath me, couldn't see up my skirt. 'Clearly, Max, you haven't grasped the concept of fear yet. And considering it's how you get your jollies, that amazes me. How long do you normally keep a girl, before raping her?'

He shrugged. 'I don't know. I don't time it. But about…' He stopped and glanced up, closing his eyes, and I wondered what he was seeing, what he was picturing as he apparently tried to give me an honest answer. 'About two hours, tops. Get them in, get them out. Quick, simple, sorted. No wasted time, no hanging about, less possibility of being caught.'

I was surprised he'd answered me honestly. '*Really*? Two hours? Is that all? That's not utilising time and fear very wisely, is it? It's not maximising your power, and that's why your power is being drained. By me – because I understand how to get the best out of people.'

'I don't have to try that hard with the women I take. They're already frightened. There's no need for me to work at it. I'm there, job done.'

I walked off the glass floor and dimmed the lights. Max didn't move and couldn't help himself from looking down again at his treasures below him. I folded my arms. 'That's why I question whether you've learnt anything. You're not going down there now and raping either or both of them. Because Eve has got to tell Bella what's coming.'

I came back and stood next to Max and looked down through the glass. Saw the leaden lump which Bella had become. Like a large crumpled bin liner, she sat messily on the floor, sobbing.

Pointing, I said, 'Which she's evidently done. Look at how Bella is now. And this is important, Max. Now, you wait. Because you need to give it time. The fear, it needs time to settle into Bella's mind and the longer she has to think about it, the worse it will become, and the more terrified she will be.'

'You can't stop me. I'm going down there now.'

'No, you're not. You really *do* have to learn this, if you want to improve your skill. I've already said it once, when I had to stop you raping Eve.' I carefully used the tone I would naturally have adopted talking to a young child: that of condescension. Breathing in slowly, I said, 'Fear, Max, is like a living thing that grows exponentially. It gets into your bones and it sets up house in your head, where it reproduces and spreads, like an infection. Bella is frightened now. By tomorrow, she'll be a gibbering idiot: too frightened to stand on her own two feet. Doesn't that appeal to you? Isn't that precisely what you're striving for?'

He refused to look at me, staring down into the playroom. 'She's frightened enough now.'

'No, she is not, Max. What are you finding so difficult about this concept? Your refusal to listen to good advice, is immature. Don't you want to be the bestest kidnapper, rapist and murderer that you could possibly be when you grow up?'

'You're not my teacher, Jess. I'm running this show.'

'Are you? Well, good luck with that.'

I stood on the glass floor and waited, while Max walked the short distance to the playroom door. Keeping my back to him, I tried not to smile. He must have been embarrassed because it was a good minute, perhaps two, before he came back to me.

'Yeah, very funny, Jess. Give me the keys.'

'No. You'll have to wait until tomorrow. We were up all last night and all of tonight.' I looked at my watch. 'It's ten past four in the morning. Why don't you go to bed, and we'll meet again tomorrow, and then we can reassess the situation?'

I could tell he wanted to hit me. He held his hand out. 'Give me the keys. Now.'

'Again, Max, no. I haven't got them on me, so there is no point in even thinking about stripping me naked until you find them hidden about my person. I do not have them on me.'

'Stripping you naked? You have got to be joking. That's all in your head, it's your little fantasy. Keep the keys. I'll do the women tomorrow and you can watch and be very jealous. You'll be green with envy, I know you will be. Because I won't ever screw you. Not ever.'

'But you'll always come back to me, Max. Because you're mine and you always will be. And that's why I've got you, not the other way round.'

I moved towards him, and he moved away. 'See,' I said. 'I think – for some reason which I haven't quite understood yet – I think you're frightened of me, and that, dear Max, is why *I* am in control. I have all the power and you will do as I say. You can't tell me what to do and you cannot frighten me. That's why I'm the one who is winning in this partnership.'

Max looked like he wanted to stamp his feet and jump up and down, furious that he hadn't got his own way. But there was nothing he could do. I put my arm on his. 'You're welcome to sleep here, instead of going back to your place – there are plenty of bedrooms. After all, if you left, do you fully trust me? With your two captured women, do you? Are you certain of my behaviour in your absence and what I may or may not do *to* them, *with* them? You must have given it some thought, Max. How much do you trust me, my sweetie-pops?'

I puckered up my lips, enjoying taunting him, but found him a disappointingly easy target. As targets went, Max could be handled with my eyes closed. It wasn't a realisation which made me jump with joy. It made me sad. Eve would be harder to control. I was wary of the homeless woman and didn't trust her. Not one bit.

Although, strangely, there was something about the woman that I admired.

It was all proving to be very intriguing.

I was brought back into the room by Max's voice. 'You're involved, Jess. You kidnapped both the women. So I know for a fact that you won't release them. You're invested in them as much as I am. Stop playing games because I'll beat you every time.'

'Carry on telling yourself that, Max. Your conceit has made you blind to reality. Conceit and ego. If you were stripped of your beauty, that's all you'd be left with: and you can't live on conceit and ego alone. You need more filling, to bulk your personality out. I can teach you.'

'No, Jess. All you can teach me is how to bulk myself out physically, and that sure ain't going to happen. Point me in the direction of a room – I'm not fighting you to get the keys to the playroom downstairs. You win.' He clapped his hands. 'As you say, the bitches will keep.' He thrust his face into mine.

'But tomorrow, my biggest and maddest fan, I shall play with them, and you'll have a front row seat. Whether you like it or not. I'll make you watch. It'll make it more fun. For me. And that's all that's important, as my conceited ego tells me. You're right, but where's your truth got you?'

He walked away and said, turning over his shoulder, 'Do I go upstairs and pick a room, any room and make up my own bed?'

Nodding at him, I felt a certain amount of satisfaction at how things were working out. It *was* my rules. Max just hadn't realised it yet.

I was self-aware enough, and honest enough with myself, that I could admit the other reason I needed to keep Max close. He brought out my true personality and that, I knew, was better than being a pathetic, bullied victim.

I stood proud and strong and knew I was my own woman.

At last.

This, my home since childhood, was bursting tonight with fear.

I looked down at the two women beneath me: Bella was clearly terrified.

And then there was Eve. She'd stopped acting now and appeared calm. I wasn't a complete fool and hadn't been taken in by Eve's earlier theatrical performance of fear at the hands of an advancing Max. She'd been playing at it, which in itself, was fascinating. It begged the question, why wasn't Eve frightened?

And of course, there was Max – he was most *definitely* afraid of me.

I considered my own personality in this unlikely quartet of relative strangers.

Eve and I are the only two here who aren't scared.

How strange and how very wonderful.

That fear which Max craves so much; I am unable to give him.

The irony of it killed me. It was strange that we'd teamed up – two misfits, unable and unwilling to give the other what they so desperately desired. If it wasn't so bloody tragic, it would be funny.

But back to the business at hand.

Fear was new to me. Shame, yes – throughout my life, I'd been plagued by it. Followed closely by humiliation and a quiet anger. But fear? Not so much. Of course, Max had succeeded in initially frightening me when he'd tied me up – but really it had been more like shock – and I'd overcome it. Because I was confident in myself.

As long as it wasn't teasing.

Fear didn't instantly resonate with me. It wasn't familiar and I didn't think I reacted to it as other people did.

Fear seemed such a waste of energy and was nonsensical. But I was aware that I'd have to be very careful about that assumption. If I was wrong, it could prove fatal.

On the whole, I decided that fear was a very human condition and one worth examining more closely. It was an emotion I thought might be intriguing if I were to develop it, examine it in more depth, with my three houseguests.

It was worth cultivating.

On an academic level only, of course.

And on a more practical level, I had to stop the rape of one or both women.

Because I am kind. Underneath it all, I do care. Really, I do.

TWENTY-NINE

Max

_____

Max hadn't bothered putting the sheets on his bed properly. His dad always did it for him, when he was at work. Bed-making had always been his father's work, after all, and Max wasn't about to start doing it now.

Flattening down the sheet, un-rucking, re-tucking and de-creasing it, he pulled the uncovered duvet up to his chin and gave serious thought to what Jessica had told him.

Really, it was the same lesson Dad had taught him when Max had been a boy. Waiting for something bad to happen, the longer the wait the better, *was* effective. Max needed to really get to the bottom of this fear thing – he'd been well-schooled in it, but he'd never fully *understood* it.

And if he was to conquer his strange fear of Jessica, he had to come to terms with it. Learn how to recognise it, and then make it worse. He'd have to seriously up his talent of scaring the shit out of women. How hard could it be? Pursing his lips, and furrowing his eyebrows in the dark, he concentrated. Hard.

He recognised he had to use fear far more wisely than he had previously. Against *all* women.

He also knew, from his personal experience with Dad, that the not-knowing when the scary shit was going to happen, only highlighted the fear until it became panic – an exhausting, leg-trembling, sweat-under-the-arms feeling that got worse and worse. It had consumed his body, settled in as easily as slipping his foot into a snug-fitting sock, and sat there, quietly growing.

And that's when you were lost. You were at the full mercy of fear itself. It was a simple equation. Fear was bad. Fear plus waiting was worse. Simple. Add in the not-knowing when the bad thing was going to happen, when it would get you, meant that when the axe did eventually fall, it usually wasn't as bad as the anticipation of it had been.

But by then, the damage had been done.

His eyes closed, Max remembered when he'd been a boy and had crept quietly into the house, not knowing where Dad was. But knowing he *was* there. Somewhere. The further into the house he'd gone, the harder it became to physically open *any* door – was Dad hiding behind it? Or under the sofa. Or worse, under his bed – that was the worst place to find him.

Max's skin would crawl, and he'd prowl about the whole house, calling out, 'Dad. Dad, are you there?'

At bedtime, especially at bedtime when monsters lurked, before jumping into bed, he'd check under it. And Dad wouldn't be there. Relieved, Max would go and clean his teeth, thinking himself safe, and coming back, he'd slip out of his clothes, bare feet on the floor, and there Dad would be, screaming at him, terrifying him. But only sometimes he'd be there. And sometimes not. That's what had freaked Max out so much. The uncertainty, the trembling fear of *not* knowing.

Max recalled the sweat which covered his forearms, and how his legs would stop working properly. He'd ended up jerking around the house after school and at the weekends, walking like a child who'd been paralysed and was learning how to move again; all stiff and awkward. His throat would click with dryness and his tongue would feel big and swollen. Sometimes it went on for hours.

Until Dad would say, 'Gotcha, you bad, *bad* boy.'

Max nodded to himself in an emphatic way. Looking back on it, his dad had been hard, but his methods had worked. It had made Max the man he was today.

He moved himself on from the past to the present, happy to forget the Whites of the Eyes game. And now, the biggest problem he had was that Jess – for reasons which were too complicated to comprehend – thought herself immune from fear.

Therefore, the other two homeless women would be his starting blocks. His practice women. He'd make them wait and wait and wait before he raped them. He'd make the not-knowing a thing that would terrorise them. He'd experiment on them, ratcheting up their emotions until they'd be as he'd been as a child: forever on the lookout. Never knowing when it was safe to relax.

Jess would be dealt with when Max had learnt this lesson properly and it had become as natural to him as breathing. As natural as his beauty. As natural as his ability to correctly label and identify women's weaknesses.

It went against his basic work ethic, which irritated him, because he'd never had to wait before, to get his women scared. They simply were frightened, because he had them.

Max convinced himself he was tweaking his methodology, and it was all his own idea. Jess had nothing to do with it. He'd just seen the opening that she'd shown him, and being a professional, had taken advantage of it. Because he was good at what he did.

Very good.

But if he was going to win this war against Jess, he had to start again, with a new modus operandi, with a proper understanding of the new rules. He'd take her by surprise. She wouldn't know what hit her. She'd be impressed by his clever and unexpected tactics. Max would use a strategy that even Jess hadn't thought of, and she'd be floored by his mind. He knew she was cleverer than him, and that was part of the problem.

Mostly, it was a psychological problem – his problem. Jess was his very own mental block and he couldn't get past her because he didn't know how to deal with her. He managed, for the time being, to put her in a separate compartment in his mind and forget about her.

Settling down into his bed, he started to think hard. It was a new thing for him – actively giving anything serious thought and not relying on his looks alone. The more he thought, the more interested and interesting it all became.

The idea of how to further terrify the two women in the playroom was slow in coming, but as it went from blurry to clear, the edges of the idea becoming definite and something concrete Max could work with, only then did he allow his smile to stretch his lips to their full width.

Nodding, he quietly laughed out loud into the silence of the large room: very pleased with himself.

He'd had a cracking idea, and it would freak everyone out.

Including Jess.

But most importantly, it excited him. And that was what it was all about.

Max sat up in bed and flexed his muscles, pleased at the definition of his biceps. He was back in the game.

THIRTY

Bella

E ventually, Bella stopped crying, but now her nose was all blocked up and she hated Eve. She hated her but needed her. Bella couldn't do this on her own. A man, a strange man, coming down to rape her. How could Eve be so calm about the whole thing?

It was all Eve's fault, and she should fix it. But Bella knew she wouldn't. Bella was on her own and it wasn't fair.

I owe Her Majesty Eve nothing at all. I need to look after number one and stuff her. Let her look after herself.

Hopefully I can have a private chat with Dominic in my head. That always helps me.

Anger, so much easier than being afraid, started to stir within her. She had every right to be angry with Eve. She wanted to make Eve pay, make her suffer for getting her into this shit, but Bella thought that might be a stupid idea. Eve was cleverer than Bella, and unless Bella wanted to beat the crap out of Eve, perhaps it would be better if they teamed up. Although that idea didn't exactly thrill the new socks off Bella's feet. It really annoyed her that she'd have to be nice to Eve, but she didn't think she had a choice.

And, she reasoned, being together with someone, *anyone*, was better than being alone.

She'd always been lonely on the streets, in her little red tent. All on her own. Maybe this was her chance to finally make friends with someone. Get a proper friend, instead of only nodding acquaintances, which was all she had, when she was out and about, and not in her red tent.

Of course, Bella had Dominic, but he lived only in her mind. She wished him real now, more than ever.

Bella didn't know what to do or what to say. Eve wasn't saying anything either. Her face seemed to have shut down and she was obviously thinking hard about something. Bella couldn't bear the silence anymore. 'So, what now? What do we do?'

Eve shrugged, lying on a beanbag, looking like a big baby in her onesie, waiting to be picked up and cuddled. She was very calm, but instead of making Bella feel better, it made everything worse.

Bella sat on her own beanbag and couldn't help but let some of her anger out. 'You got me into this, Eve. Get me out of it.'

'I'm thinking.'

'I'm here because of you, so *do* something.'

Eve sat up, picking at the blood on her face. 'What do you want me to do, Bella? We're locked in. We can't get out. Max will be coming down here tomorrow morning. *This* morning. What am I supposed to do?'

'But it's all your fault. And you're the one with the brains. *I* don't know what to do.'

Bella could hear that her voice sounded sulky and childish. But she was pissed off and thought she had every right to be a bit bad-tempered. She was scared as well. Tears welled in her eyes again, and she swiped them away, not wanting to seem weak.

Eve got up, came towards Bella and squatted beside her. 'The reason I told Jessica about you was because I was pretending to be frightened. That's the truth. All of it. I don't have any other excuse. I know that will only make you angry with me, but there's not much I can do about that, other than apologise.'

'You don't look frightened now.'

'Because I'm not. And that's something we need to discuss. It's what Max likes. He's like a parasite who feeds off the fear of others, and that's why we mustn't show him how we feel. I made a mistake thinking he'd be nicer to me if I pretended I was scared. I was wrong. We need to show him something different. Something that will put him off.'

'Put him off rape, you mean?'

'Yes, put him off rape – that's exactly what I mean. You need to stand up to him, fight him if needs be. I don't think he'll like that. He's one of those men who gets off on terrifying women. He enjoys making women quiver and quake – anything looking like strength or aggression coming at him will freak him out.'

'How come you know so much about it?' Bella got up and walked towards the bucket. 'Sorry, gotta have a slash.'

Eve waved her hand in the air, meaning she didn't care, so Bella peed, very loudly, against the side of the plastic bucket – wanting to make Eve feel like she had to go as well. Childish, but she didn't have a lot else to work with. Eve ignored her, so Bella wiped herself and went back to her beanbag.

'Go on, tell me, Eve. Tell me everything.'

'Like what?'

'Why you're on the street, nice girl like you, posh accent, what happened? And how come you know so much about men like Max. You don't look the type. Are the two linked? I mean, are you on the street because of a man? Is that it? Am I right?

That's the reason loads of women are homeless. Bloody men. I'm right, aren't I?'

'What is this? Twenty questions?'

'No, but we're stuck here, together. It might be useful if we knew a bit about each other. Tell me why you're homeless, for a start. Just general stuff like that. Give me something, Eve. We're trapped in this room with a glass ceiling and like it or not, and believe me, I don't like it, let's pretend we like each other. Let's actually really try and like each other.'

Eve sighed and wandered over to the bucket. Undid her onesie, facing Bella, and squatted, leaning forward, her breasts exposed – not embarrassed at all. Bella couldn't really get a proper feeling for the woman. She was cold, but not unkind. Just not warm.

I don't think we're going to be best friends after all. I've just got a feeling we won't be.

All buttoned up again, Eve came and sat down next to Bella. Eve clasped her hands in between her knees and stared straight ahead. 'I was with a man for five years and he used to beat the crap out of me.'

Bella was surprised. Eve didn't look like a victim; she didn't look like that type of woman – but what did that type of woman look like anyway? Putting her hand on Eve's knee, Bella patted it gently. 'Sorry. That must have been awful.'

'Yeah, well, it happens all the time. And I let it happen. So, you could say it was my fault.' Suddenly she turned and grinned at Bella. 'But I didn't let him get away with it.' And then she turned away and stopped talking.

Bella wasn't sure she wanted to know any more but steered the conversation back to her own immediate worry. Because as well as making friends, she was looking after number one and didn't want to be raped. 'Was he like Max? Did your man rape you as well?'

Eve spun her head around and glared at Bella. 'No, that's

the whole point. That's why I made a mistake with Max. I assumed he'd be the same as Oliver. But they're complete opposites. Max likes fear, and Oliver liked violence. Physical fighting, that was his thing. Quite different.'

Bella listened carefully to Eve's tone of voice – detached and cold. Like she was talking about someone else and had forgotten Bella was there. Eve freaked her out a bit. She decided she wouldn't like to get on the wrong side of her. But she wanted to know more.

'Your Oliver, he must have got off on fear if he hit you, right? I mean, men don't hit women and not like the fear they're causing. They love it. And the more frightened and the more damage they do, the better. You heard what Jessica said. "Welcome to fear".'

Eve was shaking her head before Bella had even stopped speaking. 'No, you're wrong, Bella. When I'd had enough of being beaten, and I do mean, really *enough, no more, I'm going to die*, then, and only then, I'd turn on the tears, the shaking and the trembling and the pleading, and you know what? Oliver would stop and want to make up, make friends, make love, and that was worse.' She paused. 'Much bloody worse.'

Bella didn't know what to say, so kept quiet. She thought about Eve's story and found she had to ask, 'But surely it was better when the beating stopped? Why didn't you pretend to be frightened and upset quicker, and then the violence would have stopped quicker, right?'

'No, wrong. I preferred the fighting, except when I had to admit defeat, because both my arms were broken, or my face was so smashed up I couldn't see out of my own eyes. I hated having to give up and cower and sob like a weakling.'

Eve stood up and looked down at Bella. 'The first time Oliver hit me, I was surprised. Really startled; I'd never been hit before. But luckily, my first reaction was to hit him back. It was instinctual. I didn't think about it, I just punched him straight back in the face. First time, I actually knocked his tooth out. And you know what? I liked it.'

Inside, Bella felt a bit of her curl up in horror. Not at the story – she'd heard worse. But at the way Eve spoke. Her expression when she'd talked about hitting Oliver, had taken on a dreamy quality and she'd smiled: proud and lost in the memory. Relishing it. 'I actually enjoyed hitting Oliver after that first time. He enjoyed that I enjoyed it.' She raised her eyebrows and said, 'We had a pretty sick relationship. But the bit I always hated, was the make-up, let's-pretend-we-love-each-other-again bit. The I'm-so-sorry-baby-don't-be-frightened-I-love-you-so-much part. I only resorted to using the little frightened girl who'd had enough, when I thought he might really kill me. I used my scaredy-cat routine in self-defence, and I hated every minute of it.'

Bella didn't speak for a bit until she'd thought of something to say that was a bit more practical. That wouldn't make Eve concentrate on violence. 'You left Oliver then, and ended up on the street? Is that what happened?'

Eve's eyes rounded in surprise, and she laughed. 'No, that's not what happened at all. I murdered him and went to prison for it. Came out and drifted, couldn't get a job, and it all went downhill from there.'

'You killed him? To stop him hitting you? Like self-defence?'

Bella could hear the desperation in her own voice, wanting the ending to be something that she could sympathise with, but knew, as she saw Eve shaking her head from side to side, that she wouldn't be giving Bella the answer she so wanted.

'You're not completely wrong, Bella. That's what I told the court, that it was self-defence. I got seven years for voluntary manslaughter, because of the severe provocation I'd endured, and the fact I'd acted in self-defence, having suffered from the prolonged damage he'd inflicted on me. I was severely wounded, nearly dead, but his injuries were as bad as mine: we'd beaten each other up: *a lot*. And he died. But it was worth it.' She laughed.

Bella nodded, mute with shock. It wasn't Eve's words – it was her manner. Eve grinned at her. 'But it wasn't really self-defence. I got the bastard when he wasn't expecting it. I caught him when he thought I was unconscious. He thought he'd be able to beat me up for the rest of our lives together, but I put an end to it, when I was playing possum, and he made the mistake of relaxing and closing his eyes.'

Bella offered up a wet smile and wanted to cry.

Eve bent down and put her arm around Bella's shoulder. 'Don't be upset, Bella, I survived, and that's what it's all about, isn't it? Staying alive at whatever the cost.' Eve sighed. 'But I do miss Oliver. Sometimes, when I'm bored, I do miss him.'

Bella nodded eagerly, thinking it was best to agree with whatever Eve said.

'And that's why, you and me, Bella, we'll do the same to Max. We'll trick him. We'll give him what he wants, lull him into a false sense of security, and you know what? That's always the best time to get them. When they're least expecting it. I won't be treated like I'm nothing again by a man. I won't. We'll win this one, you'll see, and I don't want you to worry. I'll always have your back. Because it's my fault you're here, so I don't want you worrying. You've got me for keeps, Bella. I promise to look after you.'

'Thanks, Eve. Thanks a lot.' Bella held her tears back and stopped herself from shaking. This was why she was always frightened.

Because you just never knew what life was going to do, and usually, all it did was turn out badly.

Bella wasn't even really surprised.

Just resigned.

And terrified.

THIRTY-ONE

Max

———

Max jumped out of bed early in the morning, wide awake after only four hours sleep, too excited to waste time not doing anything. He felt invigorated and eager to put his plan to the test. Max also found himself wanting to impress Jess. He admitted it. If he impressed her, perhaps she'd stop terrifying him so much.

But that was by the way, he tried convincing himself. Secondary to the day's activities. Today he was going to improve his technique with the ladies, with the preparation of his victims; pre-rape, pre-kill – and that in itself was a cause for celebration. There was nothing wrong in introducing something new to his modus operandi. Any skill could be sharpened and fine-tuned, and he was more than ready for the challenge.

Fuck Jess. He didn't care what she thought of him. She wasn't normal, he had to remind himself, so her opinion of him was skewed, and his view of her was definitely off-the-chart messed up. *I am* not *frightened of her. She is nothing. I am everything.*

Today he'd be doing what he did best, but because he'd

taken the time to think about the task in hand and to see the bigger picture, Jess would obey him without question and the two homeless women would do as instructed. Simple as.

Hurriedly he dressed and ran downstairs.

He slid into the kitchen on his socks.

'Morning, dearest,' Jess said. 'Hungry?'

He heard her teasing tone but decided to ignore it. 'Have you fed my women?'

Jess arched an eyebrow. '*Your* women? My, someone has a high opinion of themselves. I wasn't aware you'd adopted them. And no. Not yet. Why?'

Max collapsed into a chair. 'Well, don't feed them. I've got to go to the shops for something. A surprise. Keep breakfast till I get back. Give me forty-five minutes, that should do it. I'll get bacon and stuff, leave it to me.'

Not wanting to give Jess any opportunity to quiz him on his plans, he walked past her to the front door, and put on his coat. 'Can I borrow your car?' She nodded and got her keys from her bag. Tossing them to him he caught them. He was determined to say nothing more but couldn't help himself. Felt compelled to gain some respect from her. 'I went out of my way to give what you said last night some serious thought. About fear.'

He thought it was big of him to admit this to her and he waited, while she stood in silence, not responding in a very obvious way, in the door of the kitchen. Taunting him with her blank face. Max was surprised to find himself disappointed. Jess picked up on it instantly. 'What do you want, Max? A round of applause for thinking? I don't think so. You'll have to do better than that to get any plaudits from me.'

He didn't bother hiding his dislike of her. 'You are one nasty sarcastic bitch, Jess, and whether you like it or not, you will obey me, because I say so. You don't have a choice.'

She reared her chin back like she was working up to letting

loose a seriously long spit across the room. But all she did was look at him in mock-admiration, heavy on the mock. 'My, my, Max. Who's got out of bed this morning all extra especially manly?'

'We're doing everything my way from hereon in. You do as I say, and as an acknowledgement to you – but it's actually all my idea – I shall frighten the ladies as you suggested. Not by raping them, but pre-rape. Keep them waiting, like you said, never letting them know when I might be bad. I've got ideas. Lots of them, and believe me, they'll be crapping themselves with fear and begging me to stop.'

'What have you got in mind?'

He wagged his finger at her, as if he were telling off a child. 'None of your business. You can play along and watch. I'm sure you'll enjoy my performance.'

She simply nodded but didn't speak. Max felt a bit cheated – he'd expected more praise from Jess. Wanting her to recognise his efforts, his ideas for improvements – *not that I have to* prove *myself to Jess* – on maximising fear. Max couldn't resist giving her a clue.

'We're going to play the White Eye game.'

Still nothing from her.

'The full title is, The Whites of Their Eyes. It's a great game. A real crowd pleaser.'

'Your invention?'

'Course. Who else?'

'I'll start making tea and coffee very slowly then and await your return. Consider all your women on the edge of their seats and suitably agog with excitement and anticipation.'

Unable to deal with her disrespectful commentary, disappointed at her bitching, he pointed his finger at her. 'Forty-five minutes. See you later.'

Accelerating away in the car, away from Jess and away

from her grand house, Max drove quickly and expertly onto the main high street and parked.

Buying what was necessary, he found himself rushing, sweating, trotting in order to get back to the house. He didn't want Jess feeding the women before he got back. He resorted to queue-jumping, pushing past people and shouting at slow shopkeepers who didn't move as fast as they should – and got what he wanted. He hated Christmas, and he barged past and through the festive crowd who moved with no intent, no real goal in mind. Max wanted to kill all of them. He went to several shops, and finally his favourite one. For a prop. Finally, job done, bags in hand, he drove back.

He leant on the bell, his confidence back, and realised he now had very different props from his usual go-to stash of uniforms. What he had instead was very unique and he was strangely fascinated as he pictured how his presents would go down.

Jess opened the door and looked pointedly at her watch. 'I'm impressed. You have seven minutes to spare. Would you like to come in anyway?'

Pushing past her, he put his bags on the floor and slowly undid his coat. She said, 'I'm in the kitchen.' With Jess gone, Max got his new prop out of the bag, stuffed something in his coat pocket, and hung the other thing – the showstopper – on a hook and covered it with his coat.

Walking briskly, he went straight back into the kitchen and handed her a packet of bacon. 'I want you to serve them this for breakfast, okay? It's got that unmistakable smell and it's important all my piggies smell pork this morning. Nothing quite like a bacon sarnie to get the juices flowing.'

'You're being very mysterious, Max. I'm intrigued.'

'So you should be. And I'll be serving it up to them with no interference from you.' He looked around the kitchen. 'I don't suppose you've got any of those silver things you put over food, to cover it and keep warm, have you? You know the things I mean? You pull them off and it's like, ta-dah, your breakfast is served.'

'A cloche. Yes, I've got some. Are you going to reveal something to us all?'

Grinning, he couldn't help his expression becoming a smirk. 'I am. You'll all love it, but you as an observer – you'll be pleased to know – not a participant.' He went up and playfully smacked the back of her head. 'Count yourself lucky, Jess. This one will be better viewed from the touchlines.'

Nodding, she started to fry the bacon. 'Do you want anything in particular served with this, or is it just bacon you need?'

'Slap it in between two slabs of bread. We're going for a traditional bacon sarnie for each of them. Who'd say no to one of those?'

Jess was strangely quiet and her change in mood unnerved him. He thought about asking if she was all right but couldn't be bothered. Max had much better things to think about. Taking two Tupperware containers out of his shopping bag, he placed them carefully on the worktop, next to the fridge. Without looking at Jess, he said, 'Don't eat these.' And then he sniggered, unable to control himself. The thought of her dipping her hand in and shoving a fistful of the contents into her face, amused him.

'Turn away,' he told her. 'Keep cooking the bacon. Don't watch what I'm doing.'

With his back to her, continually sneaking glances at her over his shoulder, to make sure she wasn't watching, he prepared his own little treat for Eve and Bella. Belatedly, he realised he hadn't even thought to include Jess in his trick and hoped that wasn't a sign that he was treating her as a partner, as an equal, instead of the victim she was. Would always be, whether she wanted to admit it or not. 'Have you got four of those cloche things, babe?'

'Yes, babe, I do.'

There was her sarcastic tone again, repeating *babe* back at him, and he told himself that he mustn't encourage her by calling her anything that she might take as a compliment. He could tell she was taking it the wrong way, and she really believed they were personal terms of endearment. Jess couldn't be expected to know he called all his women these meaningless things – mostly because their names weren't important to him. Or more honestly, most of the time he never actually knew what his women were called. Because he never asked.

Wanting to get going, he fidgeted at her side, watching as the bacon sizzled and his mouth watered. 'Save some for us. For me, I mean. For afterwards. I've already worked up an appetite, just thinking about the White Eye game.' He squeezed her shoulder. 'That looks done to me. Slap it between the bread and bung it on two plates. And get a tray. And the dome thingies.' Putting his hands on his hips, he smiled nicely at her, needing her to be on side with him, not wanting to have to worry that she'd destroy his plans. 'Okay, Jess?'

'I'm fine, Max.' She quickly buttered four slices of bread. 'As I say, I can't wait to see what you've got planned.'

He put his two finished plates with their silver domes over them on the tray and added the two bacon butties under their respective cloches. Taking a third container, a large bucket with a push-down lid and a handle, from his bag, Max put it next to the fridge, on the floor. 'Again, no peeking.'

She shrugged her shoulders, as if she were finally accepting the roles as they should be: he the leader, her the follower. 'Don't worry, Max. I'm not that interested and wouldn't dream of spoiling your surprise.' Jess smiled at him and Max thought she looked more subservient than she had. Progress. All he'd needed was time with her, and he was back on top.

'You'll love all my surprises. And White Eye was Dad's favourite game.' He spoke with a voice that hinted at a fond nostalgic trip back to a happy youthful time.

Max was surprised and a little disturbed to find that when he really thought about the game Dad had played with him, actually stopped and seriously remembered it, it wasn't fondness he felt at all.

It was a sickness that sat heavily in his stomach, and turning quickly away from Jess, he re-composed his face into something that was more comfortable. It was all that over-thinking about fear he'd done last night. He remembered the White Eye game too vividly again now and breathing slowly and deeply, he picked up the tray and swallowed drily.

It was time for his version of The Whites of Their Eyes, but this time he was playing Dad's role.

He'd only got as far as the kitchen door when it dawned on him – and he couldn't really believe that he'd never thought of it before – but every time he kidnapped a woman, the time he spent playing with them before killing them, Max was always playing Dad's role.

The thought seriously weirded him out: he didn't like the too-intimate connection to his father.

He buried his thinking quickly before it took hold and turning to Jess, he smiled and said, 'Come on, babe. Let's go and frighten our guests.'

They were halfway down the hall, when Jess clapped her hand to her head. 'Forgot a knife. Just to keep you safe while I watch from the bottom step. I don't trust Eve. I'd prefer to have a knife instead of relying on my fists this time around.'

'Good idea. Catch me up.'

'Don't you worry about that, Max. I'm right behind you.'

THIRTY-TWO

Jessica

M ax must think I was mentally defective, if he really believed I wouldn't sneak a peek at his purchases. I didn't like nasty surprises.

And the constant babe-calling. Did he really think I was still flattered by it? Admittedly, before I'd known better, I'd stupidly thought it *had* meant something, but it hadn't taken me long to realise my mistake. Two days. That's all it had taken to see right through Max.

There were two containers, haphazardly crammed into my fridge. I got them out and gingerly opened each one in turn.

One of them made me jump back in shock, and one made me roll my eyes. Bending down, I opened the larger third bucket on the floor – heavy. I had to examine it more closely, putting my nose into the container before I could identify it. That proved to be a mistake. It sloshed around, heavy with liquid – the smell was putrid. Hastily putting the lid on again, I pushed it back against the wall, feeling the contents roll around inside.

The White Eye game. His father's game, as it turned out, despite Max initially claiming it as his own creation. He'd slipped up saying how it was his father's favourite game. Slipped up, because he was a fool. That didn't mean I thought his foolishness wasn't also sweet, but his idiocy needed nurturing and tending, and I was the person to do just that.

The White Eye game was hardly the height of sophistication, but I was sure the contents of the first two containers would have the desired effect on Eve and Bella. The third, larger smellier white plastic bucket hadn't been served for breakfast.

Thank God. There were limits, and I didn't think food, or anything pretending to be edible, masquerading in any other guise than something to be eaten and relished, was in any way comical. Food wasn't funny. It was something I loved. Angry, I turned my thoughts to the bucket.

Perhaps Max was planning a grand finale later in the day and would use the revolting bucket contents then.

Hurrying, I grabbed a knife and made a quick pit-stop by his coat. Inspected what hung behind it and raised my eyebrows marginally, and then checked what was tucked into the pocket. The latter disturbed me, but not overly.

I caught up with him. Max was back to being all cocksure and preening, assuming he had regained control over me and the entire situation. *Think again, Max. This is a test which I am permitting you to carry out, but believe me, I'm expecting you to fail miserably. Failing when you're with me is something you can't help doing because I have that effect on you.*

Barely able to contain his excitement, he said, 'Right, open the door and don't speak. I'll do all the talking.'

'No problem.'

He stopped. 'What are their names again?'

'Bella and Eve.'

Nodding, he started down the staircase, taking each step carefully as his hands were full with the tray. Holding the knife at my side, not seeing the point in hiding it from the women, I finally sat down on the bottom step and was genuinely interested to see Max do what he said he did best.

'Morning, ladies. How did we sleep?'

Bella mumbled that she was tired, and Eve kept quiet, watching Max carefully. She glanced over at me, and I merrily waved the knife at her. Eve did nothing merry back and continued to stand in the corner of the room.

'You must both be starving. And I bring you delights. A breakfast of treats.'

Although Max had his back to me, I knew he'd be twinkling his gold tooth at them, and now, listening to his voice, I heard it slither through the room, all oily-charm and slick with falsehoods and malice. Because that was how Max operated. Could the homeless women not hear it?

Bella had also stood up, looking uncomfortable and keen to follow Eve's lead, the big woman also tried to disappear into the corner of the room, flat against the wall. Both women eyed Max suspiciously as he laid the tray in the middle of the floor. He lifted the domes from the first two plates and wafted the smell around the room. 'Who wants a bacon sarnie?' My mouth watered, and I imagined theirs did as well.

Eve pressed herself closer into the corner. Bella's eyes latched onto the bacon sandwich, and I saw her waver. He covered them again, keeping himself between the women and his special domed goodies further away and out of reach. 'That's right, Bella,' Max said. 'It's only a bacon sarnie. Nothing to be frightened of. And I think it only fair to say at this point, I've changed my mind about raping either of you, so this is nothing more than it is. Eat.'

He walked backwards, giving them space to pick up their sandwiches. Bella couldn't resist and moving quickly towards her goal, she squatted and gently picked up the silver dome as if she thought it might bite. Seeing that it was in fact only a sandwich, she opened the two slices of bread and inspected the bacon, making sure there was nothing else lurking within. 'It's all right, Eve. It is just a bacon buttie. Come and eat.'

To prove all was well, she took a small mouthful and after a brief hesitation, chewing slowly, rolling the bread and bacon around in her mouth carefully, she started eating hungrily. I watched as her eyes closed in the delight of the flavour, and recognised the sheer joy she was experiencing.

Eve still hadn't moved from the wall.

'Not hungry, Eve?' Max enquired. 'Do you want to skip the sandwich and go straight for pudding?'

Bella ate and spoke simultaneously. 'It's a proper lush bacon buttie, Eve, I swear. Come on, it's fine. I promise you.'

'Take the cover off mine. I want to see it.' Eve's tone was totally flat, with no inflection at all. It was like listening to the voice of the dead.

Bella obliged and again separated the bread to better display its safeness. 'See, it's fine. If you don't want it, I'll have it.'

I was uncomfortable seeing Eve come forward to get her sandwich. Hunger was a strange thing, and I thought it cruel to lure her in with the promise of food. It didn't feel right or fair to me. It felt mean. The exploration of fear through these women was something I was interested in. But not teasing with food. Suddenly sweating, I held the knife tighter in my hand, not sure who I wanted to stab the most.

Food coupled with humiliation wasn't something I approved of. I wouldn't have minded a fair and true competitive mind-game of fear, but not this. You should never mess with food, especially not at the expense of a woman. Food is sacred and shouldn't be weaponised.

Eve was apparently starving, and I watched her inhale the sandwich, wiping the grease from her mouth. She didn't thank Max, and I was pleased for that. Bella, a very different person, was already eyeing the second plate behind Max's legs. He too was squatting now in an attempt to be less physically present in the room. 'Do you want more, Bella? There's always more.'

I could hear the smile in his voice and just for a minute, I wanted it all to stop. I despised food teasing; it was too familiar to me on an intimate and very personal level. But I also had to acknowledge, that if not for me and my fear-speech to Max, I wouldn't be sitting here watching him mentally torture these two women. It was a shame he'd chosen a basic human need, in this case a bacon sandwich, to use as something fearsome. I'd have to correct him on that one.

But I most definitely *did* want to learn more about raw fear. Because I had never really experienced it and was curious.

Nodding at Max, Bella stayed sitting on her ankles, waiting for him to bring her the second plate. Eve, more cautious, had also finished and stayed in place. Max put a plate in front of each of them and said, 'Enjoy.'

Part of me was truly enthralled. Everything seemed to fall into slow motion as I saw a hand from each woman, reach out to uncover the second plates. Both women were operating on very different levels: Bella was an innocent and having found there was no trick with the first food offering, it didn't seem to occur to her that the second plate might not be as nice. Eve was bolder and it was with a show of strength and a fuck-you to Max, that she unwaveringly took off the cloche.

Both women looked down and for a split second, they were both made utterly immobile with shock. Then chaos exploded into the room and I couldn't help but wince as I watched Max's entertainment play out.

Once Bella had taken the cover off, spiders spilled from the plate, scuttling and scurrying across the floor. Screaming, shouting, Bella staggered back. She flapped at herself, ripped her dressing gown off, ripped at her buttons on her pyjama top, hit out at her hair in an hysterical attempt to escape and rid herself of any eight-legged creatures. A black fleet of so many little black legs attached to black round bodies swept across the room as if the spiders had formed their own mobile curtain. Teeming, they moved and swept in a flotilla of black, eating up the floor space.

'Get them off me, Eve, *get them off.*' Bella wouldn't stop screaming and screaming and sadly, I saw the front of my father's pyjamas stain wet in the groin. Backed into a corner, her dressing gown discarded in a heap, the pyjama top unbuttoned, urine leaked down her leg and onto the carpet.

For the moment, Eve didn't react to Bella and only saw her own nightmarish gift. She had gone rigid as soon as she'd seen her plate of squirming, wriggling fat white maggots. They writhed, squirmed and wriggled from the plate as she had inadvertently knocked it with her hand. They moved and slid en masse as if they were one entity. Whitish, greyish blobs, plump and gelatinous, they fell and tumbled over each other. They seemed monstrous together and repellent individually. Eve didn't scream; I saw her bite down hard on her lip, keeping it in. White-faced, her expression shuttered down like an impenetrable veil had fallen. She walked backwards quickly and only stopped as she came into contact with the wall.

I didn't like maggots and I'd have killed someone if they'd played a trick like that on me.

I believed that Eve would kill now, if she could. She had a look that I'd never seen before.

Liking her more and more, I carried on watching.

Bella made whimpering noises now and stood, trying to disappear, staring at the spiders. Eve stamped on them. One after the other, in a very methodical way. Touching Bella's shoulders, Eve quickly examined the big girl's hair, and turned her around, swiping her hand across Bella's back, before re-buttoning her top. 'There aren't any spiders on you, Bella. Stop crying. I'm killing them all, see?'

It was like a sick and twisted dance: one minute Eve was

stationary and staring, and then stamp, crush, twist of foot, and repeat. In the end, all I could see was the squish of splattered spiders in a sticky wet clump on the bottom of her socked feet.

She looked across at me and her eyes were cold and hard. Her expression gave little away and I respected her for that.

Bella was finally quiet.

All I could hear was Max's laughter.

Turning to me, but speaking to them, he said, 'And that, dear ladies, is only the beginning of this game. I think you'll agree that it will keep you on your toes.' He bent his knees and clasped his hands. 'And best of all, I saw the whites of your eyes. A treat. Thank you.'

No one spoke.

With slightly less volume, Max said, 'I don't know why you're both *so* freaked out. It's got to be better than rape. Am I right?'

I lowered my eyes so I didn't have to see Eve.

I wasn't about to let either woman go, but equally, I wasn't prepared to be a bully. There was a fine line between bullying and frightening someone. Bullying was a step too far.

Max wouldn't understand that, but I knew he would once I'd explained the difference to him. In his world, he'd think, if I was happy to kidnap, I'd be happy to humiliate.

He'd be wrong. And I'd have to show him just how very wrong he was.

I knew then I'd got what I'd always wanted. My very own Johnny-man: handsome and cruel and stupid.

THIRTY-THREE

Eve

'It's all right, Bella. Calm down. They've gone. It's just us. You're safe.'

'I wet myself.'

'I'm surprised I didn't shit myself. Who cares? It doesn't matter. It was a sick joke and there's no reason for you to feel bad. Not in the slightest.'

Bella didn't seem to hear and went quietly about her business, gathering a wad of toilet paper in her hand. Silently, she wiped at the once-puddle of urine, which had now been sucked into the carpet, transferring bits of tissue onto the floor and making it worse. The big woman tried to hold her wet pyjama legs away from her to stop them sticking to her skin. Eve felt sorry for her but wasn't comfortable playing mother. It didn't come naturally. But she tried to be kind. Tried hard. It was relatively new to her, and she was pleased with her attempt. And did genuinely feel for Bella. Mostly because Eve was responsible for her being here.

Thinking hard, Eve knew the only way out of this situation, was through Jessica. Jessica was the weak link, although oddly, she was the strong link in the Max, Jessica duo. Eve couldn't quite work out their relationship, but there was no doubt in her mind, that Jessica was the more dominant of the two.

But not in the spider and maggot fest. That had been all Max. Eve suspected that Jessica might not have been aware of what was about to happen, or if she was, Jessica didn't like it. It wasn't how she operated.

The key, Eve thought, was finding out precisely how Jessica did operate and what she wanted from this – the capture and keeping of two women from the street. She must have a reason, but to Eve, Jessica seemed a mess of contradictions, and Eve suspected that Jessica wasn't entirely sure what or who she was either.

That in itself, wasn't great news.

I'll have to make friends with her. She already likes me, I can tell. I think we may be very alike, and we both recognise that similarity in each other. Eve snorted in derision. She didn't think anyone was like her. Eve had always felt alone, and Jessica hadn't changed that.

Tuning back to Bella, Eve made her face soft and receptive. She wanted to make Bella feel better, be stronger, become someone Eve could rely on. They'd be better as a united front, instead of two mismatched strangers.

Bella had given up cleaning urine and had turned her hand to maggot-collecting. She scooped them up in fresh loo paper and transferred them into the bucket. Checking that she'd got them all, she finally sat down on one of the beanbags and said, 'I don't understand it, Eve. I swear to God. Why can't I be more like I am on the street, instead of all weak and crying and wetting myself? It's not me. It's not who I am. I'm embarrassed.'

'You're not weak. You've just cleaned up the maggots like it was nothing. I couldn't have done that.'

Eve had been more frightened by the maggots then she'd let on. She hoped that Max hadn't seen her fear, but her skin crawled as she remembered the mass of maggots under the cloche. At least she hadn't screamed out loud.

Wanting to mentally move on, she said, 'Who are you, Bella? If you're not you now, then who are you really?'

'You know. On the street, I'm all right, I can look after myself, no problem. People leave me alone, because they're frightened of me. They know I'll beat the crap out of them, just like that.' She clicked her fingers. 'I like that people leave me alone. It's good. I'm big and strong.' She hung her head. 'But not here, not in this room. Here, I'm small and weak and I don't like that at all.'

Eve shook her head back and forth. Shook it emphatically, even though the gesture was wasted on Bella as the woman was intent on studying her own feet. Her hair hung down in a straggly mess and her shoulders juddered as she sighed. 'Why can't I be like I am on the street, Eve? What's changed?'

'You've got it all wrong, Bella. That's not why people leave you alone, because they're frightened of you. Because they think you'll beat them up. You wouldn't beat anyone up and everyone knows that.'

Bella's big head sat back on her shoulders. 'What the fuck are you talking about? I could beat you up.'

No. No, you really couldn't. 'Yes, but you won't. You're left alone and not bothered, because you're kind. You're fair, you don't cheat people, you share what you have when you've got it. People respect you, Bella, and that's much better than frightening them, don't you think?'

Bella's face cleared, as if clouds had lifted from the landscape of her face, leaving her naked and content. 'Really, Eve, *really*? Do you think that's true, or are you just being nice?'

'I'm never just nice, Bella. You should know that. But I am honest.'

'You're blunt.'

Eve shrugged. Smiled. Held her hands out, palms up. 'Guilty.'

'Do you think that? About me? Do you respect me, Eve?'

'Of course I do. You should be proud of yourself, Bella. It's not easy being popular on the streets, but you manage to pull it off, and you didn't even know. How thick are you?'

It took a few seconds for Bella to realise that last comment was a joke and she beamed like a child. 'Not like you, Eve. People avoid you.'

'Yeah, thanks for pointing that out, Bella. I know people avoid me. And I'm glad.'

'You've got a bit of a reputation, you know. Stand-offish. Aloof. A bit up your own arse.' Bella smiled to show she wasn't being cruel, but she didn't need to. Eve couldn't care less what people thought of her. She was happy as herself and didn't need anything from anyone.

'I am a bit up my own arse, but that's all right too. Because that's how I survive on the street. And that's how we'll survive here. Together. I said I'd get you out of this, and I will.'

All she needed was a plan. She had two choices as she saw it. Go for and destroy the weaker Max, or befriend the stronger Jessica. The latter was much the better option.

Max was a psychopathic rapist. Jessica was... What was Jessica?

Jessica was a dangerous woman.

Eve was a dangerous woman.

Two dangerous women against a mad and weak man.

Choice made.

THIRTY-FOUR

Jessica

I'd wanted to be on my own, but Max followed me into the kitchen, bubbling over with his own perceived artistry and style demonstrated with his ridiculous teasing game. Putting the frying pan onto the hob, I turned on the flame and laid out six slices of bacon. And I wasn't planning on sharing it. Pushing the rashers around, I ignored Max.

His punishment for being a Johnny-man. I expected more.

'Wasn't that great, Jess? Did you see Bella? She wet herself.' He laughed and I wondered at how far I'd come with this man. What I'd done to get him. And it had only been two days. *Two days*. A lot had changed. Max was still the most handsome thing I'd ever seen – that hadn't changed.

But *I* had changed. I was open to all things now. New things that before might have seemed inconceivable.

And I couldn't stop wondering at that.

Glancing over my shoulder at him, I said, 'But Eve wasn't frightened at all, was she? She didn't show you the whites of her eyes. Good luck with that one. She will never show you her whites. I doubt she's ever shown them to anyone.'

Max banged the table with his fist, startling me. 'And that's your fault, Jess. You brought me damaged women. Eve's your fault. She's a cold, hard bitch. I would never have picked her. Not in a million years. Or bloody Bella. Big, weird Bella. My women were never this mad. They were normal. They reacted normally.'

'How would you know? You never kept them for long enough. You saw them, took them, raped them, killed them. But you never knew them.' I smiled. 'Welcome to real women, Max.'

He got up and came and stood right behind me. I could feel his breath on my neck. 'You're jealous, Jess.'

Laughing, I flipped over the bacon. 'Jealous of what?'

'You're jealous of the game. You could never have thought of it.'

'Neither could you. It's your father's game. What's that make you, other than a pathetic little boy who's ripped off his daddy's favourite pastime? Yeah, Max, I am absolutely eaten up with jealousy here.'

I knew I was goading him, but Max needed to be taught that what he'd done to the women wasn't fair.

The punch when it came, took me by surprise. His hand connected with my face, his fist taking a sneaky route around the back of my head, landing on my cheek. There was no real power behind it, but I staggered, and the pan fell from the stove as I fell forward. The bacon fell to the floor.

And Max fell from grace.

Still standing, I turned very slowly around and looked at Max. Stared at him.

And thought, *Here's my chance to really play with him.*

Hating myself for doing it, I scrunched up my face and squeezed my eyes tight shut. Rubbing softly and feebly at my cheek, I raised my eyes to his. I knew I'd managed to squeak out a little tear, and I said, 'Max, please, Max, don't hurt me. I'll do anything for you.' I hung my head, as if in shame. 'And of course you're right. Of course I'm jealous. And of course, you always knew I would be.'

I desperately wanted to salvage the bacon but thought it would spoil the mood if I came out of character so abruptly. 'I don't know what I've been thinking all this time. Trying to be as good as you are at this business of getting women. I didn't know what I was doing. How could I? I don't have any experience. Not like you do.'

Max had stepped back and sat quietly on a chair. 'Carry on, Jess. Tell me how good I am, tell me how I am the best. And you are nothing. All women are nothing. All women are slags. Go on, tell me how much you need me.'

'I do need you, more than anything. Without you, I am nothing. Really, I'm not just saying that to please you. You are the best. I mean it with every inch of me.'

'That's a lot of inches, babe.'

I clenched my jaws and carried on, amazed that he was believing this melodrama. 'You took me in, and I should be grateful. I'm very grateful you don't mind me being fat. Without you, I really don't know what I'd do. Tell me how I can make it all better.'

Loathing myself now, I knelt at his feet and clasped my hands as if seeking mercy. 'I'll do anything for you, Max.' Again, I let my head hang forward: poor mortified embarrassed useless me. I peeped up at him and covering my face with my hands, I looked at him through my fingers. 'But at least we still have two women locked up downstairs. Teach me what to do. I'll do anything, honest, Max. Please teach me. Teach me everything you know, and this time I'll listen.'

I'll teach you everything I know, and this time you will listen.

I wasn't sure if I was overdoing it, but he seemed to be happily and gratefully accepting of my dramatics. Daring to make eye contact, I saw his face relax and he casually spread his legs, back to the Johnny-man I'd captured two days ago.

'You think of something, Jess, to make me keep you. You thought you were so clever, but I knew I'd beat you. Didn't take long, did it? You need to think very hard how to please your master and see if you can work your way back into my good books.'

'I never knew I was in your good books. If I was, I didn't deserve to be.'

'Hurry up. I've got stuff to do, games to play with the useless but better-than-nothing women you brought me. Fix it. Make it worth me keeping you.'

I stood up, pretending to be shaky and still rubbed at my cheek. 'You're so strong, you hurt me, and I know that wasn't even a real punch, was it?'

'That was a tap, sweetheart. A gentle pat on the cheek.'

'I really want to please you, Max. Give me a minute to think why you should keep me.'

Again he banged the table. 'Perhaps I don't have a minute to give you, Jess. My time is precious.'

Holding my hands out, as if to fend him off, I contorted my face into something that looked like it was thinking hard and frantically. And then I smiled. Putting my lips to his ear, I spoke quietly. 'Why don't I pop back to your house and pick up some of your props. You told me you have a big collection of costumes to suit various occasions. I think now might be the right time to label and terrify, pigeonhole and petrify, don't you? Do what you do best. And I can watch and learn. How about that? Please let me. And I promise I'll watch everything you do and really learn from it.'

His face tilted up, his jawline strong and his features so beautiful, it still made me stop and look. Physically, this man was perfection.

His expression softened and his eyes closed. Finally, he nodded. 'I think that's a very good idea, Jess. Good one. Then we can do it my way. With absolutely no interference from you.

Do you realise how lucky you are to still be breathing? I could and should have killed you when I first got you. Shame I didn't.'

Nodding my head, but frankly, a bit bored with this charade, I forced myself to look hopeful and grateful that he was granting me life. *Does he really believe I'm falling for this crock of shite? Is he really that shallow and self-centred? I hope so. It will make re-building him that much easier.*

He looked at his watch. 'Get going then, Jess. And hurry up. Now I know you'll be bringing my props, I'm fucking bursting with ideas. And I *will* let you watch, as you have come to accept the inevitable. I know I've said it before, but I've got to say it again – I *knew* I'd beat you.' He pounded his thigh with his fist, delighted to have been proved right. 'I was always going to beat you, because you're nothing but a woman, and women *never* beat men. It's not possible. Not in my world, anyway.'

I smiled and nodded and turning from him, I silently cleared up the congealed bacon. I didn't think he'd let me, as he was eager for me to go. But he wasn't ever going to clean the mess up. It wasn't a man's job. Covering my smile, I thought I was getting the hang of this devilishly tricky concept. His philosophy was a simple one.

Women should know their place and act accordingly.

Women could and should be kidnapped if Max fancied a plaything for a couple of hours.

Women could and should be raped, because they were only women and women didn't matter.

And of course, when their usefulness had come to an end, *after a couple of hours – that's all*, women could and should be killed, because what was the point of keeping trash about the place?

Thinking I could vastly improve on this premise, I was ready to make my departure.

THIRTY-FIVE

Jessica

As I drove, I mulled over the Max problem. He was a slow-moving car crash. I was amazed he'd got away with murder for as long as he had.

Max was deep down bad and would have been kidnapping and raping and murdering as soon as he'd thought of it. He was also a long-term bully. From forever ago. He needed to drop that aspect of himself. Quickly. The rest I could and would work with in order to get my man.

He needed a major overhaul. In my new official role as Johnny-man keeper and mentor, Max required extensive work, if he was to change to someone I could respect, and who could be proud of himself – for the right reasons, instead of his wildly twisted and warped current self-perception.

Still confident I was the right person for the job, I realised with a pleasant glow, that by creating a new and improved Max, I'd be saving countless women in the future from sadistic bullying. In the same way it wasn't a lost cause but instead an important challenge, it also wasn't a fight – it was a persuasion.

I had the brains to re-mould Max and the ability to design a far superior model. That's what us women did: we changed our men for the greater good. Satisfied, I put my foot down, eager to pick up Max's uniforms, excited to give him what he thought he wanted and needed. It was so easy to manipulate him, I almost felt no pride in my mission. Perhaps a little private boast wouldn't go amiss. Puffing up my chest, I basked in self-admiration and felt strong.

Parking outside Max's house, I was light on the balls of my feet as I approached the front door and felt as if I were dancing as I walked. So sure was I of my new role that it felt like a labour of love but a very worthy one.

As I let myself in with the spare key he'd given to me, I glanced at my watch. Half past ten. I'd expected it to be later, but I still felt the need to hurry. I had the key to the playroom on me, but I did not want to leave Max alone with Eve and Bella as I was not sure what he might do in my absence. I went straight to his bedroom. When he'd 'tutored' me on the dos and don'ts of abducting women, he'd told me about his wardrobe of fancy dress. He hadn't liked the term when I'd used it; insisted I refer to the clothes as his 'props'.

How things had changed in such a short period of time. Who would have imagined how the tables would turn in such spectacular fashion? And now, at this very minute, Max was waiting for me to come back: not realising that he was doing my bidding – not the other way around, but he'd be waiting for his own reasons. To show off, to boast and to bully our houseguests.

Ultimately, he'd learn that *he* needed guidance from *me*, that he couldn't go careering through life, behaving as he did. I wasn't willing to give him up without offering him a chance at redemption. He deserved that, at least.

Max belonged to me and I wasn't prepared to let him go without at least trying to save him and hone his natural skills. Of which he had plenty. They simply needed tweaking.

Going straight to the wardrobe, I opened the doors and

rifled through the hanging garments. There were so many it was difficult to choose. Not really caring nor thinking my selection was important – it certainly was not to me – I draped half a dozen over my arm, irritated as they slipped and slithered in their transparent plastic sleeves. I was ready to go.

Not wanting to leave Max alone all pumped up and on the wrong side of the locked door, I didn't want to dawdle. I didn't trust what he might do, now he thought I had been put in my place. Over-confidence was a dangerous thing. He didn't know it yet, but Max couldn't function efficiently without me.

Deep down he must know that. Surely? It was so obvious it hurt.

But then I changed my mind and decided to have a quick snoop. I laid the clothes on the bed, and looked around, seeing the room in a different light now as *I* was living in a different light. I shone, inside and out. I was truly happy.

Trailing my fingers over his dresser, I opened drawers at random. Went over to his bedside cabinet and opened the top drawer. I put my hand in and fumbled around, hoping to find something interesting.

I was about to close the drawer, when I saw a rectangular card in a wallet. Picking it up, I studied it.

My natural breathing rhythm actually stopped working for a breath or two. Jagged gasps puffed out from my lungs. I read the card again. Went over to the window and held it close to the light. To make sure. And yes, I'd read it correctly first time around. Staggered, I sat on the bed, holding the card. *Well, well, well. People never cease to amaze.* I put it in my bag and had another feel in the back corners of the drawer. There was another gem of a find. Might be useful at some point, so I popped them in my bag. Feeling lucky, I ran my hands under the cabinet. Under the bed.

Behind the cabinet.

And there you had it. Proof positive of Max's guilt and his idiocy. Only a very arrogant, or very stupid man would hide trophies of his kills in such an obvious place. Seven women, seven trophies. Studying them at length, I sat for some time, enthralled and appalled at what I was looking at. I was shocked. Finally, sadly, I added them to my bag of treasures and wondered what I was doing.

A quick feel under the bed again. And that's when I found something even more interesting.

I looked at the gun in my hand. It was heavy and black. Wondering if it was loaded – surely not – not even Max was that stupid that he'd keep a loaded gun under the bed, I splayed my fingers and flitted them back and forth across the dust bunnies under the bed again. Sure enough, a box of bullets. Checking further, I brought out two more boxes. I opened them all and all were full.

Don't load the gun. Leave the gun. The gun may go off and kill someone. I grinned. *But what a thing of immense power, what a vital tool to keep Max in line and receptive to my tutelage. It is the perfect find.*

It took me a while to work out how to open the chamber thingy; I wasn't sure of the correct term, but it didn't matter. Once that was done, I put one bullet in. It was more fiddley than I'd anticipated but I persevered, and eventually triumphed. *Triumph in everything has become the norm for me.* With all bullets in situ, I was ready to go. Sniggering at the enormity of my actions, I stood in front of a mirror, and pointed the gun at my reflection. *Bang, bang, you're dead.*

Good old Max. He really *was* a darling. Only he would be that naïve that he thought under the bed was a good place to hide anything. Perhaps he was going for the double bluff. But I didn't think so. He really was that stupid. I felt an unexpected wave of affection for him. He really didn't know how lucky he was that I'd come along to guide him through life.

Considering what I'd found, I made sure all his props were in order and that I had the right ones.

That's when I heard the unmistakable sound of the front

door opening. Standing still, I waited. Creeping to the bedroom door, I put my ear to it and listened. There were noises coming from the kitchen. Not secretive intruder noises, but the sound of someone moving around, uncaring if anyone heard them. Opening the door a fraction, I could clearly hear the sound of things being put onto the worktop, the fridge being opened, the tap turned on and off, the kettle switched on.

Putting the gun in my handbag and slinging the clothes over my arm, I walked softly and calmly down the stairs to say hello to whoever dared to be making themselves at home in the house I semi-lived in with Max. If I were being whimsical, I'd say it was our first house together.

And no one should be in the kitchen, doing anything.

A man's voice hummed tunelessly, a few words of an unknown song were attempted and swiftly abandoned. The kettle made its switching off noise and I pushed at the open door. The first thing I saw was a large expanse of someone's back, shoulders slightly hunched and rounded as he poured boiling water into a cup. I stood quietly and watched as the teabag was dunked and squeezed and pressed to the side of the mug. The bag itself was then spooned out, steaming, and put neatly and efficiently into the bin under the sink.

'Hello,' I said. 'And just who the bloody hell are you?'

THIRTY-SIX

Jessica

The man gasped and turned, one hand on his chest, the other holding the mug. We stared at each other, and I recognised the obvious shock on his face at finding a stranger in the house, but it was more than that: his expression was genuinely surprised and bewildered. I wondered why.

He tried to look casual but his tone was belligerent. 'I could ask the same question myself. Who are you?'

'I'm Jessica and I live here.'

'You do *not* live here. This is my son's home. Max. I'm his father, Barry.'

The creator of the White Eye game. Ooh, I'll have to watch my step.

'I most certainly do live here. I'm Max's girlfriend.' It wasn't the time to explain who I truly was – his son's tutor and saviour – so I went for the easier option. 'How did you get in and why are you here?'

'I have a key. Because I'm his dad. Because I have every right to be here. More right than you. He's never even mentioned you. And if you must know, not that I have to explain myself to you, I'm re-stocking his fridge and cupboards. I don't like him to go without.' He did a sort of

189

contemptuous sniff and added, 'Especially this being Christmas week. We always have our Christmas lunch together.' Barry looked me up and down. 'And I can tell you right now, you will not be welcome. It's always been just us boys together.'

Laughing, I shook my head, as if all this was very tedious. 'Sounds simply thrilling, Bazzer. But you're ignoring what's staring you in the face – *I* look after him. He doesn't need you for anything, because he has me now. Believe me, you are surplus to requirements. And I wasn't aware Max needed your permission to go out with me. Does he?'

'Don't get all uppity with me. Who do you think you are? If you meant something to him, he'd have told me. Get out of the house. You shouldn't even be here without Max. Where is he?'

'I'm so sorry, did he forget to give you his itinerary today? Surely he's allowed to play with his own friends without having to get permission from his daddy first.'

'How dare you? Don't you even think of messing with me. I know women like you. You're the dead spit of my ex-wife so I know the type. It's difficult to tell you two fat slags apart. Max would *never* pick up a woman like you. Never. Max is mine, I fucking made him, so I *do* have a say in who he sees and doesn't see. I'm his dad.'

'So you said.' I nodded sagely. 'His mother was fat? Like me?' I smiled. 'Now, that's *very* interesting.'

'Why's that interesting?'

'He's picking mummy-lookalikes. Bit cliche, don't you think? A bit unimpressively pedestrian, in my opinion, but I'm sure you care little for my views. Have you met many of his other girlfriends? Do they all look like me and your wife?'

That shut him up. Of course he hadn't met any of them. All Max's previous female friends were dead. Barry faltered for a moment, caught on the hop, at a temporary loss as to what to say. He made a big performance of blowing on his tea and taking a small sip.

I put a lot of sneer into my next words. 'How clingy and needy are you? Bringing him food, bringing him clean sheets, doing his ironing for him? My, how you've spoilt him. It's unhealthy. Anyway, he doesn't need you. I'm here now. I cook for him. And by the way, I didn't like your stew. Neither did Max.'

I couldn't really believe how unnecessarily and uncharacteristically mean I was being. Against my better nature, I realised I was bullying Barry – like the stick girl who'd worked in tandem with my Johnny-man. But Max belonged to me. Not his bloody daddy. 'Give me your key, Barry.' I held out my hand. 'You won't be needing it any longer. I'll let Max know you were here.'

My palm remained in space, waiting. 'Give me the key. Please.'

'Don't you speak to me like that. It's my key, and Max is mine. He's my boy, he'll always be my little man. He doesn't belong to you. You can't have him. He doesn't want you. He'll never leave me on my own. Not for you. Sod off. Go on, get out of this house.'

I hadn't moved from the doorway and he hadn't moved from the sink. When Barry moved, I knew immediately he was intent on making this a physical altercation. Without giving any thought to my actions, I plunged my hand into my bag and pointed the gun at him.

Barry stopped in mid-stride, and his mouth dropped open. Instinctively, he raised his hands above his shoulders, still holding on to his mug of steaming tea. I was pleased to note that my hand on the gun wasn't shaking, and I felt completely calm. At home and relaxed. It was almost disappointingly easy to threaten to shoot another person, as it turned out. I wondered if it would be as easy to actually pull the trigger.

Although, obviously I wasn't going to do that. I wasn't mad. I was just scaring Barry into submission.

It was with surprise when I heard myself saying, 'Are you going to leave, Barry, or am I going to have to shoot you?'

'Don't be stupid. Put the gun down. I'm sure we can come to an agreement that we're both happy with. How about it?'

Irritated that his tone had become wheedling, I said, 'Doesn't this remind you of something? Me having power over you, and having the ability to terrify you, and you, quite naturally scared? Ring any bells?'

'I don't know what you're even talking about.'

'The game you used to play with your son. The Whites of Their Eyes game. I don't suppose you ever held a gun to your darling boy, but I gather the entertainment was your creation. Max told me. Now I want you to tell me how it worked. I want to know the details.'

He attempted a laugh, but it petered out quickly. In the end, he told me all. It didn't take long – it wasn't that complicated, but it was cruel. Barry's tone became boastful in the telling.

'And then I'd jump out and shout, "Gotcha," and it would make him jump out of his socks, with his eyes wide open.' He shrugged. 'And that's it.'

'Way to go, Barry. He still plays the game, you know. You should be very proud.'

'Does he? I didn't know.' He smiled a happy smile and then remembered I was still pointing a gun at him. The smile slipped away quickly.

Nodding, I *did* smile. 'Yeah, it's funny, don't you think? And here *we* are, playing the same game, but with bigger and more grown-up weapons, and I'm better at it than you. You made a monster of your son by making him terrified as a boy, so don't expect any prizes for being daddy of the year. You disgust me.'

'Max is *not* a monster. He's not. He's all man. More man than you could ever handle.'

'Is he? I hadn't noticed. But guess what? This is your unlucky day because I'm an even bigger monster.'

Why am I doing this? Because I do want to shoot him. It excites me. Maybe that's why I want to keep Max all to myself.

Because we are the same.

We belong to each other.

All that time I'd spent dilly-dallying with the question: Would I, could I, kill for Max? Who had I been kidding? Clearly, I had been waiting to do this my entire life.

But I wasn't a bully. Not normally, but Barry had provoked me, and I'd responded in kind. By being a female Johnny-man. It didn't sit well with me, and I endeavoured to forget my uncharacteristic teasing of him – freed myself from any residual guilt that might be lurking from being so unlike my normal self.

Deciding that I had said all that needed to be said, I held the gun with both hands and pointed it at Barry. At his head.

I thought there was a definite risk that I could miss, so instead I pointed at the larger body mass of his stomach. If I couldn't hit this man's belly, I'd be amazed. But belly shots weren't often instantly fatal. They were messy and death could be slow in coming. Everyone knew that. I raised the gun a little higher. Chest height. There. That looked pretty perfect.

'Don't,' he said.

I pulled the trigger.

'Bang, bang. You're dead.'

My words were drowned out by what sounded like a sonic boom. Barry didn't answer. I couldn't hear anything. Deafened by the bang, I bent forward from the waist, not wanting to step in any blood and inspected Max's dead father from afar. It wasn't hard to see that he was dead. His eyes were open and unblinking. From where I was standing, I couldn't see Barry's chest move up and down.

There was surprisingly little blood and I felt a little cheated at that. It would have made for a better visual memory, had the man been covered in splashes of red. The only excess liquid was tea. It rather spoilt what should have been a shocking tableau, and Barry himself looked disappointingly normal. Dead, but politely clean in his death.

I waited in the abrupt silence that followed and heard my own breathing.

He was going to take my Max away. Selfish man. I had no choice. I didn't mean to do it, but I did. He made me.

I wasn't sure what to do with the body. And more to the point, what to tell Max.

Nothing. I wouldn't do anything with the body. It wasn't going anywhere, so best to leave things as they were. I would also tell Max nothing. Certainly not the whole truth. Perhaps a version of it. But later, when he was more accustomed and in tune with his new life with me. Which would be very different from his previous life. *He'd* be very different.

It wouldn't serve any purpose if I told him today, and anyway, perhaps he'd be more understanding than I was giving him credit for. He, of all people, should know that sometimes life plunged off a cliff and took you by surprise.

I have pushed Max off his very own cliff.

Barry couldn't keep Max all to himself forever: desperately clinging on and refusing to let his son go. Who did he think he was? It wasn't right. I had done Max a favour. That's what I told myself, anyway. I wasn't in total agreement with myself, not yet, because I'd just done something really bad. But I was pretty sure by the time I'd driven back home, I'd feel a lot more accepting and I would be able to fully forgive myself.

My own dreadful mother had been right. I always got what I wanted. In the end.

In time, Max will thank me for what I've done for him. I'm sure of it. I've set him free.

I waited for ten agonisingly long minutes, before leaving. No one was peeping at their windows, no hordes of staring bystanders gathered on the street, curious about the sound of a gunshot.

No one had even noticed. Perhaps they assumed it was an early festive firework set off mistakenly.

Driving away from the house, I'd successfully got the props for Max. And a whole lot more. I'd got the true me. All in all, I'd found more than I could have hoped for.

Now, it was time to be with him again. And I was eager to start our new relationship. On my terms.

And the gun would help.

I wondered what Max had been up to in my absence.

THIRTY-SEVEN

Max
_____

Max had been buzzing after his triumph over Jess. He'd finally slain the monster that had scared him so unexpectedly and now things were back to normal. When it had come right down to it, it had been easy getting the upper hand with her. *Regaining* the upper hand. He convinced himself he'd *allowed* her to have a taste of power, and now he was in charge again, which all felt very right.

But now he was bored. After the initial high, the long-awaited victory over the bitch, he felt the buzz leave him, and he didn't know how to entertain himself. Bloody Jess had the keys to the women's playroom, so he had no access.

Except for the glass floor. He had that. Smiling, he wandered around in the hall and sat on a bench, next to a coat tree and a stand for umbrellas. He thought about the bucket he had on the kitchen floor, waiting patiently to be used. He knew exactly what he wanted to do with the contents and had been waiting until nightfall. Originally, Max had thought it would be better displayed in the dark and revealed abruptly under the harsh spotlights to the homeless women. But as he sat and gave it serious consideration, he realised now would be an excellent time. The *best* time. With Jess out of the house, it would look like it was happening in real time, and that would definitely be a frightening thing for his two waiting victims trapped under glass.

Barely able to contain his excitement, he did a brisk trot to the sitting room and stood, out of sight from the women, on the edge of the glass floor. Quickly sticking his neck out, he managed to catch a glimpse of the big one and the thin one. Both were lying on their beanbags; chatting, he thought. Ducking back so they wouldn't see him, he sat on his heels.

The whites of their eyes through the glass floor: him looking down, they, up. It was perfect.

What made it even more perfect, was the absence of Jess. Her not being here, would give the illusion of authenticity. They would believe, and even that cold one, the thinner woman, would show fear. He knew she would. Even with those dead and lifeless fisheyes, she'd be very scared when she saw his creation, and he'd see her terror. It was definitely one of his better uses of a prop, and in part, he had Jess to thank for that. Although, he never would thank her. He'd rather die than show her any gratitude.

Giggling in anticipation, he hurried to the kitchen and brought the bucket out into the centre of the room. Slipping out of his jeans and top, shoes and socks, he stood in his underwear and took the time to admire his physique. He flexed his muscles because why the hell not. Max turned his attention to applying his warpaint. Dipping his hands into the liquid, he, for the moment, avoided the bulkier, chunkier things that had sunk to the bottom, and using his hands, adorned his body and face with the fluid.

Cold, he shivered, and uncaring of the mess he was creating (Jess could and would clean it up), he inspected the cutlery drawer. No, nothing suitable there. Then he saw the knife block. He took out a big chopping knife with a large flat blade – it was more like a cleaver. Fucking perfect.

Running his finger across it, he was pleased at its sharpness. Grinning as he worked, he dunked the cleaver in the bucket, making sure it was covered and would drip nicely. Lifting the bucket by its handle, he walked carefully down the hall, to the glass floor. Putting it on the edge, out of sight of the women, he hurried back for what lay underneath his coat. Grabbing that and what he'd placed in his pocket, he was soon back, ready to put on his debut and one-time only performance of Jessica's Death: he, naturally, in the starring role.

Cleaver in hand, he stepped onto the glass and waited patiently for the thin woman to look up. Her face didn't change. But the fat woman's did when she obligingly looked up. He saw her mouth open and her eyes rounded, like ping-pong balls – he could see her whites already and he hadn't even really started.

Slipping in the blood, dripping blood from the cleaver, he grinned at the women, knowing his teeth would shine white through the red. To them, he'd look demented. But he kept his face serious, with the occasional maniacal grin just for show, and proceeded to lay out the innards he'd bought from the butcher. His knowledge of anatomy was basic, but he vaguely knew where everything went. Sort of. But it would be good enough.

A brain, two lungs, a heart, a liver and two kidneys. He laid them out in a rough approximation of a human dismembered corpse. Max worked slowly and methodically, eking out the horror below as he displayed it all. Like an artist. Better than an artist, because this could fool you into thinking it was real.

Stepping off the glass floor, he took a hacking swipe at the skeleton from the fancy-dress shop, and the blade neatly sliced off the two legs and arms. He separated the two thigh bones from the lower leg to make it look more real and positioned the arms and legs around the organs. He added the skeleton hands for his own amusement.

Max stood, looking down at the carnage at his feet, and brought out the long coil of intestines from the bucket on the side. Slipping and sliding, he arranged them in the centre of his corpse, as if it had been disembowelled. He didn't like blood – but to broaden his horizons and expand on his ability to frighten, he was willing to do this. For his art.

And to impress Jess. *Still* he felt the need for her approval and it irritated the shit out of him.

His final touch was his favourite. Squatting, he picked up the auburn wig: not a bad likeness at all – it would make the women really think he'd killed Jess – and away from view, he chopped and sliced it, making wispy tendrils alongside larger tufts of hair fall around him.

Back on his stage, he threw bits of hair where the head should be and stopping, he knelt and looked to see the effect on his audience.

The big one was screaming. He could see her open mouth, and if he listened very carefully, he could hear her voice, high-pitched and hysterical, coming through and up and out of the room.

Eve – *that was her name* – stood unmoving, staring up. He thought of her relative coolness when she'd been presented with maggots. How she'd stamped and killed the spiders. She hadn't shown fear then, when she should have.

Perhaps her initial fear of him, when he'd approached her, unbuttoning his jeans, had been a sham.

And he hadn't raped her, because he'd been pulled and persuaded off course by Jess, with her blathering on about getting another woman.

It finally sunk in. Jess had stopped him from raping Eve. He had a nasty feeling that somehow the two women had united in some way and had tricked him.

Max couldn't believe it. He'd obviously known it on a practical level at the time when he'd been stopped from raping Eve, but he hadn't really considered the fact in depth. Did Jess actually want to *save* the women? Did she think she could? Were they in cahoots? He laughed at the thought. Stupid Jess with her big ideas. She'd learn. He'd shown her this morning how it really was.

Shaking his head, he refused to let thoughts of Jess spoil the fun he was having now.

At least I have her back under control. Eve will follow. I have no doubts.

Eve's mouth was slightly open, and Max was grateful for that. It was a sign that he'd at least unnerved the dead-eyed cow. She reminded him uncannily of Jess. That cold remoteness that he found so difficult to break down. At least now, he'd got an expression which was verging on frightened. It hadn't really developed from deep shock, but it was good enough.

The other woman's reaction made up for it.

Putting his voice to the glass, he shouted, 'I've killed her. I murdered Jess. It's just you two left all on your lonesome. With me. Now the fun can really start. Merry Christmas.' Laughing, he sat for a while, stroking a large piece of the hair, kissing it.

He almost frightened himself.

And wished the scene he'd created was true.

THIRTY-EIGHT

Bella

'Stop it, Bella. For Christ's sake, stop screaming. It's not real.'

How could Eve be so sure? Bella knew Eve didn't mind violence. She was familiar with it, said she liked it even, but Bella didn't. Blood terrified her. It should terrify everyone.

She couldn't help herself. Couldn't stop looking up at what remained of Jessica. 'It's her hair, Eve, how can you not see that?'

Eve tutted like she was getting impatient. Like Bella was being a great big baby. 'Look at the bones, Bella. We saw Jessica this morning, alive and kicking. What's Max done with the flesh on her bones? They're clean. Because the skeleton is a toy. See how perfect each arm and leg is? I'm telling you, it's just a plastic skeleton. Probably from a joke shop.'

'Where's all the blood come from then? You can't buy that in a joke shop.'

Eve shrugged. 'I don't bloody know. A butchers? Same with all the organs. Look at the kidneys – they aren't human size. Neither's the brain. *It is not Jessica.* I know it isn't. This is what Max does. He's trying to frighten you, that's all.'

'Well, he's doing a great job.'

'Remember what I told you, Bella. We need to fight back, not scream in terror.'

'Fight back how? What big plan have you got? Jump him when he comes down and serves us up something gross to eat? Like parts of Jessica?'

'It is *not* Jessica. I promise you. It's a game he's playing and at the moment, you're losing, by giving him the reaction he wants.' A slow, lazy smile spread across Eve's face, and with horror, Bella realised that a part of Eve, a big part, was enjoying all this. 'I reckon Jessica will help us.'

Bella snorted, angry now that Eve wouldn't listen to her. '*If* she's not dead, don't forget she's the bloody one who kidnapped us in the first place. She isn't going to help us. Jessica is as mad and bad as Max.'

'I don't think so. I really don't.'

Eve put her head in her hands and stopped talking. She was always doing that, and it was beginning to really piss Bella off. 'Can you stop going all quiet and moody on me, Eve? Fuck's sake. We're meant to be helping each other, coming up with a proper plan, instead of you being all mysterious. What do you know about Jessica that I don't?'

Eve angled her head towards Bella. 'I think she's like me.'

Bella hadn't been expecting that and was momentarily stumped. Finally, she managed, 'How do you mean?'

'She doesn't do fear.'

'What, you mean she's all cold and cut off like you. All closed down and feeling nothing. All big and fearless?' Bella couldn't keep the scorn from her voice and her annoyance. Her Majesty really had a very high opinion of herself. Thought she knew everything. Eve was making it all up as she went along, and Bella for one, didn't believe her.

She knew Eve had been lying when she'd told Bella that people on the street respected her. Eve must have thought Bella was a total idiot. *No one respects me. I don't respect me.* But Bella had nodded and pretended to be pleased, because just for a moment, she wanted to believe Eve's words.

'I know Jessica's not feeling fear,' Eve said.

'She wouldn't be, would she? What's she got to be frightened of? She's bloody Max's partner, so obviously she's not scared. What are you even talking about?'

'You're missing the point, Bella. How do you know they're partners?'

'How do you know they're not?'

Bella felt confused by the conversation and couldn't keep up with weird Eve and her strange theories. That's all they were. She was trying to be all clever, but Bella didn't believe her. Thought she was talking complete shite. Of course bloody Max and Jessica were together. 'Here's a clue, Eve. You and me are locked up down here. And they – if Jessica isn't splattered all over the glass ceiling – are together upstairs. It's us against them. What's so difficult to understand?'

'You weren't here when I first arrived.' Eve suddenly stood up and started walking around and around, throwing her hands around as she spoke. 'When Max was going to rape me, Jessica stopped him. Not overtly, not obviously, but subtly, so he wasn't aware he was being tricked. She gave me time to think of a name, you, and she persuaded him that two women would be better than one. Max didn't rape me, because she stopped him. She *helped* me.' Eve ceased walking and glanced down at Bella. 'I think she likes me. She knows we're alike and I can work on that.'

'Yeah, like how?'

'Didn't you notice how she didn't seem that amused with Max's breakfast game. Freaking us out with food, and then not food, so we wouldn't know what to expect next? Jessica wasn't happy.'

'How could you tell?'

'Her expression. Her disgust at him, the game, the spiders and the maggots, she didn't think it was funny at all. She felt sorry for us. Which means, she's vulnerable to us. As people. She's seeing us as we are. Women who are similar to her.'

'You might be, but I'm bloody nothing like her.'

'No, you're not. And maybe you should be pleased that you're not. But I am, and I'm going to make friends with Jessica. You wait and watch.'

'Fine. You do that. If she's still alive.'

And then what are you going to do? After you become best friends with Jessica, do you think she'll let us go? Or will she just let you go?

You're going to leave me here; I know you are.

You're going to abandon me.

Because you're mad and you're mean.

And my pyjamas are still wet.

Dominic, please come and rescue me. I know you're not real, but I'm desperate. I'll ring my parents and go home, I promise I will, but please let someone, anyone, *you,* Dominic, *come and rescue me. Please.*

Bella curled up in a ball, refusing to stare upwards anymore at what looked like the bloody remains of Jessica, and closed her eyes.

If she couldn't see, nothing could get her.

That's what she told herself.

Knowing it was a big fat lie.

THIRTY-NINE

Max

When Jess had left earlier, he'd believed he'd beaten her. *But I am going to kill her. It's the only way I'll ever be rid of her. But not now. I'll let her think she's won.*

When I've killed her, then I know I'll have won.

Max shook the remnants of doubts about Jess from his head and concentrated on convincing himself he *was* the director of all this: he was not the subservient one here, answering to a bloody woman. Jess was nothing. This was his territory, and he had reclaimed it. All he had to do was remind himself of his greatness, and the title of champion-of-women would be his again. Forget the bitch for now. He *would* kill her. Fucking decision made.

Standing back, he looked through the glass floor and waved at the thin one and the fat one. The thin one, Number Nine, pretended to ignore him, and he clenched his fingers, annoyed by her. There was something wrong with her. She was way too physically volatile – not what he was used to. And her personality was too similar to Jess's for his liking. Neither Jess nor the thin one knew their place.

They were the same but different. Alike enough for him to be unsettled.

Max heard the front door open and knew the bitch was back and he grinned. She'd be impressed by what he'd done. He waited, posing in his underwear, knowing he looked good, his muscles slick with blood. Making sure his thighs were tensed, and his abdomen casually six-packed, he posed, waiting for Jess to find him.

Eventually, she loomed into sight, and he spoke in short sharp sentences. *I am the boss.* 'No, stay there, Jess. Don't let them see you. Do as I say.'

She held her hands out and down in front of her, showing her understanding. 'No worries, Max.' Inching forward, she said, 'Can I have a quick peek? Promise I won't let them see me.'

He nodded. 'Go ahead. But keep out of sight.'

'Is that my hair?' She clapped her hands in delight. 'You've killed *me*. That must have been very satisfying for you.'

Sliding on his bottom, he slithered off the glass, being careful not to disturb the bloodied tableau of her death. 'You should have seen them, Jess. The big one couldn't stop screaming. I told them it was just them and me now.'

'Was Eve frightened? That's the thin one.'

Max pulled back his lips into a straight line of anger. 'She was shocked.' He lifted his shoulders. 'Better than her normal non-reaction, but she's getting there. I'm breaking her down.'

'Shocked isn't the same as frightened, though, is it? Sounds like a bit of a failure on that score. And after all that trouble you went to. How very annoying.'

He looked at her and wondered at her tone. There he was, a beautiful, almost-nude man covered in blood, and there she was, nothing special, prim and proper holding her handbag to her hip. Max studied her face. Their eyes met and he knew. 'You're back, aren't you, Jess?'

'Well, of course I'm back, silly. I'm standing right here in front of you.'

'No, I mean, *you're* back. The old Jess. You're not Jess who accepted your role as follower, when you left this house earlier. You're not my victim. The Jess you *should* be. You're back to your old you. The one I hate.'

'The one that you're frightened of, you mean? Yes, I'm back. Happy to see me? No? Well, I suggest you clean yourself up and come and have a beer in the kitchen. We can talk.'

'Fine.'

After a quick shower, Max rummaged around upstairs in Jess's parents' room and found some old boiler suit thing that he assumed had belonged to Jess's father. Going back to the scene of Jess's murder, Max was careful to keep his face neutral to the watching women below. He did a decent job cleaning up the mess and the blood. He made the glass floor gleam. He did not want a smeary, smudged view – Max wanted full visual access at all times.

As he rubbed away a final splat of blood, Max wasn't sure how he felt, knowing that Jess hadn't changed at all. She'd tricked him, and he'd allowed himself to believe. But maybe he could trick her; double bluff her – convince her he was under her rule. He could use her. She was definitely worth listening to, because she was insane. Perhaps he should simply accept her as his teacher, especially as this scenario was very, very different to how he normally operated. He'd always been a quick grab-and-rape-and-kill man. Because it worked.

But with two women, two hostages, the game had changed, and it might be worth listening to Jess.

Let her believe.

And *then* he'd kill her.

Confident he'd made the right decision, he ambled into the kitchen and waited for her to serve up lunch. She poured him a beer and prattled on about crap and he dutifully nodded and pretended to hang on her every word.

She was already stirring something in a pot. Max said, 'Do you always have a constant supply of food on the go?' He forced out a laugh. 'In case you run out?'

'Yes, actually I do. It's called batch cooking. Comes in handy when you have unexpected guests.' She turned and grinned at him. 'I'm making stew. Proper stew – not like your father made. This stew, you'll die for.'

Crazy bitch. But stew. That was perfect. He couldn't have picked a better menu for his waiting women.

She talked and he pretended to be fascinated. A lot of boring blah which didn't matter to him. He even begged her to go, to leave him alone, and she loved it all. Believed it all. Max was dumbfounded that Jess seemed to really believe that he belonged to her. She might be cleverer than he, he could admit that, but he would never be hers. And yet, here she was, playing happy families.

'You need to cover the food with those dome things,' he said, injecting his voice with some authority.

'Yes, Max. I'm aware of the importance of hiding what you are serving. Don't ever fool yourself that I'm stupid. Because that's one thing I'm not.'

She sat down in front of him. 'Shall we go over details of your next prop performance, while the meat heats through?'

'Go on, then.'

He found himself genuinely interested. Wanted to see how her brain worked. Listening quietly for some time, he didn't interrupt. And the more he listened, the more he realised what a good idea it was because it centred around him, however important Jess thought herself. Without him, the fear wouldn't exist, and as Jess laid out the next entertainment for the women, he realised she'd fallen into his trap.

Jess, so full of herself, didn't know that she was making it easier for him. Anything that had Max as the centrepiece, was as it should be. How it had always been, pre-Jess. She was thrusting him back into the limelight where he belonged, so she wasn't as bloody clever as she thought.

Max nodded politely, already excited by her plan and already deleting Jess from the vision of his own performance.

Jess was his helper, not his leader, and she was inadvertently bringing out his best. He had reeled her in, and she didn't even know it. It turned out, Jess wasn't taking over at all – she was empowering him and he liked that. He liked it a lot.

Finally, she sat back, her lips closed and she folded her arms. Like she wanted a fucking prize or something.

'You see, Max. I know how to frighten people, properly but prop-less.'

'But I *will* be using a prop. One of my uniforms.'

'But it's the preparation of it, of you, the management of the entire situation that is key. And that's what I'll be in charge of. Then…' She spread her arms, her bingo wings swaying. 'Enter Max. That show shall be all yours. Isn't that good of me?'

'No. Because you couldn't do it without me because I *am* the main attraction. You need to remember that, Jess, *babe*. Whatever you do, whatever you think, it will always be about me. And that's something you can't change, however hard you try. Now give me the plates of your fucking fantastic stew and I'll take it. To Nine and Ten.'

'I'll escort you down to the room and let you in. You don't have the keys.'

She couldn't help herself. The fat bitch always had to have the last word. Max tuned her out, concentrating his mind on giving the women downstairs a fright.

FORTY

Jessica

I *am a murderer.*
Because someone was stopping me get what I want.

I wasn't sure how killing Max's father had made me feel, but I made myself come to terms with it quickly. As a peace-offering, I'd stopped off on the way home and bought Max some cans of beer. I'd given a great deal of thought as to whether I should go back into the house as my normal self, or whether I should kowtow to Max, as his obedient servant. Both ideas appealed, but finally I'd plumped for returning as me. No trickery, no falsehoods, no pretending.

But not as I've-just-murdered-your-father me. No. That would be too harsh, and that issue needed to be handled with subtlety. Much like Max himself.

Letting myself in, I went straight to the kitchen – my refuge. It had always been my favourite place. A happy place for me. It meant food and to me, that meant self-love.

But the kitchen was covered with blood. Everywhere. Smears, splatters and splotches staining everything red.

Having seen the contents of the white plastic bucket, I didn't think Max had killed anyone. Plus, I had the key to the women, so knew they were safe. Calmly, not allowing myself to over-worry, nor be furious, I laid Max's props over the back of a chair and put six beers into the fridge.

Following the trail of blood, I walked down the hall, already knowing where I was headed. I wondered what puerile game Max had concocted; it would be interesting to see what he'd come up with as he now proudly confessed to trying to better understand the concept of frightening people.

I could hardly miss him as he lay on his side, one leg bent, his muscles hard and toned, displaying himself on the glass floor.

Stopping as Max had instructed, I craned my neck forward to better see what lay on the floor. Stepping slowly forward, with my palms facing downwards – letting Max know I understood his command – I took in the blood, the skeleton, the organs and the hair. If you weren't looking closely, *my* hair. Smiling, I did a slow handclap and congratulated him.

I watched him look at me, taking me in, and he knew. He knew I was back as me, the real Jess. Oddly, he appeared to accept it as inevitable and tried not to show how crushed he was.

Max tried to make a dignified exit but failed miserably. His shoulders were tensed up, making his neck short, his back rigidly straight and his hands tightly balled. Smiling, I returned to the kitchen and started cleaning up. I took the mess in my kitchen as a personal insult, and couldn't bear to look at it, nor did I want to leave Max to do a half-hearted and ineffective quick rinse around with a damp cloth. Keeping my handbag slung over one side of my neck, the gun next to my left hip – warm and snug and cosily weighty – I got a bucket and mop and started scrubbing.

Thirty minutes later, Max reappeared. The kitchen was back to a semblance of normality, as was he. We both sat down. 'Beer?' I asked prettily.

'Yeah. Get me one.'

'They're in the fridge.'

I watched the muscles in his jaw work: he was grinding his teeth. Realising the beers weren't getting to him by any other means than his own actions, he stood up, opened the fridge and took out a beer. Slamming the door shut, he threw himself back into his chair.

Making an effort, not wanting to completely over-state my existence, I got a pint glass from the cupboard and poured his beer for him. He took it and glancing quickly at me to make sure I was watching, he emptied the pint down his throat. He didn't even swallow. Down in one.

If I were being generous at rating inhaling beer as a talent, I'd be impressed. He burped, evidently proud of himself, and put the glass down.

Deciding to start off with a compliment, I said, 'Good idea, pretend-killing me on the glass. Better. You're improving. That's much more like fear than the teasing with the food you did earlier. I'm impressed.'

He bowed his head, in mock gratitude, but couldn't hide the genuine smile that slipped across his face. 'It was a good one, wasn't it? They actually think I've killed you.'

'And I bet you really wish you had.'

He nodded, not even bothering to hide the truth. 'Yeah, I really wish I had, Jess.' I stared at the top of his head, which he'd allowed to drop in a pretence of surrender. 'Why don't you leave me to do what I do best? On my own. Please, leave, Jess. Let this be the end. Go away. You win. Bye-bye.'

Laughing, I shook my head. 'No. Simple as that, Max, no. And one of the reasons I'm not leaving is sheer courtesy – your lack of. You need to know the women you're dealing with and act accordingly. You haven't even bothered learning their names. That's rude and means they can't relate to you – on even a very basic level. So also stupid. It means you're not taking full advantage of them.'

I crossed my legs and stared at my defeated Johnny-man. And knew he was simply going through the motions, not really engaging or listening. 'You're the one in need of mentoring, Max, not me. You don't know the difference between bullying and frightening. You need to figure that one out.'

Not meeting my eyes, he spoke to his clasped hands between his knees, his voice flat. 'But I don't need to learn their names. Names aren't important. To me, the tall one, Eve – there, happy? I remembered what she's called – and the big one; to me they're Number Nine and Number Ten. In that order.'

Sitting quietly, I worked it out. 'That would make me Number Eight. But I never went away. I'm still here. And you know what?' I leant forward and put my hand on his knee. 'I'm not going anywhere ever again. You've got me for life.'

'You've ruined my system, my system that's worked for seven previous women. The women downstairs will always be Nine and Ten, they'll never have names, and like you, I *will* kill them.'

'Someone has a very high opinion of themselves.'

'And I should. I've never been caught, and I won't be. Because I'm cleverer than you give me credit for.'

Clapping my hands, I startled him, and he reared back in his seat. I felt like shouting, 'Gotcha,' but restrained myself. Feeling vaguely sorry for Max, and frankly a little disappointed that he'd pretended to retire from the competition so easily, I gave him a chance to redeem himself. Because I knew the real Max wouldn't have gone away that easily.

'How are you going to end this charade of my death? I can't and won't stay dead for longer than today.'

Again he shrugged, making a big boohoo at how he

thought whatever he said, would be disapproved of by me. He'd probably be right.

'I've cleaned up your disembowelled corpse.' He smiled at me. 'And then I'm taking them something to eat. And of course, they'll naturally assume I'm serving them up a piece of you. They're sure to. They'll be expecting it. But it will be normal food. That's what I was going to do. Keep them guessing. Make them unsure what would happen next – would it be good or would it be bad?'

Nodding appreciatively, I said, 'That would work. But again, you're using food. Food isn't a plaything, nor a tease, nor something to be feared. It's something to be respected – it's lovely and you're spoiling that.'

Max was angry but tried to charm me. Made a big old effort, and it killed him. Good. Staring deep into my eyes, he said, 'But it will scare them, Jess, and it *will* be proper food: they'll be frightened by what it *could* be, which is the bloody point, right? So I'm not taking the piss out of your precious food.'

Not giving him the applause he wanted, I nodded. 'You can feed them in a minute – but I'll make lunch for them, just so I know they'll be getting a proper meal.'

'Okay.'

'Shall we go over details of your next prop performance, while the meat heats through?'

That perked him up. *Now* he was listening. 'Just so you know, Max. I'll be in charge of everything.' I poured him some more beer. 'I'll outline the details of which prop and how it will be used now, before you go and finish off what you started with my death scene.'

He sat quietly and listened, bending forward so he didn't miss anything. I explained what was next on the agenda and spoke for some time. Max's mouth was open and he seemed to inhale my words as if they were the gospel. I had him exactly where I wanted him.

Max was mine.

Automatically, I patted my handbag. *And I cannot* wait *to use the gun again.* 'You can't beat me, Max. Whatever you think, you can't and you won't.' I smiled at him and looked away.

'I'll escort you down to the room and let you in. You don't have the keys.'

That irritated him and I was pleased to be Queen of the show. If it didn't go through me, it didn't happen at all.

But a part of me wanted to hug my King to me. *He looks lost, so unsure of himself. Without me, he is nothing.*

But I've done it.

I've made myself indispensable to Max.

FORTY-ONE

Max

Grabbing the two plates off the tray at the door to the playroom, Max stood at the top of the spiral staircase and called down. 'Morning again, ladies.' He glanced at his watch. 'Afternoon, I mean. Doesn't time do strange things when you're waiting for something?'

Stepping carefully down the steps, he knew Jess would stay out of sight for the sake of the game. Thankfully, she was still dead to the street women, and even more dead in Max's imagination.

Hands full of plates, Max wasn't overly concerned about the open door at the top of the stairs. He had his knife strapped to his ankle in case either woman attacked him. If either of them was to be violent, it would be Number Nine. The Jess clone. Sniggering at that, he placed the plates on the floor, covered by the domes.

'Lunch is served.'

Number Ten didn't disappoint. She never did. The big one was an easy target and always gave the right reaction. She flattened herself against the wall. 'I'm not eating anything. What have you done to Jess?'

'I killed her.' He dug around in his brain and finally remembered her name. 'She had to go, Bella. But don't worry, it'll be much better just the three of us.'

'You've cooked her, haven't you? I'm not eating anything.'

'Course I haven't cooked Jess. It's just an ordinary lunch. You have my word.'

'What is it?' said Number Nine.

Max stared at boring blank face. 'Meat. It's been simmering away for ages now. It's nice and tender and juicy. You'll love it, I can guarantee it.'

'Take the cloche off,' Nine said.

'But that's for you to do. If I did it, it would be like me opening your Christmas presents, and you'd have something to say about that, wouldn't you?'

Nine shook her head and turned away. Ten copied her, still in the corner, and presented Max with her back.

Max feigned disappointment. 'With Jess gone, this is the last meal I'll be offering today, so I suggest you both eat up. While it's still warm.'

Nine and Ten ignored him and right there and then, he had to stop himself from killing them. He wanted to strangle Nine, the difficult one, and then Ten, who'd be easy and wouldn't fight back. She'd just be frightened. Even more than she was now. And that would be the perfect killing time.

Restraining himself, he walked up to Ten, with the plate held in front of him, keeping his eye on Nine. Both were in separate corners, but he was nearer the stairs. And they wouldn't dare charge him. It wasn't in a woman's nature. A normal woman. The women he picked always rolled over and accepted their situation. He'd never had trouble before, except with having to silence their screams, which was the bit he loved, and he'd never been seriously challenged on a physical level. And he didn't expect to be now.

But Max didn't trust Nine at all. Changing course, he

approached her instead with his offering. Faced the unpredictable one head-on. 'Here you go, *Eve*. Lunch.'

'Not hungry. I'll pass.' She glared at him. 'And I know you didn't kill Jessica. It didn't look real. Not in the slightest.'

You think you're so clever. Just like Jess.

'Why aren't you hungry, then? I promise you it's only stew. Nothing nasty.' He lifted his eyebrows up and down, and flashed his teeth at her, confident that she'd interpret his words as a lie. It would make her doubt the food.

'You're trying to persuade me you're serving us up bits of Jessica.'

'As if.' Max sniggered. 'What a strange idea.' He waved it under her nose. 'Can't you smell it?' Max said. 'It's delicious. Shall I leave it for you to eat later?'

He spun around and went up to Ten. 'Bella, surely I can tempt you?'

Her eyes were round and white and open and unblinking. Max breathed them in, delighted.

Job done, Max held his head high and basked in his own self-restraint. Normally, he'd have delighted in carrying this on to the obvious finish. Because Ten's response was doing it for him and that felt so good. He was grateful knowing he had that power back – there had been too long a gap after his temporary inability to maintain an erection with Jess, and it was comforting to know his manhood was working again as it should be.

He'd cleverly trapped Jess into believing that she was top of the class, when really he was in his fucking element. Everything was back on track.

All because of Jess.

Now Max had her exactly where he wanted her.

Jess was his.

To show himself that he was the bigger man, and was

intent on self-improvement, he bent and put the two plates in the middle of the floor.

He wasn't doing this self-improvement shit for Jess, but for himself.

Max wondered how long the food would remain untouched. Snickering, he put his foot on the bottom step. 'Night, night, ladies. Tomorrow, I'll bring breakfast.'

FORTY-TWO

Max

I was around midnight and Max was bored.
Considering he was the person with no power around
here, Jess was pretty understanding about letting him really put
a full stop to the food game. Max fooled her easily by saying
the piss pot had to be emptied, as he wasn't willing to work
with foul-smelling dirty women. Not forgetting the big one
needed new pyjamas, having wet herself.

Jess let him in and standing at the open door, he winked at
her, trying to annoy her by being so accepting of his lower
rank. Standing back, as she bloody should, he walked down the
stairs, new plastic bucket in hand.

Although both women were awake and staring at him, he
put his index finger to his mouth and whispered, 'Sorry to
disturb, ladies, but the bucket needs emptying. I'm run off my
feet here.'

Without looking at the woman, Max threw a pair of clean
pyjamas at Ten. Not waiting for a response from either, and not
expecting any, he went and picked up the used bucket and
running up the stairs with it, he left it next to the door. Turning
around, he danced down the staircase, enjoying himself. Max

didn't speak but was aware that both Nine and Ten couldn't stop looking at him. They were frightened, even Nine was. Delighting in that and choosing to ignore them, he scanned the room. He was just playing. Relishing the silence. He could hear Ten's breathing become more ragged as the minutes ticked by, and he did nothing but turn his head, as if looking for something that was lost.

Picking up both plates of food, he took them to the foot of the stairs. Putting one carefully on the floor, he made a performance of smelling the metal dome and as if unsure, he tilted up the side nearest to him, and sneaked a peek beneath the bell-shaped covering.

Screaming suddenly into the heavy quiet of the playroom, he almost dropped the cloche, and hastily replaced it over the food. Out of the corner of his eye, he noticed both women had literally jumped, more than startled – Max was pretty sure Ten's feet had actually left the ground. Putting his hand to his heart, he said, 'God. Stupid me. Picked the wrong one.' Laughing, he put the plate to one side and picked up the other. Revealing its contents, he sighed and muttered, 'What a relief. I'm starved.' Spooning the stew into his mouth, he licked his lips and allowed his mouth to drip with gravy, and loudly sucked up a strand of cooked onion.

Ten was bent over, her hands on her knees, as if she were catching her breath. Nine sat on her beanbag and made a point of ignoring him. He knew she was frightened. *All* women were frightened of Max, apart from the insane bitch hiding upstairs, but there was something wrong with Jess. He *knew* women found him irresistible, and that included Jess – what Nine needed was a reminder of just who was in bloody charge here.

He crossed the room to where Nine was insolently lounging, and she didn't even sit up. Showing no fear at Max's physical closeness, he moulded his hands into tight fists. Was she pretending, or was she asking to be beaten up? He knew women were a weird species and he didn't trust any of them. They were always asking for something and then complaining when they got it. Max thought that was the game Nine was playing.

Max was more used to using violence as a way of restraining his women, not hitting them for the love of it. But he could, if he needed to. Now, he thought he needed to. He back-handed Nine in the face. Hard. Then slapped her with his open palm. Backhand, forehand, backhand, forehand. Knuckles, palm, knuckles, palm. Predator tennis. *Game, set and match to me*. Nine's head jerked right and left, left and right, like curtains being ripped open and shut.

Big old Ten had cowered away into her favourite corner and in between the slaps, Max could hear her whimper. That was more the sound he was going for, instead of the grunting that whooshed out from Nine's open mouth. He smiled at the thin one.

Now Eight, Nine and Ten would all listen to him. And Max was most definitely including Jess in his numbers. She wasn't here and so wasn't watching through the glass ceiling as she was still playing dead. *His* game. But Jess would see tomorrow, the battered woman who had gone all floppy now. Panting slightly from the exertion, Max had proved there was very little lasting pleasure to be got from physical violence, and he was sorry he'd hurt his knuckles and wasted his energy on proving a point.

But in this strange new world in which he found himself, Max was surprising himself, and coming up trumps. He was excelling. Due in part to Jess – he had to credit her with the introduction of creating longer lasting fear – he was evolving and decision-making on his own.

Beating Nine would keep her in line and wipe off that snotty I'm-better-than-you air from her face – every bloody time she looked at him. As if she were all high and mighty, and he, not worthy of even a second glance.

Max had thrown the gauntlet down and no one would question his authority. He'd shown he could be violent. The risk of further physical attack would keep Nine and Ten controlled. Easily. Most people didn't like blood, himself included. It wasn't a general crowd pleaser. But it proved the point that Max wasn't one to mess with.

Having finished with Nine, he checked she was still breathing, and then picked up the remaining, untouched plate of food. Brought it up to Ten and putting his hands on her shoulders, he forced her to face him.

'Eat this,' said Max.

Ten's eyes filled with tears which inevitably spilled down her cheeks, her lips wobbling, her nose dripping as she tried to stop crying.

'Eat it.' Max screamed at her, pushing it so close to her face, that the top of the dome touched her nose. She shook her head, her eyes large and white, like boiled eggs, and Max felt himself grow hard. It would be so easy to rape her. Jess wasn't watching, Nine was unconscious and who would know?

I'd *know.*

Even if Jess doesn't know, I know, which would make the bitch right about me doing my women too soon. Not letting them wait for long enough. Jess can't beat me. I won't allow it.

Max was furious and wondered why Jess's opinion was so important to him. Why her patronising and withering words made him feel so useless. Vulnerable. Displeasing her was like angering Dad when Max had been a boy. Potentially frightening.

That thought stopped Max. And he decided to ignore the weird simile. He'd been wrong. Of course he had. Dad and Jess were nothing alike – they wouldn't even be friends. They'd hate each other.

Angry with himself, he said, 'Eat the fucking food, it's only stew. How stupid are you, Ten?'

Still holding the food to her face, Max knocked off the cover and dipped a spoon into the food and started eating. 'Cold, but nice. Eat it.'

Ten eventually started taking little bites, swallowing food, but tears remained, trembling on her lower lids, her eyes staring white and bright.

Turning from both women, sexually excited but ignoring his erection, Max left the room.

Tomorrow, things would be very different. They were playing his type of game, and he would triumph and really come into his own. Because it's what he did best, and Jess had suggested it.

Just went to show how wrong she was. Jess had no idea what she was letting herself in for, allowing him to appear in one of his uniforms. What did she really know about anything, anyway?

After he'd frightened Nine and Ten, Max decided on a date to kill Jess.

Immediately after his prop performance tomorrow afternoon. Then, things could return to normal.

FORTY-THREE

Eve

'What time do you reckon it is?'

Eve said she didn't know, but thought it was the morning. She didn't feel like talking and her face was sore, her eyes were puffed up and her neck ached. She was also bloody furious and couldn't wait to see Max. Even if he beat her again, the next time Eve would make sure she hurt him.

She also wondered when Jessica would put in an appearance. It was difficult to navigate time with no real daylight, but Eve thought it was definitely the next day, and didn't think Jessica would be prepared to carry on with the pretence of being dead. Eve thought she wouldn't want to miss anything, and so would happily reveal herself today.

After Max had left them last night, Bella had cried herself to sleep. Eve had regained consciousness just before Max had left, watching through swollen eyes, as he'd forced Bella to eat. Angry that he'd got away with being such a bastard, Eve sat in silence this morning, letting her mood steep, like tea in a pot. It only got stronger as it brewed. *You never really know what life has in store, and then it throws shit at you when you aren't looking. Sometimes I hate bloody life.*

But sometimes I love it.

Hearing the door, Eve and Bella both turned their faces up at the sound, Eve hoping it would be Jessica.

And it was. Despite her fury, Eve couldn't help but smile to herself and had to admit that there really was something about Jessica that she liked. Recalling the meal Jessica had cooked for her after bringing her here, Eve remembered the conversation they'd had. Perhaps they'd recognised something in each other then, and as had been said, under different circumstances, they really might have been good friends.

Eve laughed quietly to herself, as she saw her kidnapper come down the stairs, carrying a tray. With not a cloche in sight.

Not bothering to explain her un-dead state, Jessica wafted delicately down the steps, and walked towards each of them, holding a tray. She nodded her head, indicating that they take what she offered: a bowl of porridge and toast and marmalade and a cup of tea. Eve couldn't help but notice Jessica as she did a classic double-take on seeing Eve's battered face.

So, she didn't know that Max had beaten her last night. Eve was surprised when having taken what she wanted from the tray, and put them on the floor, Jessica knelt and cupped Eve's cheek. Neither woman spoke, but Eve saw Jessica's eyes harden and her lips thin with anger.

In the sudden silence, Bella said, 'I thought you were dead.'

Jessica swivelled around, keeping a tight hold on her handbag which she'd slung over her neck with the strap across her chest. She let her hand rest on it. Picking up the tray from the floor, she approached Bella who took her food. 'It was one of Max's great jokes, killing me, while I wasn't here to defend myself.' She laughed and added, 'Take no notice. I'm not dead and I'm here with important news.' Glancing up the spiral staircase, Jessica lowered her voice. 'I wanted you both to know,

I've called the police and they're on their way. Everything's going to be all right.'

Bella stopped eating mid-mouthful and Eve could see into her mouth as it opened in surprise. Eve said nothing and made no reaction because she wasn't quite sure she believed it. That this whole kidnap would be so easily resolved, with no further violence, seemed extremely unlikely. It didn't feel right. Why the change of plan?

Bella found her voice. 'Really? What have you done to Max? He'll go apeshit.' She lowered her head, clearly remembering her ordeal last night. 'Bloody bastard. He beat up Eve as well as making me eat stuff I didn't want to. He's a nutter.'

Jessica nodded but didn't say anything more.

'Come on, Jessica,' Eve said. 'What's going on? Where's your partner?'

Jessica's expression changed for an instant, and a dreamy look softened her round face. 'We're not partners in the biblical sense, if that's what you meant by the term, "partner". We're more like business partners, but now I find we don't share the same business values. He can't be allowed to carry on.'

'But it's your fault as well,' Bella said. 'You brought me and Eve here. It's your fault as well.'

'I know it is, and I'm prepared to take whatever punishment I have coming, with grace and deep shame. I know the word "Sorry" isn't enough, but so you know, I really am. Sorry about everything.'

She's lying, thought Eve. *Everything she's just said about calling the police is a lie.* Eve couldn't help but be disappointed in Jessica and surprised at how easily her fat host had tricked her. Eve had believed that there was a weird sort of shared, unspoken camaraderie between them, and had genuinely thought in some way, that connection and that relationship between them, would be the thing that would ultimately save her.

How fucking wrong am I?

Both Eve and Bella had been sitting on their beanbags, ready to eat. At the mention of *police*, Eve had stood up. Keeping her tone flat and refusing to show how upset she was, Eve said, 'Where are they then? The police, where are they?'

'They're on their way. As I said.'

'Where's Max?'

'He went out. I sent him shopping on some pretext and off he trotted. It never occurred to him that I'd betray him, but judging by the state of your face, it's just as well I did. I can't control him anymore.'

Eve glanced up at the door. It was closed, instead of pushed to. 'What happens if Max arrives back before the police get here, and what's taking them so long anyway? If you really told them there were two kidnapped women in a cellar, then where are the hell are they? It would be an emergency. You're bullshitting.'

'I assure you I'm not.'

Jessica was sitting in her usual place on the bottom stair, and Eve walked closer to Jessica, seeing her hand tighten on her handbag. It was like the bag was surgically attached to the woman and now Eve thought about it, she wondered what was so precious that Jessica wouldn't be parted from it.

'What's in the bag, Jessica?'

'Usually the keys to this room. I didn't want to leave them around so Max could use them and get at you whenever he fancied it.'

'What's in it now?'

'Not the keys. I've left them upstairs, hidden under the mat in front of this door. The front door is open. I told the police to look for the glass floor and to shout when they got here. We'll hear them.'

'What else is in the bag?'

Jessica stood and said, 'What's your point, Eve? What do you think is in the bag? A gun?'

Eve watched Jessica laugh and then she stopped quickly, tilting her head to the side. Holding her finger to her lips Jessica said, 'They're here. The police are here.'

The three women stood in a loose huddle; their necks tipped back.

They all saw a pair of black soled boots and the trousered legs of a uniformed man, walk across the glass.

Jessica shouted, making Bella jump, and waved her arms in the air. 'Here, we're down here.'

The face of a man peered down at them; his cap pulled down low on his brow. Eve saw little else of his face, as the stiff collar of his coat was turned up and his hands held it tightly to his chin.

But Eve knew. And turned away, not wanting to give anyone any warning of her sheer bloody rage. It was just a stupid game and if this was the punchline, Eve was disappointed.

Jessica shouted, 'Get the keys and open the door.'

'Give it up, Jessica,' Eve said, hearing her own voice tight with anger. 'You're not fooling anyone. I'm surprised at you. I would have expected more thought to have been put into a disguise. Am I meant to not know who it is?'

'Of course I expect you to know, Eve, but let Max have his fun. He has a very small brain, although beauty in abundance. And there *is* a surprise. Just you wait.'

After unlocking the door, the big boots on the feet of the uniformed man walked slowly but steadily down the spiral staircase. Reaching the bottom, he said, 'Are any of you hurt?' He didn't even bother disguising his voice, and as he looked around him, he suddenly laughed, pushing back his cap and letting his collar fall away, allowing his coat to flap open. 'And where is Max? The great and beautiful Max. Where the fuck is he? Who am *I*? Why, I'm a policeman come to save you all.' He bowed. 'You can thank me later.' He held his hands out at his sides, standing proud in his uniform and gleaming boots.

Jessica joined in with his laughter. 'Girls, it gives me great pleasure to introduce Detective Sergeant Max Chisholm, serving officer with the Metropolitan police.'

Max saluted theatrically, and then stopped and faltered. He glanced quickly at Jessica, confusion covering his face. His jaw hung slack with bewilderment.

'This wasn't the plan, Jess. What the fuck?'

'What's wrong, Max?' said Eve. 'You look like you've had a nasty shock.'

Jessica rolled around the room, nimble on the balls of her feet. 'Max is under the impression that I don't know who he really is. He thinks I am convinced he is wearing one of his inspiring uniforms, that he refers to as "his props". What he doesn't realise, until now, is that I *do* know who he is.' She tittered. 'Or should I say, I know what he is.'

Bella said, 'What is he?'

'This isn't one of his many fancy-dress uniforms he uses to gain the trust of women: like a priest's dog collar with Bible in hand, nor a doctor's white jacket with a row of pens in his pocket and a stethoscope around his neck. No. This is far more interesting. This is Max's *real* work uniform. Your tormentor *is* actually a detective sergeant. I have his warrant card in my bag. Care to see it, Max?'

'You bitch. You stupid crazy bitch.'

And yet, despite his shock at her betrayal, he couldn't stop himself from preening just a little, holding himself straighter, and strutting as he shouted out his protestations – pulling down on his jacket, flattening out his collar, pulling at his cuffs. He recovered quickly. 'So what, Jess? I'm a real copper – and a damn fine one.' He twirled. 'Don't you think my uniform suits me?'

Feeling like she was watching all this play out from far away, even Eve was shocked at Jessica's next move. Dipping her hand into her handbag, Jessica brought out a gun and pointed it at Max-the-real-copper, which Eve *hadn't* expected, and said, 'Gotcha.'

Max's bragging vanished and he stood open-mouthed.

Eve cheered up.

FORTY-FOUR

Jessica

Max semi-crouched in the middle of the room, his hands up in an automatic response – like father, like son.

'Frightened?' I enquired.

'Put the gun down, Jess. You don't know how to use it. Put it down now.'

I absolutely do *know how to use it, and I did exceptionally well shooting your precious daddy, considering it was my first time.*

'That's my gun, right?'

Pretending to examine it carefully, I waved the gun around, looking down the barrel, turning it upside down and round about. I enjoyed the effect it had on everyone in the room, ducking as the barrel swung their way. Eventually, I said, 'Doesn't have your name on it, Max, so no. It's mine.'

Walking up to him, I placed the gun right in the middle of his forehead. 'When I say walk, Max, you walk. To the top of the staircase. Off you trot.'

Interestingly, I saw his Adam's apple bob up and down in his throat, but his eyes were squinted – perhaps he was too well-schooled in concealing fear when taken by surprise – so the all-important whites of his eyes weren't coming out to play.

'Go and sit on the top step.' I waved the gun, indicating the direction he should take, and he crab-walked to the spiral staircase, still managing to look exceedingly handsome in his sergeant's dress uniform. Glancing over his shoulder, his face had lost some of its arrogance. 'You've lost it, babe. Come on, it's me. Max. The man you've wanted forever and now you've got me.'

Eve, Bella and I watched as the most beautiful man in the world sidled and stumbled up the spiral staircase. 'Yes, I have you. The question now is, do I still want you? Eve, open my bag and take out the handcuffs. There are two pairs of them taken from Max's little bedside collection. We'll follow him up and you can attach him to the railings, okay? Don't worry. He won't struggle. Not with a gun pointed in the middle of his pretty face.'

Eve grinned in reply. 'I'm not worried in the slightest. I'm *hoping* he'll struggle.'

Bella's face remained neutral.

Under my guidance, although it wasn't strictly necessary, Eve secured Max to the third step down, his body having to arch around the curve of the stairs. His hands were cuffed and stretched behind his head to the metal railing at the top, and one outstretched foot fixed to another lower rail. It was an uncomfortable and awkward position, but he wouldn't pose any physical threat, tangled and trapped as he was. I relieved him of his mobile.

Satisfied, Eve and I came back down, and I told the two women to sit and enjoy their breakfast, while I thought about what came next.

Eve and I liked each other. I wasn't sure why we did – not yet – but thought we'd have time to make friends properly now. I could hardly believe it. A man and a friend – all in the space of a couple of days. I should have made more of an effort at this socialising lark before now. Seemed I was quite successful at it. Had I started earlier in life, I'd be swamped by both boyfriends and friends alike. A missed opportunity.

Finding out Max was a detective had deeply shocked me but now, if I really thought about it, I wondered why I'd been surprised. Perfect job for a perfect psycho.

Although, frankly, I was surprised he had the brains for it.

Relaxing into a beanbag, I repositioned the angle of the gun, and said, 'How many times do you pick your very own uniform to wear, instead of the others, Max? I'm referring to when you're out and merrily kidnapping, under the guise of your highly sophisticated labelling, pigeonholing and identifying scheme.'

'I *do* use lots of my other props. I only use this if it will work well with a particular subject.' Max attempted to look offended. 'I don't abuse my uniform. And this is my dress uniform – for official police functions, like funerals and awards. Normally, I'm in civvies.'

'And how many awards have you won?'

No response.

'I think you're being coy, Max, about wearing your police uniform. I'm sure it's used an awful lot more than your other "props". Because it's easy and you're lazy. It would never occur to a woman that a policeman was anyone other than a person in authority who'd help them. They'd never imagine they were, in fact, dealing with a man who was intent on raping and killing them. And that, to me, well… it feels a bit too much like cheating.'

'I agree,' said Eve, smiling. 'That's not playing fair at all, Max.' She made a sound of derision. 'Max is a real honest-to-God copper. Who'da thunk?'

'Jess, you know I always play fair. I can't help it if women are stupid enough to fall for me. I reckon I could be naked and they'd still come home with me.' He leered, like a cartoon man, although in order to see us, he had to twist his neck uncomfortably. 'I label them, and guess what? Mostly I can pigeonhole them as instant Max-lovers. There isn't a woman on this planet who doesn't find me irresistible. I can't help it.'

'I've got a gun pointed at your head, Max. Don't show off. I'm not very good with guns,' I lied.

'You won't pull it, Jess. You're obsessed with me. You're in love with me, so I think I'm pretty safe.'

Shaking my head sadly, I spoke with an element of true sadness. 'I haven't fallen out of love with you, Max. On the contrary. Although the term, *in love*, isn't quite right, but we'll go with whatever makes it easier for you to believe.'

He found a laugh. 'I haven't been able to get rid of you, babe. Don't lie because you've been caught out. You can't imagine a life without me now. Admit it.'

'I admit it. And I'm more invested in you now than ever before. But I can't ignore the fact that you're essentially a very beautiful but stupid and conceited man, drowning in your own vanity.'

'So?'

I smiled, not wanting to say out loud what the point was.

Max was *my* very beautiful, stupid and conceited man.

I owned him. He was my trophy Johnny-man.

I liked that. I liked that a lot.

Not bothering to answer, I let Eve take the floor. She finished her toast and started on her porridge before speaking. 'You mean he picks up women on the street, wearing fancy dress, or as it turns out, his copper's uniform, and then what? Takes them home and rapes them? Kills them? Wow, impressive, Max.' She laughed and for the first time, he started to look unsure.

I said, 'He does all of that, Eve. But mostly what seriously annoys me, Max, is that you're not giving any of your chosen women a fighting chance, are you?' I shifted around on my beanbag, my bottom sinking deeper into it. 'It's not only your charm that you rely on, as you had me believe, but your very real authority. Most women wouldn't dream of *not* getting into a car, if told to by a policeman.'

Looking down at his gaggle of women, Max's lips moved, but his voice lacked volume. 'I didn't need any uniform for you, Jess. You begged me to give you a lift. You nearly flattened me, getting into my car so quickly – I couldn't have stopped you.'

'Yes, true. My mistake, I don't deny it. But there you sat in your cosy little house, teaching me how to recognise the needs of your victims and all the time, you'd been taking short-cuts. No charm required. Just bung on your uniform and job done. I don't believe you ever use your other "props" at all. Not until you've got your women tied and gagged in your bed. Then you play dress-up, and that's really rather a bit pathetic, don't you think?'

'Did he kidnap you?' Eve asked.

I laughed. 'That question is up for debate. Let's leave it at: I was stupid and desperate and made a very big mistake. But frankly, who could blame me? Look at him, look at his beauty. I wanted it, wanted him all for myself, and now I've got him.' I rested the gun on my bent knees and tilted the barrel upwards. 'And now I have to think how best to deal with him.'

Us women were all quiet for a moment, and all looked proudly up at what we'd captured.

Bella still remained quiet and seemed upset. For the moment, I left her to it, and said, 'Just for the record, Eve, I had every intention of frightening you both, by allowing you to think it was a real policeman and then surprise, surprise, it would have turned out to be Max, as he'd scrubbed off his make-up, taken off his wig which I bought at great expense today, and lastly, he would have peeled away a very small but realistic moustache. He would have looked unrecognisable, and therefore the shock of it being Max would have been terrifying.'

I crossed my ankles. 'But I changed my mind, and that would be your fault, Max. Don't think I didn't realise you thought you were really the one in control. Your conceit was plain to see, as was your condescension of me.'

'I have every right to be conceited. Look at me.'

I shrugged. 'It doesn't matter. For now. But you need to know *why* I spoilt it all for you and decided to capture you instead.' Angry now, I heard my voice rise. 'I permitted you entry into this room last night to give Bella her new pyjamas and to fetch the bucket. That was it. Nothing more was required.'

Fiddling with the chamber of the gun again – I still wasn't as adept with it as I'd have liked – I let it fall open and made a point of examining it closely. I smiled as if truly content. It wasn't an act, as I genuinely delighted in the power the gun gave me. Bringing it up close to my face, I pointed it at him again and closed one eye as if taking aim.

'Your mistake was that you wouldn't stop with the food bullying. I told you not to play with your food, that food was off limits, but you couldn't resist. You forced Bella to eat, making her believe she was eating me, and you even bragged to me about it afterwards. You couldn't stop yourself. I don't like food and bullying and fear in the same place. I fucking *hate* it.'

Max remained silent. I could feel the memory of all the fat shaming and food jokes I'd been on the wrong end of. Shaking with fury, I moved on, my voice struggling to stay controlled. 'You also took the time to needlessly beat Eve and showed me your bruised knuckles, as if you thought I'd be impressed. You abused my kindness, Max, and you disobeyed me.'

I realised I should have brought a cup of tea for myself. My mouth was so dry I could hardly swallow. Licking my lips I said, 'I've decided that it's time for you to learn the difference between bullying and frightening, because it's an important distinction.' I waited a beat. 'We'll concentrate on fear.'

I turned to Bella and Eve. 'If I'm being completely honest, I *am* interested in fear. The whole concept of it. Because I don't feel any. I am fearless. Unlike Max, who *is* fascinated with it, but doesn't understand it, and therefore wastes it. Doesn't know how to really create it. I wanted to know what frightens people and why, so was happy to go along with this farce.' I smiled at both of the homeless women. 'And that's my guilty secret.'

'You're as bad as he is,' said Bella. 'I don't think it's funny. I want to go now. Please.'

Shaking my head, I admitted to myself, happily, that I at least felt guilt. Which meant I wasn't totally emotionally incontinent. 'I can't let you go, Bella. Not yet. Because I kidnapped you, and you'll go straight to the police.'

Eve spoke to Bella. 'Don't worry, Jessica won't hurt us. If we do as she says. Look on the bright side – at least she's not going to rape us.'

'No, I won't hurt either of you. That's not my intent at all.'

'What are you going to do, then?' Bella's voice was angry and I thought she had every right.

'I'm really not sure. But together, I thought it might be amusing if we all, as three women, who were all nearly victims of DS Max over there, found out how he likes being on the wrong end of fear.' I glanced up at Max, as if he were an afterthought. 'Okay, sweetheart?'

Getting up from the beanbag, which was difficult to do with any style, I stretched my legs, and walking slowly up the black staircase, gun in hand, I stopped when I got to Max. Dipping my hand into his pocket, I tutted and tried another one, until I found the keys to the playroom. 'You sit there, Max. I'm sure the girls won't kill you in my absence. If you feel in danger, just scream. I'll only be a jiffy.' I opened and closed my mouth. 'I'm absolutely bloody *gasping* for a cup of tea. Wait here, babe, and I'll see you in five minutes. Tops.'

I left the room and locked the door.

Walking across the glass, I glanced down and smiled.

What an interesting turn of events.

Now I had kidnapped *three* people.

If you'd told me this would be the case a few days ago, I'd have laughed.

As it was, I still laughed.

FORTY-FIVE

Max

_____

Max had definitely been frightened when the bitch had brought the gun out – his gun – but he thought he'd hidden his fear well. Now he was also worried how long he'd be kept in this position. He knew he couldn't maintain it, without suffering cramp.

Or being shot.

He was also worried, full-bloody-stop. The bitch had beaten him, on the very day he'd decided to kill her. *I can still appeal to her soft side, her I-love-Max side. Jess adores me. She even still admits it.*

But that Number Nine, she'd back up Jess every time. That wasn't good – not from where he was sitting. Together, Nine and Jess were a lethal combination. One would egg the other on. He should know because the one thing he was an expert on, was women.

And of course he didn't always wear his bloody uniform. *Course* he didn't. He loved using his many and varied props, but Jess was too dim to understand that. Again, proving his point, she was unable to see past the uniform, to the man wearing it. And that was what his whole system relied on. The stupidity of women and their blindness to the wrapping he presented himself in.

Although in his case, whatever cloth he decided to hide behind, once women saw how handsome he was, they realised he was even better than his chosen disguise. A rare thing. Presents, once opened, were always a disappointment. Beautiful wrapping paper – crap gift. Except in his case. He always went down well, and the ladies were always thrilled to find the nugget of gold that was Max.

There was only one immediate and obvious positive to be taken from his current situation. At least Dad wasn't here to see his shame. His defeat, as Dad would see it. He'd always been so good at frightening him, that Max had been armed for life – he couldn't remember the last time he'd experienced true fear.

Except for Jess. Strangely, and weirdly, Jess still frightened him. Beyond his comprehension.

Dad would be disappointed if he could see Max now. He'd say Max hadn't terrified them into submission when he had the chance. As Dad had done to him, and the White Eye game had done him no harm at all. It had made him stronger and the man he was today.

Although, weirdly, after he and Dad had stopped playing the game, Max had still come out triumphant. The bigger man. The man who Dad so desperately wanted to be loved by. *Everyone loves me – it must be a natural talent that I was born with.*

Nine's voice interrupted his thoughts. 'What's to stop me coming up there, Max, and beating you around the face, just because I can? Tit for tat, if that's how you'd like to think of it.'

He heard Bella's voice. 'Don't, Eve. It's not right. He's tied up, it's not fair.'

Nine laughed. 'You're kidding, right? After what he put us through, you want me to be *fair*?'

'Jessica put us through it as well. Why aren't you angry with her? She kidnapped us, not him.'

'But he might as well have done. He'd have any woman; it just happened to be us. And if not for Jessica, we'd be in a much worse situation. What's wrong with you, Bella? You should enjoy being given the chance to get your own back on Max. After the way he treated you, I should have to be holding you back.'

'If it wasn't for Jessica, I wouldn't be here. If it wasn't for _you_, I wouldn't be here. If Jessica is so great, she should let us go.'

'Don't be stupid. How can she? You'd toddle off to the police and tell them everything. We have to give her a reason to trust us.'

'Like what? Beat up Max. Torture him, mentally? I'm not like that.'

Max smiled. Already there was dissent amongst the ranks, and Jess had only been gone five minutes. That's because she had no concept of control. _Which I have in oodles, even when I'm handcuffed._ He'd never have considered he'd be potentially saved by the big one. Careful to use her proper name, Max said, 'Bella, don't listen to either Jess or…' His mind went blank and he panicked. What the fuck was Nine's name?

'_Eve._' He almost screamed out her name in his excitement at remembering it. 'Don't listen to either of them, Bella. You're right. I knew you were different to the other two. You've got common decency, which neither of them have.'

'I _am_ decent. That's how my parents brought me up. Honest and decent.'

Max's neck was aching from having to keep it upright, so he relaxed and listened to Eve's laugh. 'Get a bloody grip, Bella. He's tricking you, can't you see? You can trust Jessica. And maybe she will let you go. Eventually.'

'I don't want to be involved with anything nasty,' the big one said.

'Concentrate on being nice to Jessica then. Forget Max.

Max is a rapist, Bella. Which bit of that are you forgetting? He's also a murderer. Be honest and decent with her, not him.'

Max had to stop himself from laughing out loud. It was that easy to get women on his side – even women who he'd been more than happy to rape and kill. If Jess hadn't stopped him. Gritting his teeth, and raising his head, he did what he did best. 'Hey, Bella. Do me a favour, would you? I can't hurt you from here, so there's nothing to be frightened of. Just listen.'

'What do you want?' she answered, her voice all quavery and unsure – exactly how he liked women's voices to sound: tremulous and child-like. Even trussed up and incapable of doing any serious damage, Max still had the power to enthral and captivate women. It was in his DNA and he couldn't not do what he did best. 'Don't let Eve and Jess hurt me, Bella. It's not fair, and if they really hurt me, you'd be held criminally responsible. You'd be an accessory.'

Eve's voice cut into his dialogue, ruining it. Breaking the spell Max was casting over the big stupid one. 'Bella, stop talking to him. *Now.*'

Angling his head painfully, Max saw Eve approaching the bottom step. 'If you don't stop talking to Bella, I'll come up and make you stop. And don't even bother entertaining the notion that I won't. I've done it before and I'll do it again.'

Bella raised her voice, obviously scared that things were getting out of hand. She was on his side, Max knew. He'd have her to rely on, to stop the other two crazy bitches from getting him. 'She's telling the truth, Max. Eve likes violence, she told me. She killed her partner by stabbing him to death. And she went to prison for it. Eve's not joking, so everyone needs to calm right down right now.'

That was news worth knowing, Max thought and found that it unsettled him. Eve and Jess together. Trust Jess to bring him a murdering woman. Fucking typical.

Max heard the door unlock and closed his eyes. He wondered if Jess knew Eve's background and whether it was even true. Something told him it was. There'd always been something very off with the thin one with her empty eyes.

'Miss me?' said Jess as she stepped over him. 'Remember how you said that to me, when you'd left me tied to your bed, Max? Now it's my turn to ask you. How much did you miss me?'

'I didn't. But I have news for you.'

'I'm all agog – surprise me.'

Max wished he could sit up and be more comfortable but resigned himself to again relaxing his neck muscles and stared at the ceiling, disappointed that he couldn't see Jess's reaction to his words.

'Did you know that in this one room, there are two killers? Me, obviously.' He couldn't help but let out a puff of pride. 'Do you know who else?'

'Tell me, Max. Have your moment.'

'That maniac woman you brought to me. Eve. She's also a killer, did you know?' Despite the pain, Max lifted his head, unable to resist seeing the bitch's face. He was pleased to see that she was surprised.

She turned to Eve. 'Is this true?'

'Yeah, although it's not something I usually talk about, but Bella-big-mouth did the honours and repeated what I told her in confidence.'

'Who did you kill?'

'My abusive partner, Oliver. Got seven years in prison for it.' She shrugged. 'Served three and a half. Now I'm out.'

Bella spoke again, obviously pleased at being the one with something interesting to say. 'Eve said she enjoyed killing him. She likes violence so you better all watch out.'

Jess glanced up at Max and their eyes met. He tried to give

her his twinkly look, but was hampered by his head position and having to stare downwards.

But he saw Jess's mouth split into a huge smile. She was delighted, not frightened. Well, Max wouldn't expect Jess to be frightened at that. *He'd* never been able to frighten her, but he'd hoped she'd at least be shocked that there was another killer in the room.

'Well, well, well,' Jess said. 'What are the chances? And sorry to burst your bubble, Max, but you're wrong. There aren't two killers in this room – there are three. Isn't that extraordinary? We should form a gang.'

Putting his head down, Max listened to Jess's peals of laughter. The sound echoed around him, and he finally acknowledged he might be in serious shit.

FORTY-SIX

Jessica

Things were going quicker than I'd anticipated, but that was all to the good. I wasn't in a hurry, but equally, was keen to get started. I was sure Max knew it was me who was the third killer and would wonder who I'd killed. But it was Eve who spoke, not being one to tiptoe through any conversation. 'Who did you kill, Jessica?'

I put the tray down: my mug of strong tea and a brewing pot bedside it, along with a plate of custard creams for all. Except Max. I didn't feel like sharing my favourite biscuits with him. He'd probably spit them out just to annoy me. There would be no more shaming of food, or the people that ate it. Never again.

Answering Eve, I said, 'That would be *my* secret, Eve. For the moment. Always keep something fascinating back for shock value. It's good to keep you all guessing.'

'Fair enough,' she said.

Max's voice floated down to me. 'Knowing you, Jess, I wouldn't be surprised if you'd killed a newborn child. Because you're an evil bitch.'

Not bothering to answer him, I offered the biscuits around.

Bella took a handful and said, 'Sorry. I didn't mean it, Eve. I shouldn't have told your secret, sorry. I'm just freaked out.'

'No problem. Wasn't a secret, anyway. Forget it.'

The two women and I all sipped and nibbled in a friendly silence. Max's quietness was like a sonic boom of misery and anger, and it upset what would otherwise have been a nice morning of tea and biscuits, between a group of new female friends. Sitting and licking the cream out of my biscuit, I studied Eve and decided our meeting on the street hadn't been accidental, nor coincidental. It had been inevitable. My whole life had been friendless but now I realised I'd subconsciously picked a woman who'd reminded me, of me. Even though homeless and alone, she'd radiated an inner strength and a certain something else, which I wasn't sure I could identify, but whatever it was, I trusted her, and knew she trusted me.

Good to have an ally in this situation.

Brushing crumbs from my lap, picking up the gun I'd laid beside me on the floor, I got up and checking my watch, said, 'Will you look at the time? It's *that* time already. Watch and listen, Max. This tutorial is for you.'

Bella immediately stopped cramming her mouth full but didn't say anything. Her eyes spoke for her. I wanted to assure her she'd be safe, but I was too busy maintaining my cruel, cool girl-about-town, wielding-a-gun look. I thought I had it down pat.

'Ready, Max?'

'You can't teach me anything, babe. But you carry on. Try your hardest.'

'I'm going to teach you what it is to be frightened. Or should I say, *remind* you about fear. Take up where your father left off.'

'Are you like Eve, Jessica?' Bella said. 'Do you enjoy violence as well? That's not normal.'

'Which of us is normal?' I answered. 'What is normal, Bella? Are you?'

'More normal than anyone else around here.'

Bella was sulky now, but I felt sorry for her. 'You'll be fine,' I told her quietly and as I passed her, I squeezed her shoulder reassuringly. 'Leave it to me.'

Walking towards the stairs, the gun in my hand, I found I was really looking forward to this and felt really rather wonderful. I embraced it.

'No, stop. Please stop. I want to speak before you do anything.' Bella's voice was firm but crammed full of concern and worry, unable to disguise the panic. She deserved a hearing, so I stopped.

'You and Eve are wrong. I don't know what you're even thinking, Jessica, but Eve isn't scared at all. She's *enjoying* this. And that's not right. You both think you're so great and powerful and strong. You're not. It's wrong, what you're doing. It's very wrong.'

'You don't know what I'm doing, Bella. Don't fret.' I spoke quietly but with assertion, not expecting her to carry on.

But she did.

'I know you're going to do something awful to Max.'

I stopped feeling wonderful. Although eager to get going on my new mission, I was interested to hear what Bella had to say, and guessed Eve was as intrigued. Bella didn't usually venture her opinion, unasked, and there was something about her views on life, that I thought were worth listening to.

I sat on the bottom step and said, 'Go on, Bella. Tell me what's upsetting you.'

She made a snorting sound as if I were an imbecile. 'What's upsetting me? This whole thing is. People *need* fear. It's the same as needing to feel pain. Both of those things protect you. If you don't even understand what it means to be frightened, you can do anything you want. Anything bad.'

I watched Eve come around in front of Bella, and she, as I did, watched and listened.

'You and Eve, you might as well be two loaded guns, just cruising through life, waiting, until you decide to pull the trigger. Whenever you want: because maybe you feel like it, or maybe you want something, or just fancy a laugh – it doesn't matter what the reason is – the point is, you can cause damage by just being you. You have no idea what everyday people feel.'

Bella gulped at her tea as if the custard creams had sucked the moisture from her mouth. Her face remained fierce. 'Fear's a good thing. It makes you behave right. It keeps you safe. If you're not frightened of fear, you're totally fucked.' She twizzled a piece of her hair around a large finger.

Eve said, 'Of course fear's a good thing to have. In its place. But Max's blend of torture doesn't frighten me. What do you want me to do? Pretend? I wouldn't give him the satisfaction.'

'But you and Jessica are carrying it on. You're enjoying creating fear. I'm different. I'm normal. I have loads of fears. Apart from the fear of being raped, and who isn't frightened of *that*?' She showed her teeth in a fake smile. 'I'm also scared of spiders, and of strange big men.' Bella glanced at both me and Eve. 'And strange women.' She shrugged. 'Fear of the unknown. Fear of the known. I'm afraid of everything and since I've been here, kidnapped, I've learnt that I'm glad I'm a great big scaredy-cat. It's what makes me human. It's also what makes me nice.'

She stared at us and frowned. 'You two aren't nice. At all. You're mental.'

I wanted to cry. It wasn't supposed to be like this, but it was, in part, my fault, and I stood and listened to my punishment.

'I'm afraid of you both.' Bella stated flatly, pointing her finger at us. 'Neither of you is normal. Fear, being able to feel it, makes people normal. It's a good thing and you're taking advantage of this situation, which by the way, Jessica, you bloody helped make.'

I was losing my patience. 'Max needs punishing. Don't you want me to show him that his behaviour to all of us is unacceptable? To show him that he can't go around abusing women?'

Bella shook her head. 'You're the same as him. Both of you are. You're not better than him, you're worse. The three of you are cold and dead inside. I don't know what you're going to do to Max, but I know it's sick.' Folding her arms, Bella drew her knees up to her chin. 'You're all mad. And horrid, and I'm happy I'm not like any of you. I'm happy I'm me.'

'Mad and horrid and mental.' I repeated and didn't know how I felt about the criticism. Disappointed, overall. Bella was missing the point. Pushing myself away off the step, I stepped closer to Bella, and she shrank back. I put my hands out, in a placatory way. 'It's all right, Bella. I'm not going to do anything to you. I wouldn't dream of it. Really, I wouldn't. I'm not even going to hurt you. I never was going to.' I paused. 'Not really. Deep down, I know I couldn't ever hurt anyone.' I wasn't sure if that was a lie, but it was true now – well, true-ish, if you didn't include Max's big old daddy – so I felt no guilt.

Eve stood next to me, and we both looked down at Bella. Eve said, 'I told you, Bella, you don't have to worry. I'm on your side. You don't have to be frightened of anything. Definitely not us.'

I remained silent.

Bella was right. She had no idea what I was going to do to Max.

Even I thought it was a bit mean.

But I told Bella the truth. 'I'm doing this for you, Bella. You, and Eve and me. For all women. It's what we do: we have to manipulate our men into what they should be, and not allow them to be what they were. And if they're bad, their behaviour should be corrected. I want Max, but I want him on my terms, and he needs to learn a few simple facts of life.'

I raised my eyes to my imperfect man but couldn't see his face from this angle. 'I really am doing this for us. Trust me, Bella. I swear, you'll thank me in the end.' For some strange reason I felt like weeping. 'Very handsome men like Max need special care and attention: a woman's touch, if you like. Without help, beautiful men become bullying bastards and I'm not allowing that.' Taking the time to breathe slowly, I forced myself to calm down. 'Teasing leads to bullying which leads to frightening. *That's* not right.'

'He's more than a bully, Jessica,' Bella said. 'He's a rapist and murderer.'

'Which I'm trying to fix. Give a girl a break here, will you? He's my first relationship – I'm doing my best. Max is a work in progress, but I'm a quick learner. Let's hope he is.'

It was my duty to save Max from just being another pretty face. It was my job to make him worthy of his beauty, and a better person than your run-of-the-mill Johnny-man.

I was ready to cure him and make him flawless.

FORTY-SEVEN

Jessica

I sat on Max's free leg, his other still cuffed to the railing. My weight came into its own, and I was happy I was fat. It gave me physical advantage. He couldn't move at all, and he gazed into my eyes. I gazed straight back.

'Strange, that it's come to this, isn't it?' I said.

Max rolled his tongue around his teeth. 'What do you mean? You sitting on me? It's not the most outlandish outcome, considering your size. It had to happen at some point.' He laughed.

'Old joke, Max.' I bent forward and whispered in his ear. 'I know why you like your women fat, so don't die laughing just yet.'

'What do you mean?'

Shrugging prettily, I brought the gun up and in between our faces, the barrel pointing towards the ceiling. 'Don't you want to know the game we're going to play?'

'Tell me, babe. As I'm your first proper relationship…' He rolled his eyes and tried to look modest. 'And I'll be your last, in case you were wondering. So, yes, tell me. I think I deserve to be in the know.'

I cocked the hammer. It made a satisfyingly grown-up sort of sound. It had taken me several goes in the kitchen when I'd been making my tea, to get a better feel for the gun. Now, I thought I understood it better.

'We're going to play my version of Russian roulette.' I wanted to twirl the cylinder of the gun – cowboy-style, but the internet said it could damage the chamber, so I restrained myself from the theatrics. Anyway, desired effect already achieved: Max's eyebrows had risen several notches.

He laughed. 'Yeah, right. The gun's empty. How stupid do you think I am? You wouldn't put yourself at such risk. You're not that mental, whatever Bella thinks.'

He laughed again, this time with more belief. I sat on his body and let his laughter run its course. Eventually, it fizzled out without any help from me.

'Do you want to go first, or second, Max? I'm giving you the choice here, which is generous of me.'

'Give it up, Jess. The gun's empty. I know it is.'

I aimed it at him and then with a straight elbow, I moved my arm out to the right, so the gun was pointing at the wall. And pulled the trigger.

Guns really do go *Bang*. There's no other way to describe it.

I went deaf again. I assumed we all did. But I wasn't worried about that. I was intent on Max's face. It drained of colour and went a nasty, sickly white. As if someone had turned off his blood supply, and it had drained from his cheeks, in one great big evacuation.

'Fuck me, Jess. You are really mental.'

I rubbed my ears with my free hand, trying to drum up some audio and spoke even though my ears rang in a festive bell-fest, chiming out the Christmas spirit – ding dong, merrily on high.

'And just so we're clear, Max – the gun has the capacity to hold six bullets, as I'm sure you know. I've discharged one. I've left one more in the chamber.' I grinned. 'And who knows where it is?' Max didn't grin back. I couldn't help but notice there wasn't a lot of reciprocity going on here. I outlined the last detail in case I'd misjudged his stupidity. 'That means there's a one in five chance of me blowing your face off.'

'Don't, Jess. Please don't. I'll do whatever you want, but let's not play this game. It's stupid. You could kill me.'

This time *I* laughed. 'Yes, dear Max, that's the fucking point. I could kill you, or I could kill myself. Either, or. Interesting, don't you think?'

He seemed at a loss, so I explained the other part of the game, which was equally side-splitting. 'Before each shot, presuming we get down to the last click of the trigger, you get to ask me two questions about who I killed. I can only answer "Yes" or "No". Okay?'

Max shook his head from side to side. 'I couldn't care less who you killed. Why should I care? I'm not playing. And please put the gun down, Jess. Please.'

'If you don't play the "Yes, No" game, I'll sit here and fire the gun at you until the one bullet goes off, bang and you'll be dead, so believe me, you *will* be playing the who-did-Jess-kill parlour game. Yes?'

He nodded. 'Yes, I'll play. Okay, I'll play.'

'Good. You'll have two questions per pull of the trigger. Do you want to go first, or second? I'm not asking again. I'll just pull the trigger without asking you. And I can tell you now, given the choice, the first one won't be pointing in my direction.'

Max was silent for a while and then he smiled. 'You must think I'm really thick. Of course I want to go second. That way, you'll have more goes than me. More chance of you losing. Are you sure *you* want to play?'

He sniggered and I could tell he still didn't really believe I was going to go through with this.

Out of the corner of my eye, I saw Eve manoeuvre herself into a better viewing position beneath me, so she wouldn't miss anything. Far away, in the background of the noise in my head, I heard Bella whimpering, 'No, no, no.'

Yes, yes, yes.

'Okay. I'll go first.' I held the gun to my temple. 'Like this, Max? Or should I point it at the middle of my forehead?'

'The temple is fine.' His voice was flat and unsure, and his beauty shimmered in my eyes.

I closed my eyes and put the gun to the side of my head. 'Oh, oops.' I screamed out a shrill giggle, making Max jump. 'Silly me. You need to ask me a Yes, No question first. Two questions – one after the other.'

I lowered the gun and waited.

His eyes skittered around in his face and his mouth opened and shut several times. He nodded slowly. 'Okay. Who did you kill?'

'Jesus, Max, this isn't the difficult part of the game here. I'll give you another try. It has to be a question, requiring a Yes or a No answer. For example, "Have you killed more than one person?"'

'Fine. Have you killed more than one person?'

Tutting, I put the gun back to my temple. 'No. And this time you can ask your own question. I'm not playing this game for you. Question two, is?'

I gave him time to gather himself. Eventually, he spoke, his voice croaky as if he were coming down with something. Like uncertainty about life. 'Did you use my gun on this person in order to frame me?'

'Ooh, good one. Now you're getting into the spirit of it.' I pretended to give it some real thought. 'No.'

Glancing down, I said, 'Eve? Want to play?' I waited for her to respond, which she did with an eager smile. I added. 'Feel free to ask your own questions. Anything you like.'

'Did you enjoy killing this person?'

'You're not getting to the "Who" of the game, but that's fine. I'll answer.' I pressed the gun harder to the side of my head, reminding Max, that we were still Russian rouletting. 'I enjoyed the result of them being dead. The actual, very physical nature of the killing, was shocking.'

'That's not a Yes, No answer,' said Max.

'Eve's making up the numbers, here – prolonging the game and broadening up the topic. She doesn't have to follow the rules. You do.'

And then I pulled the trigger.

Click.

I breathed out and smiled. Wiped my brow with the back of my wrist even though there was no sweat. 'Your turn.'

His face was angled towards me anyway, looking over my right shoulder, so his temple offered itself up naturally. 'Ready?' Not waiting for his reply, I placed the gun to the side of his head. His eyes were closed, scrunched up tight. 'Open your eyes, Max.'

For a moment, I thought he'd passed out, so stiff and totally immobile his body had become. But then, like an avalanche starting its descent, I felt his steel girder legs begin to shake. I knew it was an involuntary movement, and I didn't enjoy the sensation. It seemed... a smidge cruel. But hey-ho. I let his shaking continue, assuming it would pass, but no. It carried on. And then I heard a strange sound and couldn't immediately place it.

It became apparent fairly quickly. His teeth were chattering.

Without speaking, his head shook and I felt the vibrations of his body dancing up through my own fat. I steadied his face with one hand held firmly on his chin, and repositioned the gun. 'Questions first.'

He could barely speak. Putting my hand on his chest I tried to calm him. 'Come on, Max. Any questions will do.'

'Was it a man or a woman?'

I closed my eyes in exasperation. 'Yes, Max. Next question.'

He was confused, but something finally clicked in his brain. 'Did you kill a man?'

'Yes.' Without taking my eyes from Max – I was worried about him – I said, 'Eve? Your question, please.'

'Was there a lot of blood?'

'No.'

Slowly, I cocked the hammer again, for dramatic purposes only. I tried to be gentle, although it was a difficult ask while holding a gun to a man's face. 'I'll count you down, Max. On one. Three, two… one.'

Another dry click. Strangely it sounded almost as loud as the bang. Waiting patiently, I sat there until Max opened his eyes. He looked around him, as if disbelieving that he was still here. 'There, that wasn't so bad, was it?' I grinned at him. 'Unfortunately, it's my turn again. The more times I pull the trigger, obviously the risk of getting shot, increases. Nasty. Whatever madman came up with this torture?' Putting the gun to my temple again, I said, 'Questions?'

This time, Max kept his eyes open. 'As much as I hate blood, Jess, I hope I see it when you pull the trigger this time.'

'Again, good for you. One has to have faith, however misplaced it may be.'

'Wait.'

'Unfair. I'm preparing myself here.'

'Why aren't you afraid?'

I lowered the gun into my lap and looked at the man who'd changed me. Brought out the real me. Shrugging, I shook my head in wonder, as I realised the truth of my coming words. 'You want me to be honest? I'm not afraid, because if I die, then I die. What's to be frightened of? Death doesn't scare me. I don't know why. Probably, because it's inevitable, in whatever shape it comes.'

I waited for my questions.

FORTY-EIGHT

Eve

E ve was edgy. She enjoyed anything with *edge*. That's what
Jessica had – edge. It was a strange word, but it summed
up Eve's outlook on the world. Edge – a knife edge, a balancing
act with an associated sharpness, a cliff over which you could
fall. *I am living on a razor blade and I love it.* As she looked up at
Jessica holding the gun to her own head, Eve thought, this
couldn't be edgier.

She willed the gun not to fire, and asked her next question,
wanting to go first. 'Did killing this first person, make you want
to kill again?'

'At last, a Yes, No question. I hope you're taking notes,
Max.'

Eve watched Jessica's eyes as they glanced up, as if she were
looking into the past and seeing the murder she'd committed.
'No, not really. In fact, no. Emphatically no. This person had
to be killed, and now it's done, I can't imagine *wanting* to kill
again. But I might *need* to. And that's the truth.'

Grinning, Eve held two thumbs up and remembering Bella,
glanced over at her. She'd taken up her position in the corner
of the room, curled like a cat with her back to the room. Even

through the dressing gown, Eve could see the muscles in her back were rigid.

Then came Max's two questions.

'Was it a young person you killed?'

'Depends on your definition of young. Age is relative. Another wasted question. I'd have thought you'd have been in your element with this game, Max, bearing in mind your job. Surely you've conducted Q and A interviews before, to ascertain the lies or truth of a possible suspect?'

'I wasn't limited to bloody Yes, No answers, was I?'

'Try another one, babe. Make it a good one this time.'

'Did you kill out of jealousy?'

'Better, but you're meant to be trying to find out who I killed, not why. But, let me think. Jealousy.' I let the word rest on my tongue and tasted it for truth. 'I'd have to say, no. It was more out of necessity.'

Eve wondered if Jessica was enjoying tormenting Max. She didn't think so, and thought Jessica looked more confused and slightly disappointed, rather than actively taking pleasure from this fascinating entertainment.

Now, they all waited for the bang or the dry click of the gun. Four breaths were held in anticipation of either sound.

Click.

Part of Eve was disappointed. Not because she wanted Jessica to die, but because she wanted a more instant thrill. Something to actively *deal* with. This was all a bit drawn out for her liking – not her style of operation at all. She'd have gone with the gun, and left out the questions altogether. Eve was more of a hit and see what happens type of woman. Instant gratification.

Giving moral support from the sidelines, as the only spectator, she said, 'Good for you, Jessica. Hope this next bullet blows the bastard's brains out.'

'Thank you, Eve, for your participation and support,'

Jessica said. 'I think little old Max needs someone cheering him on. I don't wish to take all the limelight from him, with you so obviously on my side.'

Eve turned in a full circle, looking up and down, and held her hands out to her side in fake despair. 'Sorry, no takers down here. The man's on his own.'

'That's true, isn't it, Max?' said Jessica. 'Apart from dear old Dad, you don't have many adoring fans, do you? Certainly not as many as you clearly think you deserve.'

Eve, despite being a more hands-on physical woman, had to give it to Jessica. As psychology 101 went, this was basic, but basic was what Max needed. Eve didn't think he had it in him to do, or admire, sophistication in whatever guise it came.

Despite the Russian roulette, Eve realised she was bored. Even being allowed to join in with the questions. It felt as though Jessica had invited Eve to a party but hadn't asked her to join in with any real personal involvement. The point of it all still eluded Eve. Equally, Eve didn't think Jessica herself actually knew what the point was yet. Perhaps Jessica was relying on Max's response to his situation to guide her. That felt right. Felt like something Eve might conceivably do. At a push. Go with the punches and see where that got her.

But still, Eve wanted to be *more* included. To be the one helping Jessica make decisions. It would pass the time, apart from anything else.

As the party had progressed, it had become apparent this was something very personal to Jessica and her strange obsession with Max.

All the same, knowing she was intruding on a very intimate weirdness between Max and Jessica, Eve still relished the participation she'd been granted. She'd have preferred things to have been more physical, but she accepted the rules as they were.

Keeping her eyes on the two figures on the spiral

staircase, Eve watched Jessica turn the gun on Max again, but this time she didn't speak and allowed the silence to lengthen. It was almost as if Eve could imagine hearing the hands on a clock, ticking and tocking. For a long time. Minutes went by.

'What are you playing at, Jess?' Max's voice sounded breathy as if he were having trouble inhaling and exhaling normally.

He was panicking.

Still nothing from Jessica. *Good tactic,* Eve thought. Let the terror seep in and take root. Even from here, Eve could see that like Bella, Max had tensed up, his body inflexible as it waited for an answer.

The gun swung down and around and faced Eve. 'Anyone else hungry, around here?' Jessica asked. Eve held her hand up, but Bella didn't stir. 'Yes, I'm famished,' Eve said, in case her hand shooting up in the air like an eager schoolchild desperate to answer a question, and get praise from her teacher, had gone unnoticed.

'Good. Do me a favour, Eve. I made some fresh sandwiches for brunch earlier, and whatever the time is now, it's brunch-time. Would you mind collecting them from the fridge and bringing them down for me? I think we all deserve a little time-out and food always cheers everyone up. Food is a real crowd pleaser.' She glared pointedly at Max. 'Or it bloody well should be.'

This was a test, being allowed out of the room. It was also a risk. Jessica was relying on Eve to return from the kitchen and not to just keep on running. It made Eve want to laugh. As if she'd leave now, just when it was getting exciting.

Bella said, 'What? You can't let Eve go, what about me?'

'I'm not letting Eve go. I'm letting Eve get the sandwiches. Isn't that right, Eve? The keys are in my bag. You'll have to dig them out. My hands are all full of gun.'

'Are you fucking insane, Jess? Eve won't come back. She'll go to the police.'

'In which case, Max, you'll be saved from all this. But do you *really* want the police coming round now? Really? It'll be my word against yours, and all us girlies here, will all testify that you're the baddie, you're the rapist and you're the killer. I have more proof I've yet to share, Max.' Jess grinned. 'In fact, Eve, why don't you give the police a call. Tell them what's happening here. But bring the sandwiches down first.'

'Fuck, fuck, fuck, Jess, I fucking hate you.'

Eve flew up the stairs, around and around until she got to Jessica. It was a tight squeeze at the top with three people crowded together. Opening Jessica's handbag that was slung around her shoulder, Eve found the keys. 'Won't be a minute.'

Even as Eve left the room, she could hear Bella wail out her distress, her fear of being left alone spiralling up the stairwell before Eve shut out the noise as she closed the door. *I'll never leave you, Bella. I owe you – I haven't forgotten it's my fault you're here.*

Hurrying, she walked across the glass floor and looked down. Quite a different view, literally and metaphorically, from this standpoint. She caught Jessica's eye and a knowing look passed between them. Eve had no bloody idea what they both knew, but they both knew it, and that was good enough.

Relying on memory, Eve found the kitchen and opened the fridge. A plate piled high with sandwiches sat centre stage on the top shelf, with cling film wrapping them in a neat mound. Picking it up, and some side plates laid out on the worktop, Eve turned around and walked down the hall and back across the glass floor. And felt like laughing. She was really enjoying herself now.

Looking at the sandwiches, Eve wondered if Max would choose the egg mayonnaise and cress, the smoked salmon, or the ham and cheese.

She also knew that Max and Bella would not understand

her coming back, voluntarily, instead of taking the opportunity to run. Only Eve and Jessica knew what bound them.

It was simply a question of identifying their bond, although Eve wasn't that bothered. In the grand scheme of things, it mattered little. Not a lot mattered to Eve, except what she was confronted with, in the here and now. Anything else got lost in the background. Unless it was in front of Eve, it wasn't important. The past had been, was gone, was done. The future, who knew, so why worry? The immediate now of any moment was what did it for Eve. If it was confrontational, all the better.

And what she was confronted with here, was fun.

And sandwiches.

FORTY-NINE

Max

_____

One more bullet left. And now it's my turn again. I'm going to die.

Max was man enough to admit he was fucking terrified. Had never known fear like this. It made Dad's White Eye game seem like pass the parcel by comparison. He reminded himself he was man enough for anything. Like Dad had always told him, it was important he remember how great he was, because it was all he had now. His own self-belief. And naturally, his dad's. Dad believed anything and everything that Max told him. Because Dad adored him.

But Max also had his looks. Which had been the thing that Jess had been drawn in by. She couldn't take away his beauty.

She can, if she shoots me in the head.

Max concentrated on what made sense. He could still appeal to Jess's obsessive love for him. There was no way in this world that she'd actually put a bullet in his head. She was joking. She must be. She was mad, but she wasn't that mad.

Was she?

Max tried and failed to forget that Jess had always frightened him, because she really *was* that mad. She'd even admitted to killing someone, the insane bitch. And thought he gave a rat's arse about who it might be. Like he cared. Whatever she'd done before he'd met her, had absolutely bloody nothing to do with him.

He didn't get the point of the stupid questions.

The leg Jess was sitting on had gone numb. 'Come on, babe. Give me a break, here. I can't feel my leg.'

'You won't be feeling anything by the end of the next two shots, sweetheart.'

'How do you know you won't get the bullet?'

'Because I've rigged it. I've made damn sure I know precisely where the bullet is in the chamber, so I can't lose. Bummer, right?'

Instinctively, Max attempted to lurch upwards in order to hit her, but his hands remained cuffed above his head and he only managed an ineffectual body flop. He was fucking furious. To his horror, Jess's face loomed closer to his and she kissed him on the nose. 'Shh, baby, don't get all upset. You're a bad man and you're being punished, but hopefully you'll learn from this experience.'

That stopped him and made him think. That meant he'd live through the Russian roulette, if she hoped he'd learn from it. He couldn't learn if he was dead. Jess had slipped up and he smiled at her.

'It's a bit early to be smiling, Max. I said I know where the bullet is. I didn't say who the bullet was for.'

He did what he hoped would come out as a disbelieving snort of a laugh. 'Yeah, right. Like you'll kill yourself. What will I learn from that?'

'If I was the one to get the bullet, you'd learn that you're one lucky bastard.' She sat back on his leg, adjusting her weight so that it pinned him down even more. Softly, she placed the gun in between his eyes, and tapped it rhythmically, as if she was knocking out a tune on the bridge of his nose.

'And do you really think you're that lucky? With me holding the gun? I make my own luck. And I'm a very, *very* lucky person. Especially, when I know where the bullet in question is nestling. I'm very organised and I don't make mistakes. So, stop smiling and sit tight. We'll eat and then we'll see how lucky you really feel.'

The *bitch*. She always confused him with her lunatic words, and he still had no idea what drove her. Why was she doing this? Admittedly, he'd been a bastard, but not enough to warrant this behaviour. From a fat bitch who adored him. Who the fuck did she think she was? Playing with him like he was some kind of idiot.

The next bullet could kill me.

God, help me.

He lay there, waiting. Saying nothing. 'See?' said Jess. 'You're learning right now, this minute. You're thinking and that's good. That's what I'm talking about, Max. You're learning all the time about yourself, when you're with me. I'm making you experience real life with real people, and that's what will stay with you.' Giving a final rat-a-tat-tat with the gun, she said, 'If you're still alive, that is.' Her gaze rose to the ceiling. 'Good, Eve's back.'

Max closed his eyes, heard the door open and shut, and felt Eve lift her legs over him as she politely apologised at the inconvenience caused. By mistake, on purpose, she kicked him in the ribs in passing, sorry-ing all over the place. Eve was as bad as the bitch. It wouldn't surprise him if Jess and Eve had some lesbo thing going on. There was something weird about them, and he hated them both.

He was terrified of Jess, and Eve came in at a close second.

But he'd rather die than ever admit that to anyone.

I might die with the next bullet.

Max refused to show gratitude as Jess slid off his leg, and

quietly carried on breathing in and out, hoping he'd come up with a great plan to escape all this.

Don't think about the gun.

Painfully lifting his head, he looked down and saw that Bella had come out from her corner and was sitting on her haunches, bending over a plate of sandwiches, practically dribbling. Enough sandwiches to feed a million. Greedy bitches. How could they even think of eating at a time like this?

Max couldn't see a way out. Two crazy women and a pathetic big one. The only one who appeared to feel any sympathy for him was Bella. Perhaps he could get her on side, although he didn't see how. Not with the other two crazies on constant watch. He was fucked.

But now he believed, *almost* believed, that Jess wouldn't kill either him or herself with the one remaining bullet. What would be the point? It would be game over, and if he knew anything, he knew Jess wanted to win as much as he did.

You can't win if there's no one to see your victory.

And by no one, he meant himself. If he was dead, Jess wouldn't be victorious: she'd have no one to gloat to, no one to show off to and say 'Look at how clever I am.' More importantly, she'd have no one to love. She'd be alone with two homeless women: a tall one and a big one. Jess would want more than that, he was sure of it.

Jess wanted Max.

That was what drove her. It was that simple. It wasn't complicated at all. Like all women, Jess was besotted by him, and all he had to do, was give himself to her. He could do that, if it meant he'd live. No problem.

Jess's voice floated up to him from down below. 'Max? What sandwich do you want, darling? Any preferences?'

Swallowing down a sudden desire to vomit, he filled his voice with a charming warmth; the words dripping from his mouth, velvet sweet. 'Whatever you've got, I'll have one of each, thanks, babe. I'm starving up here.'

'You're teasing him,' Bella said.

Good, she is *on my side, stupid woman.*

'Precisely, Bella. And I hope Max appreciates the irony,' Jess said.

'I thought you were against teasing?' the big one said. 'Anyway, why would you care if Max eats or not? You're going to kill him because, according to you, *he* was going to kill all of us.' Bella stopped for a bit and then spoke again. 'Maybe you're right. You don't give good food to an animal like that.'

'You do, if you're normal. Which I am. Food is a basic need, and we've got enough to share,' Jess said, although Max could hear her words were clogged with bread, making her sound nasal. 'Only a sick animal would deny him food. I'm bullying him.'

After listening to wet eating sounds which made Max feel sick, Jess piped up again, sounding all school-teacher-ish and superior. 'That is the whole point. Max is finally learning what bullying is. And I have every intention of feeding my man. What sort of woman do you think I am?'

Max could only hear a mumbled mouth-full-of-food response from Bella. Bloody useless woman.

'Take him up a selection, Bella. I was going to because I'm not a monster, but you want to feed the beast, off you go, with my blessing.'

There was an uncomfortable silence, and Max knew Bella wasn't moving. Heard her next words and wanted to scream in fury. 'No, it's all right. I'd prefer to stay here, thank you. You take them.'

Max heard footsteps on the stairs, and Jess stood above him.

'Bella wanted to feed you but changed her mind. So, as requested, my sweetie-pops, a selection. Enjoy.'

'I can't feed myself. My hands are cuffed.'

'Shit. Tough luck.'

Breathing in from the bottom of his lungs, Max managed a smile and even flashed his gold tooth at her. 'Why don't you hand feed me, Jess? That would be nice.'

'Why don't I peel you a fucking grape, while I'm at it?'

He maintained his smile, and made his eyes fill with self-pity and handsome boyishness. Most of him still believed she'd succumb to him – as all women eventually did, sooner or later. He hoped for sooner. 'Please, Jess. I'll be eternally grateful. Honest, babe. Please. Be nice.'

Squatting next to him, Jess unceremoniously shoved a sandwich into his mouth, pushing it in so far, that he gagged. 'Want another one, baby? Egg and cress?' This time, she folded the triangle so it was double the size and crammed it in. 'There. Nice? See, Max? You shouldn't ever fuck around with food, and I'm sure you'll agree, this is a whole lot better than maggots, spiders or chunks of pretend-me. Mind you, doesn't the smoked salmon look like human flesh? It could be, but who knows? Now, come on, one more bite for Mummy.'

Max closed his eyes, desperately swallowing and trying not to choke.

Bite quickly, chew and swallow.

Smile, Max, smile. Show her you're not worried. Carry on smiling. And biting and chewing and swallowing.

'Just one more sandwich, Max. You can do it. You're a big boy. A big boy with lots and lots of luck.'

He heard her laugh and carried on frantically chewing, feeling his throat clog up. His breath became panicky, his eyes felt as if they were bulging from his sockets, and the bitch carried on shoving food down his throat.

Patting him on the head, Jess said, 'There's a good boy. Finished them all up. My, you must have been hungry. It must give you an appetite, being such a complete bastard.'

Still chewing, gagging and spitting out bread, he watched the back of Jess as she walked down the stairs.

I should have killed her when I first picked her up. I really should have.

Now, I might have left it too late.

FIFTY

Bella

The longer Bella was in this room, trapped under a glass ceiling, the more she hated all of them.

During the gun game, Bella had curled up in a ball, keeping her back to what was happening, and she'd screwed her eyes tight shut – as tight as tight could be. Concentrating, willing herself away from the madness around her, she'd focused all her attention on images of her pretend boyfriend. She'd managed to picture him more clearly than ever before. Bella could almost reach out and touch him, hear him, smell him. Desperately, she allowed herself to be fully submerged in the fantasy, in him, safe in his arms.

She made him *real* because she needed *some*one to help her.

However deeply she'd buried herself in everything-Dominic, Bella couldn't drown out the clicks which sounded out loudly, interrupting her mental escape. Bella see-sawed between the clicking reality, to the fuzzy fantasy, teetering into one world and then the next, until she had difficulty in knowing which was real.

She'd heard, with relief, Jessica take a break from the horrible game, when she'd asked Eve to fetch sandwiches.

Bella had been bloody dumbfounded. Eve could have escaped just now, instead of collecting stupid sandwiches. If Jessica had asked Bella to go to the kitchen, Bella would have been straight out the door, and no messing.

She couldn't understand any of it.

They were all bad and mad.

Bella wanted to speak to her mum. She wouldn't tell her what was happening: she only wanted to hear her voice, telling Bella how much she was loved and missed. Bella wished she'd gone home years ago. Her pride had turned out to be a nonsense. It had stopped her reuniting with the people she loved best in the whole world.

And Dominic, a voice reminded her, whispering in her head. *Dominic loves you.*

It was only now that she realised what a pathetic excuse of a woman she was. A girl when she'd left home, and now a washed out, plain and bigger girl. Older and sadder.

But just as thick.

And with a very real but pretend made-up boyfriend. *That* was an improvement.

'Eat up, Bella. There's plenty for all of us,' said Jessica.

Bella didn't answer but took another sandwich anyway. She'd decided that she wouldn't speak to any of them anymore after her talking to Jess about feeding Max. There wasn't any point. They might as well have been living on a different planet. She hadn't liked Jessica forcing Max to eat. It had been disgusting and cruel. Couldn't understand Jessica, or Eve and Max. Bella knew that of them all, she really was the only one who was truly sane.

And *that* was a frightening fact.

Jessica and Eve were punishing Max. It wasn't their place, wasn't their job to do that. Bella was as afraid of the two women, as she was of Max. She'd only stuck up for him, because that's how she'd been brought up. To be fair to people, even if they'd done wrong. That didn't include murder, obviously, but still… Bella didn't like the way things were going and knew the whole thing would end badly.

If Dominic was here, he'd sort them all out, no bloody question. Wipe the smug smiles from their faces. Even a made-up person was more normal and dependable than any of these people. *And he is here. I can hear him talking to me now. Thank you, Dominic.*

After the force-feeding, Jess had come downstairs again. Bella shifted on her beanbag and watched Jessica and Eve sitting on theirs – all of them had splayed their legs out in front of them like they were having a children's tea party, and they sat like straight-legged toddlers on too big chairs. Jessica had the gun next to her on the floor, and slipped her hand into that huge fucking bag of hers, the bag that was always full of terrible things.

Smiling, Jessica shuffled squares of what looked like photographs in her hand. Then, like a magician, she spread them out in front of her on the floor, in the shape of a fan.

'Seven photographs, Max,' Jessica said, directing her voice up, but including Bella and Eve as well. 'Look at them, girls. Pictures of terrified women.'

Despite herself, Bella couldn't resist looking, and had to stop herself from gasping. Seven frightened faces of seven fat women, who all could have been related to Jessica. Bella was too embarrassed and scared to point out the odd similarity.

'They all look like you,' said Eve. 'Are these women Max has killed?'

'I can only assume so. I don't know their names, because they are only numbered on the back – one to seven. I know I'm number eight, because Max told me,' Jessica said. 'That they're all dead, is certainly the conclusion I'd draw. Max, care to enlighten?'

'You shouldn't have gone snooping, darling. What's mine, is

mine. Not yours. And yes, of course they're all my women. Now ex-women. So what? You knew that's what I do, so why act all outraged now. You offered to kill for me, baby. Remember? Kept quiet about that little fact in front of Nine and Ten, haven't you?'

Bella drew her knees up, scared and wishing she couldn't see or hear any of them. To her surprise, she heard Eve's laughter, her voice harsh but with something like respect in her voice. 'You were ready to kill for him? Fuck me, Jessica, what were you thinking?'

'I wasn't thinking. And it was only a passing whimsy. It was an aberration, now thankfully, and hopefully…' Jessica glanced at Bella. 'I've managed to repair my kidnapping mistakes, by saving you both from Max.'

Bella was furious. Leaning forward, her neck thrusting forward, she said, 'Save me some more, Jessica. Let me go. Now. I don't want to be with any of you. I won't go to the police, I promise, swear to God, on my mother's life, I won't go to the police. Please let me go, Jessica.'

'I can't.'

'But it's wrong. What you're doing, it's wrong. What are you going to do with me and Eve?'

Jessica was quiet for a moment, staring at the seven faces of dead women displayed like the beginning of a card trick. 'He took a photograph of me too, you know.' She didn't look up at Bella. 'I'm not included in this display, because I'm alive. I escaped Max. Kidnapped him straight back.' She grinned, and finally raised her eyes from the dead, and said, 'I don't know yet, Bella. I suppose it depends on how wrong I turn out to be.'

Jessica turned away from Bella, as if her answer had been good enough. Or more like, as if Bella wasn't important enough to deserve any extra time on a better explanation. Bella felt very alone. As if she were the only person sitting under the glass ceiling, realising no one would save her.

Don't forget Dominic. I have Dominic.

Eve was the same as Jessica, pulling the photographs nearer, so she could better study them. She actually picked them up and held them close. Bella couldn't properly read Eve's expression: the nearest she could come to identifying it was *fascinated*. Like she was looking at something rare and special. Bella supposed, dead women would probably fit the category of a rare sight, but *she* didn't want to see them again. Once had been enough for Bella.

'But why no names, Max?' Jessica said.

'The names don't matter, I've already told you.'

'Surely their names appeared in the papers, the news, the radio? You must know what they were called.'

'Probably, if you reminded me, but I prefer the numbers. That's all they were to me. And you, Number Eight, you ruined it all. Now, I'm all out of sequence. I've got Nine and Ten here, but I haven't got rid of Eight yet.'

'Sorry to be such an irritant.' Jessica held one of the photographs in her hand and waved it at Eve and Bella. 'Can you believe, Max hid them behind his bedside cabinet? If it was me, I'd have hidden them far, far away, somewhere utterly remote and obscure. Only Max would have hidden them so openly.' She turned back to him. 'Such arrogance. Did you think no one would look behind your dresser? Or are you so conceited that you didn't think anyone would ever even look in the first place?'

'No one suspects me. I'm a copper. I didn't take all my women from the same patch – they're from far and wide. And over a long period of time. Their bodies are scattered all over the place. In fields, rivers, ponds and woods. In and out and around London. They'll never be found.' There was a small whisper of a laugh from the top of the stairs. 'They haven't even been connected, so, yes, I like to keep my pictures close to me. I take them out and remember each and every one of them. As I say, their names aren't important. Just how they look. That's good enough for me.'

'They're all fat,' said Jessica.

'It's how I like them.'

Bella was suddenly sick of the conversation. The fact they were even *having* a conversation about dead girls wasn't right. She kept her voice neutral, but was unable to hide the fear from her voice as she said, 'They all look exactly like the same person. Why do you like fat women so much?'

Jessica clapped her hands, making Bella jump. 'Good question, Bella. Why indeed? What's your theory on that, Max?'

'I don't have one, babe. I don't care, I only know I like 'em fat. So, kill me.'

Eve asked Max, 'Do they represent a girlfriend who dumped you, and you're getting your revenge on all who resemble her?'

'No.'

His short answer sounded an honest one, Bella thought, but then he laughed. That spoilt it, because it sounded a bit forced. As if he really *was* a bit bothered about the fat-women questions. He was obviously also unable to forget Jessica might kill him and he didn't really find that funny at all.

Bella hated the way Jessica smiled up at him, and seemed to be enjoying all of this, every single second, as if it were some great big old competition, and not really about real people, real dead people and real live people. *I'm real and I'm still alive. Someone needs to care about me.*

Jessica said, 'Not a long-lost girlfriend then, and you forever avenging her. Good.' She paused a moment before saying, 'As long as you haven't got a mummy complex going on, that's okay. You haven't, have you? Is your mother fat, Max?'

There was silence from above. Bella could only see his twisted legs as they curved round the spiral.

Max didn't answer.

'I think she was,' said Jessica. 'Which is kind of fascinating. In my humble opinion, should you even care what I think.'

Jessica knew something and that made Bella afraid but she didn't know why. Groaning to herself, she watched as Jessica got up and started for the stairs again. 'Here I come, Max. Time to finish our Russian roulette – one way or another.'

Bella returned to her tightly wound-up ball-shape and this time, put her fingers in her ears. And tuned into her boyfriend.

Conjuring up the love from inside her head, Bella allowed herself to get completely lost in the perfect world that was Dominic. She drifted away, easily connecting with him, and forgot the cold, hard reality that surrounded her.

Dominic meant safety and protection and trust, and most of all, Dominic meant true love.

FIFTY-ONE

Jessica

I thought that all parties present assumed I was enjoying this. But I wasn't. If nothing else, I'd discovered that physical threats weren't my thing. Nor psychological taunting, which amounted to good old-fashioned bullying. No surprise there. Only relief, but definitely not surprise. Why would I enjoy inflicting something I'd been on the wrong end of my entire life? Answer was, I wouldn't.

I wasn't enjoying anything about this. Doing the demeaning of another human being was as despicable as being the demeaned. Both were uncalled for and required cruel punishment. Unwittingly, I conceded, I had become my own punishment and felt shame at what I was doing to Max. It made me no better than him or any Johnny-man who'd fat-shamed me.

But I had to finish it. It was the only way I'd get Max to be properly mine. However I got him, in whatever new situation we found ourselves – created by me – I still wanted him. Which made me a very sad woman.

Assuming the position on Max's legs, again I felt his muscles beneath me flex in fear. I couldn't blame him, and I really didn't want to carry on, but had no choice. Anyway, this way I would be certain of getting him. He just didn't know it.

He still believed.

My stupid, handsome boy.

The hope was, that by the end of this bullet game, coupled with the Yes, No questions, he'd see life from a very different perspective. *I am trying my hardest here to change him for the better. Perhaps my methods are unorthodox, but they'll work.*

Putting the gun back at Max's temple, I settled into his lap. 'Here we go again, darling. Questions?'

This time, his voice was more resigned, and he spoke flatly, his eyes open and not veering from mine. 'Did this person deserve to die?'

Managing to shrug and still keep the gun in situ, I said, 'Very philosophical. Which of us is without sin? Did all your women deserve to die?'

'I'm asking the questions.'

Raising my eyes in mock surprise, I said, 'Okay. Let me think. Yes, they did.'

'You didn't even have to think about it.' He smiled. 'If I could hold your hand, Jess, I would. We're alike, you and me. Lots of people deserve to die. Especially women. It's the way of the world.'

'Don't dare to presume we share an ideology on life and the benefits or not, of existence itself. The answer is, yes, this person deserved to die; it required no serious thought. Next question.'

The gun slipped and I saw that Max was sweating. And I didn't mean, gently perspiring, but excessively sweating, as if his life depended on it. Which it did, as far as he knew. His face wasn't only slick with sweat, it was awash with it, as if a river had washed over him, making his cheeks a puddle. I watched a bead of perspiration hanging from his eyelash. Fascinated, I thought how beautiful it was.

Still he stared at me. 'Do I know this person?'

'Yes.'

Our eyes were locked together in silence, and strangely it seemed neither of us knew where the key was, to undo us.

Eve broke the absence of sound, although not mine and Max's gaze. 'My turn. Do you enjoy tormenting others, Jessica?'

Finding Eve's questions easy to pre-empt now, understanding the way her brain worked, I had no need to give any real thought to the answer, but it was still an honest response. 'No.'

Max's voice sounded as if, like his face, his mouth was clogged with sweat. Like he was drowning from the inside. His words were barely coherent, swimming in fear as he was. 'Then why, Jess, are you doing this? *This* game is bloody full of torment.'

'And I've just said, I don't enjoy being the tormentor.'

'Stop it now, then. I'll forgive you. I can love you. We can get rid of these two and be together. Make a real go of it. That's what you want, isn't it? I can make it happen.'

Sadly, I shook my head. 'Sorry, no can do, Max. I've started, so I'll finish.'

'I have another question,' said Eve, loudly. She was over-excited. This was clearly exciting her. I was deeply upset. At the whole bloody thing. That my life had come to this.

I nodded down at Eve, gratefully disengaging eye-play with Max.

'Did they put up a fight?'

'No.'

'Did you want them to beg and plead for their life?'

'No.'

Watching her, the gun to Max's head slip-sliding around at the side of his eyes, I realised Eve almost looked as if she were experiencing some sort of sexual pleasure from all this. She held her hand in the air and counted off on her fingers with the other. 'You killed a man, you inadvertently admitted to using that gun, which you got from Max, and he knows the man.' Even from here, I could see she'd worked it out. Not necessarily the who, but the fact that Max must be able to work it out now, with the new facts she was exposing. Slowly, she lowered her fingers. Said the words out flatly. 'Did you kill this man, *after* meeting Max?'

'Yes.'

I'd gone back to eye-gazing and saw Max's open slightly. Not in fear, but in genuine shock. 'Really?' he said.

'Really.'

I closed my eyes and pulled the trigger.

Click.

The sound of a gun firing, with no bullet, has a very dry and final sound. Not as final as a bang, but it emphasised the end of something. It usually signified something good for someone, or downright terrifying for another person. Depending on the situation.

This situation left me emotionless.

Although, I had to admit, I'd never been full-to-brimming with emotions in the first place. Had had them bullied right out of me.

Looking at Max, I first recognised the relief that the gun hadn't gone off, then the dawning realisation, that I would be dead, were I to pull the trigger again. That made his face light up with victory and lust. His blabbering about 'I could forgive you and love you,' I'd known to be a lie, but there was no need to be quite so bloody obvious about it. He wasn't even trying to hide his glee that he thought I'd be dead in his lap in a minute.

I watched as he put it all together. Last to put in an appearance on his face, was knowledge. I'd killed someone he knew. Peering at his expression, I wasn't convinced he'd made the connection yet, but I'd give him a minute. I gave him several minutes. *This connection will be experiencing some delay, due to unexpected stupidity of the driver, and the wrong sort of emotion on the line.*

I carried on staring at him, and there was nothing. No sudden and great understanding. No outrage, sadness, grief, shock – pick an emotion, any emotion – Max wasn't showing anything.

He was too thick to work it out and I found that astonishing.

All Max was concerned with, despite his declarations of our future together, was watching me put the gun to my head. He couldn't see past that.

His eyes were too full of triumph at beating me, and it had made him blind.

He didn't care who I'd killed.

For him, it was more important that he saw me die.

FIFTY-TWO

Max

If Max had been able, he'd have done a bloody cartwheel. He'd have laughed in Jess's face, his nose pressed against hers and his spit landing in her mouth as he shouted out his fucking great victory. He'd beaten her in the gun game which meant he could now happily watch her die. Pulling the trigger herself made it all the better.

Bursting with delight, he instead tried to keep his joy under wraps. Not give Jess the bloody satisfaction. Play it cool. Like it had never entered his head that he may ever lose to the bitch in the first place. At least now, she'd never know how much she'd freaked him out.

After the gun killed her, Max would still be handcuffed – alone with the tall one and the big one. Nine and Ten. Ten might uncuff him if he asked nicely. The keys to the cuffs must be in Jess's fucking handbag, which so far, had everything else in it.

As Max carried on staring into Jess's eyes, he caught her expression of confusion. As if he'd done something, or failed to do something. Keeping his face blank, he worried at it.

It must be the question game, although Jess didn't know

anyone he knew, so why should he care who she'd killed? *After* she'd met him: Eve had stressed that word. Did that make any difference? What was he missing here? Anyway, more importantly, *when* could she have killed anyone? She'd barely had the time. He mulled it over in his head and came to the conclusion that her only opportunity would have been when she was out getting Eve, when she'd left him in his house alone.

His stomach did a strange somersault, like a pancake being tossed unexpectedly in the middle of a forest, at exactly the same time as an idea popped into his head: totally out there – right alongside the pancake.

She'd also had the time when she'd gone out yesterday to collect his props from his house.

There was only one person who Jess might have met when she'd been inside. Someone who'd let themselves into his house with a key.

He must be right. Jess wouldn't be making all this fuss if she'd killed a stranger. Max had worked it out.

The knowing struck him, as if someone had jabbed two fingers into his eyes.

'You killed Dad.'

'Is that a question? Sounds more like a statement to me,' Jess said.

'Before you blow your brains out, answer me. Am I right? *Did* you kill Dad?'

'Yes.'

Max was aware of a shattering stillness in the room. Like all the women were holding their breath, waiting for his reaction. He didn't do anything, simply allowed the information to settle in his brain, where he found he didn't know what to do with it.

He didn't want Jess to win at confusing him, making him look stupid at taking so long to work it out, so instead of questioning her about why she'd killed Dad, he'd thought he'd have the last laugh and see out the other game instead, the Russian roulette, which would take away her ability to win at *any*thing ever again. He couldn't wait to be rid of the smug expression on her face. She wanted to see his reaction to her confession of killing Dad – never. He wouldn't give her the pleasure. He didn't really have a reaction, anyway, so it was a pointless game. *Chalk that one up to me.*

'Pull the trigger, you bitch. I don't care you killed Dad. Do it now. Shoot yourself.'

'You don't care I killed your father?' She made a performance of covering her mouth with her hand. 'Are you being serious?'

'Yeah, pull the trigger.'

Nodding in defeat, she held the gun to her temple and said, 'All that for nothing. Well, goodbye then, darling. It's been fun. Congratulations. You beat me, after all.'

He laughed, wanting it to be the last thing she saw, his beautiful golden smile, taunting her.

The click of the gun when it came, took a while for him to register.

Rage rumbled from deep within him, like a building earthquake cracking through a hard crust. Splintering into great chasms. He shook with the force of it. Fury spewed out of him like a flame. 'You fucking bitch. You *cheated*.'

'What do you think I am, Max? Stupid? Course I cheated. Or I'd be dead. And not to labour the point, I can't believe you'd have preferred me dead rather than ask why I killed your father.'

'Uncuff me,' he said.

Peering at Jess from his now very painful head position, he repeated his instruction. 'Fucking uncuff me now. You've still got the gun, so take the bloody cuffs off me.'

'I've also got an empty gun, which is no good at all.' He watched as she slowly took a box of his bullets from her giant bag and started methodically to reload the gun. Six bullets. Made a point of showing him the full box and shook them so they rattled, before returning them to her bag.

Shaking her head at him as if he had failed again at some test, without speaking, and pointing the gun at him, she rummaged about with her other hand until, smiling gently, she brought out the tiny handcuff keys. 'I'll set you free,' she said.

Jess rolled on top of him, stretching her hands up past his head, to reach his cuffed hands behind him. She was going to release him. He exhaled loudly as she lay on top of him, and waited as she writhed about, grunting like an animal. Max tried not to smell the sweat which clung to her armpits as they lay across his face.

He heard her sigh and slowly, Jess wriggled off his body and sat back on his knees. 'That would be stupid of me. Fiddling with teeny keys, releasing you and holding a gun at the same time. An impossibility to carry out the two tasks successfully. Eve, come up here and undo Max, please. And his leg.'

'Is that wise?'

'Yes, it's bloody wise. I've got a gun. Do it.'

Jess stood and he presumed she went to wait at the bottom of the stairs, allowing Eve to come up. Jess was still thinking clearly, had a fully loaded gun and she had *cheated*. She'd also killed Dad. He felt like weeping with frustration.

He couldn't get over how she'd tricked him, pretending there was another bullet. The *bitch*.

Again, Eve took the time to physically hurt him, kicking him in the groin, before she undid his hands and ankle, and nimbly, skipped back down the stairs. Stretching his neck, arms and legs, Max sat and rolled out his shoulders, cramping everywhere. Three pairs of eyes watched him, and he realised how much he hated all of the women in the playroom.

He managed to control his temper before he spoke.

Knowing he had to get this right, he tried out a few practise phrases in his head. *Why did you kill my father? What did he ever do to you? I loved him. I'll never get over this. I'll kill you. I'm devastated – I can't live without my old dad.*

None of the sentences sounded right; they were too forced and sounded completely unreal. Because they *were* all completely unreal. He felt nothing. Nothing at all.

He listened to nothing. There was nothing to hear. He thought over everything Jess had said. How she'd be teaching him a lesson. How she wanted to change and improve him. Max could play this game. All he had to do was lie.

Going for the safe and easy option, trying to tinge his words with sadness, he said, 'Why did you kill my father, Jess?'

'Because he would never have let me have you, that's why. And that's why you picked me up. Because I look exactly like your mother. Your father told me how fat she was, how she and I look so alike. As do all the seven women you killed. What's that mean, Max?'

Letting his head fall into his hands, Max gave that a lot of thought. Dad had been an irritant in his life. He'd white-eyed him into being perfectly behaved as a child, and he'd found it easier than not, to carry on that behaviour. But he didn't love him. He'd *never* loved him. He'd given him what Dad wanted – perfection, and as an added bonus, he'd been beautiful. In return, Dad had doted on him: cooked, cleaned and catered for him.

He was angrier that not only had Jess had the bloody cheek to kill his father, but she'd fucking cheated at Russian roulette. How dare she? His fury made him tremble, and the sensible part of his mind realised he could use this to his advantage.

It would look like he cared about Dad's death. Shaking, manoeuvring his face into something that he thought mimicked sorrow, his eyebrows lifted slightly and creased, he raised his eyes and looked out, not engaging with Jess. As if too upset.

And then he stopped.

What had Jess meant, *we all looked exactly like your mother?* What was she implying? Dropping his face again, he concentrated. Hard. After a bit, he realised what the bitch must be getting at. All his victims were fat like Dad said his mother had been, which meant Max was killing her, his mother, every time he murdered a woman. That made him want to laugh. As fucking if. He had to stop himself laughing out loud. He was getting better at understanding how Jess's sick brain worked.

He looked at her, giving Jess her chance to taste victory. However short-lived.

Making his voice sound quivery and crumbly, he said, 'You think I really wanted to kill my own mother, when I killed those girls? Is that what you mean, Jess? Because she abandoned me when I was a baby. Me and Dad – Mum left us both.'

Max saw the triumphant smile spread across Jess's lips as if she'd made him jump through a hoop, and he'd successfully landed on the other side, standing tall but a better man for it. Through her stretched and upturned mouth, she said, 'Don't you think it coincidental that all your victims are visual replicas of your mother? I don't think so. That's not luck, that's an unconscious act on your part that you were probably unaware of. You had a very warped and complex issue with her. To spell it out, you suffer from a fear of abandonment. By women. Fat women.' She rolled her eyes. 'So, you kill them. Bloody mothers. They've a lot to answer for.'

Was she letting him off the hook here? Max was confused and irritated. 'What are you even talking about, Jess? I'm sure she loved me before she went, and probably had a good reason to leave. But Dad looked after me, and you killed him. That's your shit.'

'And your shit is that you're not even upset. You're not

anything, and that's more than worrying. That's very disturbing.'

He puffed out his lips, admitting to being temporarily stumped. Because he really didn't feel anything at all, hearing his father was dead. He tried again. 'Dad was a very nice man. Don't try and paint him as a weirdo or something. He was… nice.'

'Nice? Really? Is that the best you can come up with? Fucking *nice*?'

'Yeah, Dad was nice. It's not a word you'll ever hear me say again. *Nice*. The world isn't nice. I'm not nice and women aren't nice. With the possible exception of my mother, but we'll never know, will we? She could have been nice. I suppose.' He grinned down at her. 'I'm fucking gorgeous, but that's not the same as nice, is it, Jess?'

'Your father isn't so nice now, Max. Not now he's dead. It took that nice sparkle right off him. You should have seen him. Bang, and then he was gone. Laid out flat on your kitchen floor looking decidedly un-nice.'

He shook his head, uncomprehending. 'You really are madder than me, Jess. You killed my dad. You're a murderer. And you did it because you wanted me. That's a bit desperate.'

He snickered and decided, *So what if I feel nothing about Dad's death? All he did was tell me I was great. I got it. I am great. Job done. I can move on.*

'What have you learnt from today, Max? From the games we've played. What have you taken away from all that?'

I've learnt you're even more besotted with me than I thought. I've learnt that I couldn't care less about Dad.

Or anyone.

Jess still had the advantage here because she had his gun. He needed to get this right. He knew he'd failed at responding appropriately to his father's death, but if he didn't feel it, he couldn't pretend.

He decided to be honest and tell the truth. 'What I've taken from all that you've done, Jess, is that you fucking cheated at Russian roulette. You made me wait for the gun to blow my head off, and all the time, it was just a sick joke. I'm angrier about that than my bloody dad. *You* can cook and clean for me. You can take his place. You want me, you got me.'

Jess's face didn't show any expression at all. He still didn't know what more she wanted from him. He thought he should make her feel like he'd been worth all the trouble she'd been to. 'You can carry on telling me how great I am. It's all Dad did. You and me. Together. We'd make a killer team.' He put on his sweet expression. 'How about it, Jess?'

He slowly came down the steps. 'Do we have a deal?'

As he approached the bottom of the stairs, a thought popped into his head. *Am I on a fucking roll, or what?* He suddenly realised why Jess had always frightened him so much.

It was because she wasn't afraid of anything. Not even her own death. He'd never see the whites of her eyes and he knew it didn't matter anymore. He'd won.

Now he knew the punchline, he could play the game. He'd give her what she wanted.

And *then* he'd kill her. *Finally.* He still had his knife strapped to his ankle. He could win this because he was stronger.

'I'm glad Dad's gone, Jess. Now it really can be you and me. And no one else can get in our way.' He smiled his most beautiful smile and Jess smiled back.

FIFTY-THREE

Jessica

'Stop right there, Max.'
He was still smiling at me, and I hadn't quite got rid of my own smile which I'd pretended onto my face, as I'd listened to his fake we-can-finally-be-together speech. I was affronted that he thought I was so enamoured with him, that I'd fall for his pathetically transparent teaming up suggestion. But I'd play along.

For about a second.

Eve and Bella were both sitting upright on their beanbags, knowing that the end, whatever that end might be, was near. Bella spoke first. 'You're wicked, Max. Jessica killed your dad and you don't even care. How could you be so mean?'

'Shouldn't you ask, how could Jess have killed my father? Isn't that as important?'

Bella shrugged at him, and I went to her. It was difficult not to. She was like a whipped dog, unloved and alone and at the moment, utterly out of her depth. I had to finally accept that as things stood, Bella was the nearest thing to normal in the room.

'Don't worry about it, Bella. Ignore Max. Ignore me.' Her eyes were looking up at me, but they were unfocused. 'Bella?'

Slowly, she came back, as if she'd been somewhere nicer. Somewhere cleaner and saner. 'What were you thinking about, Bella?'

'I want to go home.'

A simple enough request.

Max was hovering ever nearer and thought I hadn't noticed. 'I said, stop, Max. Sit down and sit there in your nice shiny uniform. On the floor. Stay.'

'Babe.' He spread his arms apart as if to embrace me. 'It's me. Your other half. We came through this. We're on the same side. You don't have to point the gun at me anymore, Jess.'

He laughed softly and I angled the gun above his head and pulled the trigger. Everyone ducked. Everyone held their hands to their ears, and everyone closed their eyes. Except me. I had the advantage of knowing it was coming so I watched them all. I'm sure I blinked when the gun went bang, but other than that, I had the pleasure of seeing Max's face. Utter disbelief and total incomprehension that it was I who was the victor in our relationship. In his eyes, I'd beaten him. In my eyes, I'd only beaten myself.

He quickly sat and crossed his legs, his hands on his ankles. Eve was the first to speak. 'Got what you wanted, Jess?'

'No. No, I really don't think I have.'

'Anything I can do to help?'

I considered her offer, but I wasn't even sure what I wanted to happen next. I had a bloody good idea, but it needed some decent grouting around the edges, because at this stage, the coming act would fall apart pretty quickly if not properly cemented into place. Eve persevered. 'What did you want to happen?'

'I genuinely wanted to change my man. But I haven't. I've failed. Failed on a huge scale.'

Max, still under the illusion that he could manipulate me, said, 'What do you even mean, Jess? I *have* changed. You did that. You're responsible. I understand now.'

I was filled with a sad disdain for him. And for myself. My eyes settled on his face. 'What do you understand now?'

He showed me his gold tooth and went into his cute little-boy-lost routine. 'I know I should be sadder about Dad's death. I get it. You taught me that I'm not normal about grief and loss. About death. And I understand that all my victims were fat. Like my mother. And that's weird, right?' He did a sort of chuckle and a roll of his eyes. 'And I *know*, I know for a fact, that it's not nice to tease. Like you did with the gun. That wasn't nice. You taught me that, Jess. It's wrong to cheat. And it's wrong to bully.' He flashed his teeth at me. 'But mostly it's wrong to trick people.'

I wanted to put a bullet right through the middle of his blue eyes, but how could I kill my beautiful but cruel man? Max thought he'd fooled me again with his lies, and for the moment, I was happy to let him live with that fantasy. I was too busy coming to terms with my own very ultimate and final humiliation.

There was something worse than failure. There was shame. I'd shamed myself. All those men out there who'd fat-shamed me my entire life, and bullied me for the hell of it, now I had done it to myself. I'd me-shamed. On a spectacular level.

Certainly, I'd managed to get myself a Johnny-man, but he was monstrous. He was cruel and mean, and even though I was wholly responsible for shooting his smothering father, I was neither cruel nor mean. I was desperate. And I was pathetic. But I still had the capacity for kindness and empathy.

Eve and Bella sat there, unintentionally making me feel worse by their very existence. They highlighted how very unsuccessful I had been in getting myself what I wanted. I'd subjected them both, no… not both. I'd invited Bella into a game which I'd started, and subjected her to horrendous atrocities at the hands of Max. In my defence, I'd tried to shield her as much as possible.

Eve needed no shielding from anyone. I'd have to invite her to *leave*.

The question now was, what was I going to do next? I knew what I wanted to do, but wasn't sure I could achieve it. Another failure at this point would really upset me, and with a loaded gun, being upset wasn't an option I'd immediately plump for if I was standing anywhere near me.

I told Eve to stand up and I went and stood behind Max. Put the gun to the back of his head. 'Eve, get the knife strapped to his ankle, would you, please? And Max, do not even consider that I won't pull the trigger. I killed your father, but you're not what I hoped you'd be, so believe me, I will also shoot you.'

The deflation of his shoulders was a very physical thing as he realised I hadn't fallen for anything he'd said. But still he couldn't help himself. He slipped his fingers up his trouser leg and reached for his knife. He stopped when I cocked the hammer.

I had discovered that guns made the best noises ever. When I'd been upstairs, what seemed an age ago, making tea for myself and sarnies for later, I'd given myself a quick but thorough lesson on how to load a gun with something more than guesswork. I'd learnt how to put one bullet in the correct chamber, having worked out it turned clockwise when I'd dry fired it, making sure it would fire first. Simple but risky but executed perfectly. I learnt how to cock the hammer. Everything about guns made exceedingly good clicky, gunny-type noises – all of them lethal sounding.

Deciding I liked guns, I held out my hand to Eve to collect

the knife in the palm of my hand and pressed the revolver harder to Max's head. 'You've learnt nothing, Max. Nothing at all. All you've proved, is that you're a sick bastard, and I'm a pathetic one. But not an unkind one with no feelings, as you'd like to think.'

He tried to laugh, but found he was all out of them.

Without moving, I spoke to Eve and Bella. 'You can both go now. The clothes you came in have been washed and dried and folded. They're in the utility room next to the kitchen.'

Bella's eyes were all over the place as if she weren't entirely sure where she was. Finally, the meaning of my words got through to her. 'Really? We can go? Just like that?'

'Yup. Just like that. And please do accept my apologies.'

Max stirred and I pressed harder with the gun. I said, 'I swear to God, Max. You move, and your pretty head will no longer be a pleasure to behold. Even for me.'

Eve remained standing. 'What are you going to do, Jessica?'

'Have me some fun.'

'Can I stay and watch?'

'No. It wouldn't be right. But thanks for offering. Was it help you were offering, or something else?'

Max interrupted. 'You can't let them go, Jess. They'll go straight to the police. For fuck's sake, what the bloody hell are you thinking? I told you, we can be together. What more do you fucking want?'

Eve spoke as if Max hadn't. 'I was offering help, but I also wanted to watch. You know…' She shrugged. 'For fun. To see him die. I want to stay for that.'

'No, sorry. Max is mine, after all. You just heard him say so. Let me have him to myself.'

'Shame, but okay. It's been a blast though.' She laughed. 'Except for the maggots. I could have done without those.'

'Where are the keys to the door?' Bella said. She looked wild and instead of relaxing now that she was being set free, she appeared to me as deranged as the rest of us, in her panic to leave. Perhaps it was the anticipation of her release that made her eyes shine so.

'Where do you think the fucking keys are, Number Ten?' Max shouted. 'They'll be in Jess's fucking great big handbag, where else?'

Again, it was as if Max hadn't spoken. 'Thanks, Jessica,' Eve said.

'What for? I kidnapped you.'

'Yes, but you also saved me. And Bella. You didn't have to save either of us, so I'm grateful.'

I handed her Max's confiscated mobile, and my own, and finally the keys which had fallen to the bottom of my bag. I watched as she walked up the spiral staircase. Bella was already there, and Eve let her out and stood looking down at me, her hand on the door. She smiled. 'I like you, Jessica.' Holding her hand up in farewell, Eve added, 'And don't do anything stupid. Like not killing Max.' Already she was halfway out of the door, and I heard her say, 'I'll miss you.'

'Don't forget to lock the door,' I shouted.

'Will do.'

The door slammed shut.

Standing there, with the gun in my hand, I wasn't sure anyone had ever said that to me before. *I'll miss you.* Three simple words. My eyes filled with tears as I absorbed the full tragedy of that fact. No one will miss me except a homeless woman whom I have known for three days.

What an unmitigated disaster at life I'd been. Mummy would crow at my downfall and say I deserved my misery. Perhaps she was right.

Running, I chased after Eve. Banged on the door. Heard her say, 'Hang on.' After a lot of key-turning, the door opened. 'What's up?' she said.

'Does it hurt?' I whispered.

'Does what hurt?'

'Sex. Does it hurt the first time?'

'Yes, usually.'

And this time I let the door remain shut and locked.

FIFTY-FOUR

Jessica

I watched as Max lounged on a beanbag, his legs spread wide, his arms folded. 'Finally, you have exactly what you want, Jess. Me. All to yourself.'

His stupidity matched his beauty. Both were endless. His stupidity was as astonishing as his face. Both were absolute. And inside his perfect covering, there wasn't anything there at all worth having. Not really. After all I'd been through – I'd tried to persuade myself I was getting what I wanted – but I had been very wrong. It seemed I still had precisely what I'd started with. Precisely nothing.

Except visually. Max was still a treat on the eye, and I never tired of looking at him.

Perhaps that made it worth it. A fleeting victory. I had me a handsome man who belonged only to me. I accepted that for what it was.

Not a lot.

And now it had really come down to it, I wasn't sure I wanted to have sex with Max. With *any* man. The thought of me not knowing how to do it properly, made me awkward and sweaty. Simply *thinking* of the fumbling, the doing something wrong, squeezing too hard, not squeezing hard enough, the noises I may or may not make at all the wrong times, all of it made me cringe. When we'd kidnapped each other, I'd been swept up with the thrill, the excitement of the capture. Ironically, I probably could have done it then.

But now?

Not so much. Now I felt big and fat and ugly and useless. I didn't know how to do stuff and Max would delight in that. He'd tease and taunt and destroy me with his scathing words.

Anyway, he wouldn't be able to perform. I wasn't frightened. He could only get it up with the help of seeing white-eyed terror.

Instead, I accepted I'd die a virgin and so bloody what? There were worse things. I went back to playing the default game to which Max and I always returned. Raising my eyes at him, and vowing never to tell him of my virgin-state, I waited for him to say something Max-like, knowing I'd never be disappointed on that score.

'What now, babe? Now you've got me, fancy sex?' He rolled off the beanbag, feigning hysterical laughter at the very thought. A little part of me shrivelled with a familiar dread. Was the thought of sex with me *that* ludicrous?

'Let's stop playing who's bigger and better than the other, Max. It's boring and pointless. Just stop trying to be the alpha personality here. I think we can agree that neither of us has actually lost that particular battle. We're on a par. We are as good and as bad as each other.'

His laugh was harsh and bitter. 'Are you fucking kidding me? Apart from the fact that women cannot, they can*not* be alpha personalities, *because they're fucking women*, of course we've lost. Both of us have. We're trapped and we can't get out. Which of us has won what? Do tell. I'm all bloody ears.'

'Don't be like that. Let's not argue. I'm tired of the game. There is no winning.'

'What are you going to do with me, with your big old gun? Blow my head off? Kill the one man who you love like no other? Really? As mad as you are, Jess, I don't think you have it in you to destroy me. Imagine it, no more beautiful Max to fawn over, to adore. No more craving his touch.' He laughed. 'You're buggered, love. You don't know how to finish it.'

'I know, Max. Because I'm not as shortsighted as you. I've always seen the bigger picture. You, however, can only see as far as the end of your own perfectly formed nose, and that's why you should be very afraid now.'

He leapt up and walked towards me. Instinctively, I stepped back, holding the gun between us. 'Don't push your luck, Max. I *will* shoot.'

'And then what? We're locked in, thanks to you making sure bloody Number Nine locked the door, you moron. Why would you do something so stupid?'

'Because it's always been about the two of us. Not anyone else. Not even your father, although he had the dubious honour of having helped create you and he reared you. No, it's just you and me, Max, and that's how it will end.'

Ignoring me, and running around me, he leapt up the stairs and ran his hands around the door frame. 'There must be some way out of here, Jess. Right? Like this is a trick, isn't it? You're giving me a taste of what you say you hate so much. You're fucking teasing me, trying to make me believe we're both going to die down here.' He started pressing at the surrounding brickwork, testing for some structural weakness. 'You wouldn't let yourself die down here with me. You love me too much.'

He stopped checking for hidden escape routes and secret tunnels, and said, 'Come on, Jess, babe. Stop messing about.

You've got another key, haven't you? In that bloody bag.' He clapped his hand to his head. 'Of course. That's it. You're definitely teasing me. Good one. You really had me going there for a minute. Give me the other key.'

'Course I've got an extra key, Max. You know me so well, I can't expect to pull one over on you. You see right through me.'

There he stood, at the top of the staircase, whilst I gazed up at him. It was a real Romeo and Juliet moment. But he should have been down here, serenading me, up there. But I could still orchestrate the perfect ending to our imperfect relationship even if I couldn't get the love scene right. Max might not see it that way, but he'd have time to come to terms with it. And I knew, deep down, he'd eventually see it my way.

Because he really had no choice at all in the matter.

'Come down here, Max. And please don't think of rushing me, attempting to get the key, because I'll shoot you before you get anywhere like close enough. Why don't we pretend we like each other. Just for the hell of it? Aren't you tired of all this constant bickering?'

Bounding down the stairs, he stood approximately six feet away from me. 'No, I'm not tired at all. Give me the keys, Jess. I'm not asking again.'

'No, you're not asking again.'

I shot him in the leg. Well, I say that like it was with the first shot. It took three bangs before the third landed. The first two simply stopped him in his tracks – unable to grasp that I'd had the cheek to really shoot at him, the duo of booms paralysed him and rooted him to the spot. The third brought him down.

'There, Max. I did tell you, but you wouldn't listen. Now look what's happened. You shouldn't play with a girl with a gun. How many times did your father *not* tell you that little life-saving tip-of-the-fucking-year?'

Max's face had gone white and sweaty and he clutched his

knee or thereabouts with both hands. Lucky shot. At least I hadn't hit him in the thigh, so little chance that he'd bleed to death. No, his death would take a long time, and it would give him time to reflect on how not to treat women. 'I did try to teach you, Max, that you should really be nicer to women and not take advantage, but you refused to hear my life lessons. Thus, here we are. You on the floor with a bullet in your leg, and me, standing here with the spare keys in my bag. All ready to leave you to it. Good one, right?'

'You mad bitch. Christ almighty.' His teeth gritted, his jaws clenched and his brow dripped with perspiration.

'Not mad, Max. Never that. Just stupid. But unlike you, I have the ability to learn from my mistakes and adjust my plans accordingly. You, you are beneath contempt and think yourself above everyone. Being beautiful doesn't give you a free pass. Well, it does, unless you meet someone like me, who wants to change the fairy-book ending of handsome prince getting his beautiful fat princess. Because it never happens like that in your world, does it, Max? Not happily, anyway. Never happily for all the fat women.'

I thought he was trying to speak, but it was difficult to tell. Too much grimacing and groaning going on to differentiate between speech and utterances of pain.

'Sorry it's all turned out like this, Max. You had a million chances to make it right and be nice to me – that was all I wanted. But it was beyond you. This is how it ends. Are you paying attention? I wouldn't want you to miss the grand finale.'

'Do what you want, bitch. You're doing the old "If I can't have you, no one else will" crap, aren't you? That's a bit disappointing, Jess. I would have expected something more sophisticated from you.'

'How about this?'

Steadying the gun, I straightened my arms and pointed it

at him. His ineffectual but very beautiful hands flapped up in front of his face as if he could ward off the bullet.

'Bye, bye, Max.'

Adjusting my hold on the handle, I took aim carefully and pulled the trigger.

FIFTY-FIVE

Max

The gunshot still echoed in Max's head, and he lay there, blood pooling around his leg for a good five minutes. It took him a while to understand what had happened.

The mad bitch hadn't shot him. She'd shot herself.

Wincing with pain, his hands slipping in his own blood on the carpet, he pulled himself over to Jess. Ripped her handbag from around her neck. It had always irritated him how she'd worn it like a bloody satchel – keeping it safe.

Now it was no longer safe from him. And inside was the key.

He could hear a noise in the background and realised it was him, gasping and panting and yes, fucking whimpering. Max told himself to calm down. *Find the key, find the key.*

It was quicker to upend the whole bloody bag onto the carpet. A whole bunch of completely random stuff made a messy heap on the carpet in front of his shaking hands. A second box of bullets rolled out, a banana, loads of tissues, lipstick, hairbrush, a second pair of handcuff keys, a pen, a small notepad, two chocolate bars and a packet of crisps. No mobile.

No key.

Where is the fucking key?

Panicking now, Max tore at the inside of the bag, ripping the lining. His hands shook and finding nothing, he returned to the pile of rubbish which lay, looking like a mound of nothing-he'd-ever-wanted-in-his entire-life. Ever. Nothing. No key. He sat back and felt tears fall down his cheeks.

I am going to die down here.

Jess had well and truly fucked him. She'd cheated him *again*. Tempted him with freedom, and snatched it away, and he hadn't even had the opportunity to kill the bitch.

Max lay next to Jess for a long time. He could have moved to a beanbag, but he couldn't be bothered. He didn't care that he lay next to a corpse and anyway, dead Jess was way better than the live version had been.

She'd brought his whole world to a stop.

And in the end, she'd shown him who was boss.

He'd always known she would beat him. When he'd lain in bed, and freaked out about her, he'd *always* known she'd win. He'd always known and had only ever been kidding himself that he had any chance of winning against her.

Max leant forward and smoothed down his hair and smiled, imagining his gold tooth showing itself off to no one.

It wasn't wasted on him. He was as entranced by his good looks as all his women were. Slowly shaking his head, he knew no women would ever have the pleasure of seeing his beauty again. Dad would never comment on his extraordinary handsomeness, as he had every time he'd seen him, because Jess had killed him. Dad had been his biggest fan. That's all Dad had ever been. And now he'd never comment on Max's perfection again, his virility, his manly looks, because fat bitch Jess had taken even that away from him.

Lying in the middle of the room, he knew Jess had nicked a

main artery in his leg. He'd lie here until the blood had drained from him. Killed by a bloody useless *woman*.

Unless he had the last laugh. Anger kept him breathing although he was aware he was getting sleepy. He picked up the gun. It wasn't a difficult decision to shoot himself. Jess would have assumed he'd be too cowardly, and simply lie here, waiting for death. Well, he'd show her.

He should never have kept it: shooting people was a bit too impersonal for him. Too removed and remote. He preferred bringing death to women by using skin on skin, hands on neck. It was more friendly and intimate. More him.

Max held the gun to his head. And stopped for a minute. To think.

It occurred to him that if he'd never got the gun from some nameless young white male who'd been fleeing a burglary and had dropped it, desperate not to be caught with it, none of this would be happening. The twenty-something man Max had been chasing, had thrown it behind a wall. On reflection, it had been a fatal error of judgement when Max had seen the tossing of the weapon, and decided to let the young bastard go so he could pocket the gun for himself. For a rainy day.

Now it was bloody pouring.

His partner had puffed up behind him and hadn't seen Max pick it up. 'He got away,' Max had said and his side-kick had believed him. Because Max had spoken with authority and why wouldn't his partner believe him? Max prided himself on his lying abilities, his abducting women skills, his art of killing. He was best at everything. Dad had total faith in Max and always commented on it. Every bloody day. He would miss hearing how proud Dad was of his son, and Max supposed that must be part of the grieving process.

He snickered. Nah. Not grieving. More like royally pissed off at the whole Jess thing. It was all her fault.

She'd even changed his game. That's why he'd lost. He

hadn't been able to label and pigeonhole. That's where he'd come unstuck. The bitch had taken over and brought two women who had always been the completely wrong type of women. Because *he* hadn't chosen them.

Bloody shame that he'd end up in a fucking glass box, his dead body rotting down here: his remains waiting to be found, scraped up and bagged and tagged and buried.

I wonder how many people will come to my funeral? He smiled. *Loads of bloody women, that's for sure.*

Before he closed his eyes, he glanced up and saw the tall one, Eve. She looked down at him, laughing, and gave him the thumbs-up.

He smiled back and gave her the finger.

Glancing quickly down at himself for the last time, Max was proud to be dying with his uniform on with his gleaming buttons and his polished black shiny boots. He really was a picture of authority and he liked the irony of being in command of his own death. It was his final duty, his show of respect to his service as a policeman. It had been an honour.

He was an honour to all the women *he'd* serviced.

No one beats me. Definitely not a woman. Never that.

Max pulled the trigger.

FIFTY-SIX

Eve

'Wait, Bella. I'm going to watch. We owe Jessica that much.'

'We owe her nothing. We don't owe either of them anything. I don't care what happens to them.'

'Aren't you interested? Even a little bit?'

'Nope. I'm getting my clothes. Do you want me to get yours as well?'

'Yeah, whatever.'

Eve wasn't really listening to Bella, but then she remembered. Tearing her eyes from the theatre below, Eve said, 'And don't worry, Bella. I haven't forgotten.'

'Forgotten what?'

'That I owe you. For getting you kidnapped. After this has finished…' She pointed at the glass floor. 'You should really come and watch – I'm trying to guess what Jessica will do.'

Bella's expression didn't change and Eve couldn't fathom why the woman was so disinterested in what was going on in the room below. 'Don't you want to know what happens?'

'What difference will it make?'

'None. But it's fun. Jessica's going to beat the bastard. And that's something I am *not* missing for anyone.' She grinned but got nothing back from Bella. Eve shrugged, vaguely irritated with Bella. 'I was going to say, I haven't forgotten that I need to re-pay you for involving you in all this.'

'No, really. You don't have to do anything. I don't want anything from you. Honest.'

Desperate to get back to watching through the glass, Eve spoke quickly. 'When this has finished, and it won't be long, you and me can go back to our little red tent. How cool will that be? You and me. And I can protect you forever, so there's no need for you to ever be frightened again. I'll look after you.'

'But it's *my* tent.'

Eve smiled at her. '*Our* tent, now.'

Bella didn't speak again, and Eve gratefully and immediately went back to watching, her nose pressed to the glass. She wondered what Max was looking for in Jessica's handbag. Eve had seen Max running up the stairs and had had to move to the opposite corner of the floor to watch him feverishly touching the door frame and the surrounding wall, as if he were patting it down, searching for something.

Then Jessica had shot him. That had made Eve laugh. Good old Jessica. Eve had never doubted her. They were like a strange pair of sisters, reunited after a lifetime apart – nothing had needed explaining between them. Each of them had instinctively known what the other was doing and thinking.

But then Jess had turned the gun on herself. And pulled the trigger.

That had shocked Eve.

Not as much as it had shocked Max. He'd been stunned. Eve had laughed at his confusion. And then watched his desperate and frantic searching of the handbag.

He's looking for a key. Jessica's told him there's a key in her bag. But I bet she's lying. I'm sure she's lying. It's what I'd do.

Eventually, Max had also come to realise there was no key and he'd lain back and looked up. Eve was just loving this. It brought it all back – her and Oliver. All the beatings, all the violence, the sick twisted behaviour which had led to murder. This was almost better, and it had given Eve the itch back. The itch to come down on the wrong side of the razor's edge. For no reason other than it fascinated her. She missed things being wrong and off-kilter and acknowledged her role in the darker side of life was voluntary. It's who she was. Nothing complex about it. It was simplicity itself.

And look *what I am witnessing here. It's box office gold. Just take a fucking look. Life didn't do this unless you made it happen.* She silently applauded Jessica.

Most people needed punishing in some way, and Max had been punished. Eve perhaps would have eked it out a bit longer, but she'd respected Jessica enough to let her do it her way.

In a way, Eve wanted to be like Jessica, but she conceded that Jessica had a softness and a kindness that Eve wasn't convinced she had. She *thought* she had the capacity to empathise and be generous, but she didn't *know*.

Stop it, Eve told herself. When she and Bella left here, it would be the perfect time to help the girl with the tent. It would be a testing time for Eve – kind and caring? She'd give it her best go. And Eve had promised Bella she'd look after her, and she was a woman of her word. Eve absolutely wouldn't allow Bella to drift away all on her own, terrified of the world. Bella needed Eve and it would do Eve good – to do something selfless.

She told herself over and over again as she watched Max bleed out, that she would look after Bella forever, but she kept on forgetting, so fascinated was she in the engrossing death of Max. She didn't want to miss Max actually dying. 'Do you reckon I'll be able to see him breathe out for the last time?

From up here, I mean? Am I close enough, Bella? What do you reckon?'

Pressing her face so hard to the glass, she thought she might break her own nose, Eve saw Max pick up the gun. He looked up at her but didn't see her.

Unable to take her eyes off him, Eve watched as he lay there with the gun to the side of his head. He waited. Eve couldn't imagine what for, but then he looked up and saw her. Laughing, she gave him a thumbs-up. He smiled back and gave her the finger.

And pulled the trigger.

There, done. She was surprised he'd had the nerve and felt slightly disappointed at the speed of his death.

'He's shot himself, Bella. Who'd have thought he'd be brave enough?' She sighed. 'It's over.'

Eve turned around and realised she'd been speaking to herself. Bella wasn't there. Tutting, Eve lay down once more to savour and have a final look at the room which had housed her. Thought about the experience she'd been living for the past few days. She wouldn't miss it, because ever onward and all that, but she *had* enjoyed it.

She felt, rather than saw, Bella sit down next to her, and was aware that Bella sat with her back to both her and the glass floor, refusing to watch. She was dressed in her own clothes and placed a pile of Eve's clothes next to her, along with her orange rucksack.

'Thanks, Bella. Give me a minute, while I get undressed. Then we can leave, okay?'

Bella didn't answer, and Eve, uncaring at the non-response, pushed herself off the glass like she was doing a press-up.

Eve tore herself away from the tragedy that had been Jessica. An intellectual tragedy, as it failed to reach her on a personal level. For her, already the playroom and its last two occupants were things of the past: been, gone, done. Eve was all about the moment, and already this moment had gone. So on to the next.

Mentally, Eve packaged away all that had happened here: she was no longer present. The kidnapping and everything that had followed might as well have happened to someone else.

And that's why Eve doubted she had the kindness that Jessica had. Eve had already as good as forgotten her.

Shrugging, she concentrated on the next thing. The looking after of Bella.

Smiling broadly, she stood up, her back sore from bending for so long, and stretched. 'Hand me my clothes, would you, Bella? I can't get this stupid onesie off. One of the poppers is stuck.'

'Course. Yeah. Here you go.'

It was only a small thing, but something was wrong with Bella's voice.

Eve spun round and was quick enough to see it coming.

FIFTY-SEVEN

Bella

'But it's *my* tent.'

Eve had smiled at her. '*Our* tent, now.'

Bella couldn't get over it. *It's* my *little red tent. It's the only thing I have. It's mine.*

And the very last thing Bella wanted was to share it with Eve. Eve was a nutter. She pretended she wasn't, but she was. Leaving Eve behind, all excited at what was happening under the glass floor – Eve really shouldn't be watching, it was disrespectful – Bella wandered back into the kitchen.

She wasn't hungry. She wasn't tired. She was nothing. It had all been too much, so Bella took the time to sit and be quiet and listen to the sounds of the house.

And conjured up Dominic. He hadn't really left her again, not properly, not since the gun game. He'd moved permanently into her mind now, and Bella had welcomed him. It was like he'd moved into her house, and they hadn't even slept together. That thought had made Bella laugh and blush with pleasure. Perhaps she could take him home to Mum and Dad's for Christmas. It wasn't long now. What, a week or so?

Sitting at the kitchen table, Bella thought she'd not only lost her sense of time since she'd been kidnapped, but also a big piece of herself. She couldn't quite identify what it was she'd lost, but she felt bereft. Like a death had happened. And she didn't mean the death of any of *them* – they didn't matter – but of someone she loved. But no one had died that she knew.

Perhaps she was grieving her own innocence which had been taken from her, by *all* of them. Max and Jessica and Eve. They were all spiteful and nasty and she didn't care what Jessica did to Max or what Max did to Jessica.

It's nothing to do with me.

Finally, she moved and got her clothes. It was nice to be in something not pyjamas. Bella picked up Eve's clothes as well, which had been folded neatly and left, like Bella's, in a tidy stack. If Jessica expected thanks, she'd be waiting a long time, Bella thought. Especially if she was dead already. That made her giggle and bend double, laughing hard. She had to stop for a moment, before she could carry on taking the dressing gown and pyjamas off.

Back in the kitchen, she opened the fridge, closed the fridge and opened and shut drawers and cupboards. Not really knowing what she was looking for until she found it.

When she did find it, she knew, without questioning it for a minute, that it was perfect. And not only perfect, but there was a bit of that teasing to her using it, that Jessica would approve of. Smiling, Bella practised with it a few times until she felt confident.

Dominic reassured her all the while that she was doing the right thing and that he'd be there, waiting for her. Always.

Wandering back through the house that had so intimidated her when she'd first arrived, she reached Eve and the glass floor. Eve glanced at Bella, and asked Bella to pass her clothes. Eve banged on about something stupid like a popper being stuck. That also didn't concern Bella, but being polite, she answered anyway.

'Course. Yeah. Here you go.'

Bella knew instantly she opened her mouth, that her words were so dull, her tone so flat, that she might as well have been dead. There was no feeling at all in her voice, because she was all felt-out. Bella was in doing mode. Maybe Eve had recognised the tone. Probably. That would be just like Eve – able to pick up the first scent of danger, before it was even a real thing. Before it had happened. Before Bella had realised she'd even thought it. Because Eve was a nutter and was clever like that.

Dominic's voice in her head had changed. It was still kind, but different. It was sort of more spiritual, guiding and all-knowing. Like a guardian angel. He told her he was her saviour and he was so easy to listen to, so easy to believe, that she felt a part of him. Or was he a part of her?

But it was such a relief to be looked after, Bella didn't care that he was with her now forever. Nothing else mattered. It was enough that he was hers.

His words flew and swooped around inside Bella's head: *If you don't kill her now, Bella, Eve will eventually kill you. Because that's what she does. She's a destroyer. That's why she was friends with Jessica. She has no heart, but she will take yours. Be quick, Bella, be quick.*

Hurry, before she takes your tent.

The thought of her tent being taken over by Eve was enough to bring forth a roar from Bella's lungs. A sound she'd never uttered before, but she would not allow this, and Dominic said it was okay. It would be a fitting punishment. *No one will* ever *take my tent. Not even Eve.* Especially *not Eve.*

The cleaver swung through the air and more through luck than judgement, the blade landed exactly where Bella was aiming for. It sliced Eve's throat and for a moment, Eve's eyes were wide open and extra round looking as they gazed momentarily into Bella's.

Bella could see the whites of her eyes and couldn't care less.

She wasn't quick enough to avoid the blood, and now she'd have to find something else to leave the house in. She could hardly turn up at her parents' house for the Christmas holidays in red-stained bloody clothes.

Humming, Bella didn't need to check that Eve was dead. She knew she was.

Once she was all cleaned up, she would go back to her red tent before going home, and be thankful it was all over.

She didn't mind Dominic coming with her.

Dominic would always be with Bella now.

They were inseparable.

Also by Jocelyn Dexter

Mother Said So

Shh

Uninvited

Bad Company

Acknowledgements

First, and as always, a huge thank you to all the Bloodhound team, who could not have been more supportive, nor worked any harder on this book. My sincerest gratitude.

A very special thanks goes to Our Trish, who came up with the brilliant title, The Playroom – for which I can take no credit at all, *(Damn)*, and for her help in finessing a large portion of the book, vastly improving the narrative, dialogue, etc, pre-edit. The help was invaluable and generous as always. Ta ever so.

And yet again, many thanks to my editor, Clare Law – whom I literally couldn't edit without. A great job and much appreciated.

And mostly, as always, thank you to Francesca.

For everything.

A note from the publisher

Thank you for reading this book. If you enjoyed it please do consider leaving a review on Amazon to help others find it too.

We hate typos. All of our books have been rigorously edited and proofread, but sometimes mistakes do slip through. If you have spotted a typo, please do let us know and we can get it amended within hours.

info@bloodhoundbooks.com

Printed in Great Britain
by Amazon

58271326R00189